Delia Suits Up

Delia Suits Up

AMANDA AKSEL

BERKLEY
NEW YORK

BERKLEY

An imprint of Penguin Random House LLC

penguinrandomhouse.com

Library of Congress Cataloging-in-Publication Data

Names: Aksel, Amanda, author.
Title: Delia suits up / Amanda Aksel.
Description: First edition. | New York: Berkley, 2021.
Identifiers: LCCN 2020045192 (print) | LCCN 2020045193 (ebook) |
ISBN 9780593201619 (trade paperback) | ISBN 9780593201626 (ebook)
Subjects:
Classification: LCC PS3601.K74 D45 2021 (print) | LCC PS3601.K74 (ebook) |
DDC 813/.6—dc23
LC record available at https://lccn.loc.gov/2020045192
LC ebook record available at https://lccn.loc.gov/2020045193

First Edition: August 2021

Printed in the United States of America
1st Printing

Book design by Kristin del Rosario

*For Heather
and
all the Pink Power Rangers*

AUTHOR'S NOTE

When I started my career in the financial industry, I couldn't help but notice there were so many men in the business but only a small percentage of women. Not only that, but women are paid less than men for the same jobs. I remember meeting with a female colleague who said, "In this business, being a woman will get you in the door, but you'll have to work harder to stay there." So I started to pay more attention to how men and women are treated differently.

With this book, I wanted to explore the idea of taking on a new form and how that might inform the way the world sees us and, more importantly, how we see ourselves. As Delia's story evolved just like mine, I knew it was an opportunity to bring attention to sexism in the workplace. So much has improved in the last century, but there's still much more to do. I sincerely appreciate all the women of the past and present who have worked and fought toward the goal of building an equitable society.

Delia Suits Up explores themes of sexism, self-confidence, and empowerment. As she literally walks in another man's shoes, I would be remiss not to recognize that gender identity is not one size fits all. Everyone has their own experience of their gender identity, and each person's individual experience, expression, and identity is valid.

It's my hope to leave you, the reader, emboldened to be the truest version of yourself, to follow your heart, and to have some fun along the way.

Delia Suits Up

CHAPTER ONE

Stay positive. That's everyone's advice, as if enduring optimism is some kind of elixir. Lately, positive doesn't cut it.

The antique clock's ticking pulse fills the room. It's been thirty-two seconds since he's said a word. I watch his reflection on the sleek mahogany desk scan my resume up and down. Up and down. What's he looking for? Waldo? We've already established I'm well qualified for this position. I cross my fingers, keeping them hidden beneath my padfolio.

This guy's view of the city stretches all the way to the East River. The window alone is half the square footage of the apartment I share with two roommates. He shifts again in his plush leather chair, grazing his bristly mustache with his fingertips. Twelve seconds later, he peers over the rim of his glasses and draws in a slow breath while I hold mine. Monty Fuhrmann is one of the top investment banking firms in the world. Landing a position here would mean being a part of larger-than-life deals with a paycheck to match. It's more than a job. It's a dream come true.

Okay, Delia. Stay positive.

"Mrs. Reese," he says, sliding the stiff paper forward.

"It's Miss, or you can call me Delia. It's very important that you know I'm a Miss. I'm not married. No children. I don't even have a boyfriend. Who needs the distraction? Am I right?" I say as if handing him a good-ole-boys brandy.

I clear my throat, resenting the fact that as a woman in this industry it's better for me to admit that I have no life. And no prospect of having one either. He's probably wanted to ask me ever since my resume came across his desk. But legally . . . he can't.

He says nothing.

Maybe if I tell him that I've spent the last three nights in bed with a pint of Häagen-Dazs, he'll hire me on the spot.

"What I mean to say is that work is my life, and I will make this job and this firm my life if you hire me." My fist falls softly on my padfolio. I wish I had the balls to bang it on his shiny desk.

He raises his brow. "Right . . ."

Right.

Of course that's all I get.

It's typical in this industry for men to dismiss women. To them, we're temporary fixtures around the office, bound to meet and marry Prince Charming, experience the miracle of childbirth after a miserable nine months of sobriety, then ultimately crumble under the pressure of balancing mommyhood with an intense career. We're gone as quickly as we arrived; off to spend our mornings watching cartoons with small people, cleaning messy faces, and running bake sales with the other career abandoners. But that's not me. I have as much potential as the applicants wearing neckties. And I'm dedicated. The most dedicated, in fact, and yet, I have to sit here beaming pleasantly and plead my case.

Mr. Mustache returns a smile. "Your resume's very impressive. Any firm would be happy to have you on."

That sounds promising.

"It was nice to meet you, *Miss* Reese. We'll let you know."

Right. Translation—we're not interested. I catch myself frowning and immediately force a smile. Staying positive is like a full-time job in itself. I was optimistic after I was laid off, hopeful when I went on my first five interviews. But I'm not sure how much longer my bank account will stay positive.

He rises and extends a hand. I jump to my feet so I can meet his eye line, or meet it as best as I can. These heels give me an extra three inches.

I muster my solid *I'm as good as any man* handshake like it makes a difference. "I'll look forward to your call."

Walking back through the polished waiting area, I see nothing but suits and ties. The only other woman is the receptionist behind the front desk. I swipe my lips with a fresh coat of Fierce Crimson on the elevator ride down to the thirty-second floor. That's where I'll find Eric. He's my friend and colleague from the Howard Brothers Group. We were laid off along with a bunch of others after the merger. That was four months ago. Eric's been employed here for three. Rows of desks set up with bright LED monitors and ergonomic keyboards fill the floor. Young underwriters talk into their headsets while typing away into sophisticated software programs. I catch tiny fragments of their conversations—*capital*, *prospectus*, *issue price*, *shareholder*, *syndicate*—dialogue that always energizes me. That's how this industry is. Never a dull day. For a moment, I forget I'm not one of them anymore and hold my head high. This is my playground.

When I was little, Giggles candies were my favorite—especially the watermelon flavor. Every paper wrapper had a silly saying written on the inside, almost like a funny fortune cookie. My favorite one said, "A bank is a place that will lend you money, if you can prove that you don't need it." Out of all my fourth-grade friends, I was the only one who got the joke, which made me feel special. Granted, my dad is a financier with his own firm.

He took me to the Giggles candy factory once for a private tour. I sampled so many sweets that day that I couldn't stomach dinner. Dad explained that it was his company that helped Giggles grow so big that lots of kids like me could enjoy those funny treats. His eyes radiated pride as we walked the factory lines that day. That's when I decided that I wanted to help companies grow too. And I wanted to be the best at it because if I were the best, maybe he'd look at me with the same pride. That's why I came to Wall Street, to play with the big boys, which now that I think about it doesn't leave much room for big girls like me. And my current circumstances are proof of that.

Eric peeks around his own monitor, catching me with his alluring eyes. My breath gets stuck in my throat. I don't usually go for the whole blue-eyed-blond thing, but he makes my temperature rise like a bull market.

"Hey, Delia!" There's something thrilling about the way he says my name. I could listen to him say *Delia* all day long and never get sick of it. "Did you kill it? You're starting Monday, right?"

Kill it?

Sure. A little piece of me dies every time I have to fake it twice as much as any guy interviewing for the same position.

"It was all right," I say, attempting a casual lean on his desk, but my sweaty palm slips off the edge. I recover quickly, wiping it on my tailored Kate Spade skirt. Between interviewing for the job of my dreams and being close to my crush, it's not just my palms that are damp. "Is it warm in here?" I fan my face.

"Um, feels fine to me." He rolls a chair over from the neighboring desk. An empty desk that would be mine if only things were different.

"Why don't you sit down for a minute? Take off your blazer." He scoots his chair so close to mine that we're practically in the same breathing space. I slip off my jacket, revealing bare shoulders, but his eyes don't fall below my chin.

Why do I torture myself with him? I've been doing it since the moment we met more than two years ago. I don't think he wants me. These days it doesn't seem like anyone wants me.

"Tell me about the interview," he says.

I sigh. "I'm pretty sure they're not gonna hire me."

"Why not? You're perfect for this place! You're smart, driven, dedicated." See! Eric gets it. He gets *me*. "Every time we've encountered a problem with this IPO we're working on, I always think, Delia would know how to fix it." He leans in on his elbows and my heart beats faster. If he gets any closer, I might take off more than my blazer.

I push the floor with my black pumps and roll back a couple feet, tucking my arms in just to be safe. "Thanks for the vote of confidence, but you know how this industry is."

He arches an eyebrow, and I find myself biting my lower lip. "You mean the good-ole-boys club."

"Exactly." The term makes me cringe. When has there ever been a good-ole-girls club? I shrug and glance down at his freshly polished shoes. "Maybe I'd get the job if I were applying to be an analyst or, I don't know, a receptionist."

"Hey, look at me. You should stay positive." There's that word again. "I have a good feeling about this." He smiles, a gleam sparkling in his eyes. Wish I were feeling as bright. "Besides, if it's not this firm, another one will scoop you up."

Scoop me up? Why can't he scoop me up, like ice cream, and lick me all over until I completely melt away? That would be very positive.

"Maybe, but I can't keep going like this much longer," I say.

"What does that mean?" His eyes try to connect with mine, but I don't look into them. I know he'll see what I've been hiding from him all this time.

I pick at my unpainted fingernails. "I'm running low on reserves. This city isn't cheap, you know?"

"So, what, you might leave New York?" He lifts my chin and I breathe deep, subtly taking in all I can. Calvin Klein has never smelled better on anyone. He drops his hand after only a second. My body tingles in the wake of his touch. Everywhere.

"Yeah." I shiver, looking over his shoulder past the gray cubicles to the wide window that frames the city skyline like a panoramic postcard—*If you can make it here . . .*

The thought of moving back home with my tail between my legs makes me want to vomit the PB and J I ate for lunch. Especially after working so hard to get into an Ivy League university and making my way to this metropolitan mecca. I can't count how many high school parties and nights on the beach I missed with my friends so I could study at home and make more of myself than just another one of my father's employees.

"You're not thinking of going back to Boca Raton, are you?" he asks. I wince and smooth my hair at the thought of South Florida humidity. That place is my living hell. So much worse than living unemployed in the Big Apple.

"I might not have a choice. I have to make money, and there's a position waiting for me at my dad's investment firm." My desperation increases every day I'm out of a real job. Otherwise, I wouldn't even consider retreating.

"It's none of my business, but couldn't your dad just lend you the money until you get another job?"

Man, he'd love that. I can hear him now. "Delia, I don't know why you have to make things harder on yourself. I told you that you should've stayed here and worked for me and your brothers. After all, we're family." That's the problem. In the family, I'm the youngest. And female. They treat me like a little girl at home, and they'll treat me like a little girl in business. I'm not a little girl. I'm a fucking woman.

"I don't think so. It's complicated," I say.

His eyes narrow and his tongue peeks between his lips. I love his thinking face. If only he were thinking about putting his tongue between my . . . um, lips.

Geez. I don't know what I need more, to get a job or to get laid. Both would be fantastic.

"Well, if I ever get the chance to put in a good word for you, I will."

"Thanks, Sinatra. I appreciate you trying to help." I dubbed him with the nickname after being bewitched, bothered, and bewildered by the sparkle of his ol' blue eyes one night while we were enjoying a few after-work cocktails. He laughed, saying despite those eyes, no one had ever called him that, but he liked it. I've been using it ever since, mostly for the more sentimental moments. Sentimental to me, at least.

He puts his hand on my naked shoulder, and this time I can't look away. "The truth is, I'd miss you if you left the city." His words set off what feels like a swarm of butterflies fluttering around my insides.

"You would?" Is this it? Is this the moment I should tell him? What do I have to lose besides my longtime friend and what's left of my dignity?

My gaze trails to his hand still resting on my shoulder, and he gives me a playful shove. "Of course! You're one of my best friends."

All the winged creatures flapping in my stomach drop dead. I'm not sure which is worse: being rejected for a job because I'm a woman or being rejected by a man because I'm a friend. I slouch back into the chair, lowering my eyes to the floor again.

"You okay, Delia?"

I look up at his concerned face. "I'm fine. Why?"

"You just don't quite seem like yourself lately." Maybe that's because I don't feel like myself when I'm not doing what I love. "You seem . . . deflated."

"Deflated?" And here I was thinking I've been doing a pretty good job of staying positive.

"It's understandable. I know it's been a rough few months.

But . . ." He casually slides his chair back and retrieves a small white box from his desk drawer. "I got you something that might cheer you up."

I spot the bakery logo on the side. "Is that a Brooklyn blackout cupcake?" My cheeks flush at the thought of him buying me a gift.

Donning a sweet smile, Eric sets the treat down and reveals a tiny white candle. "Your favorite. It's for your birthday tomorrow."

I smooth my flyaways back behind my ear and grin like I've just been hired at Monty Fuhrmann. "I can't believe you remembered my birthday."

"That's what best friends are for." A small flame sparks from a lighter in his fist as he mimics a vocal warm-up. "Me-me, me-me, meee."

"Wait!" I wave my hand over the unlit candle. "What are you doing?"

He lets out a small laugh. "Warming up my pipes to sing 'Happy Birthday.' What does it look like I'm doing?"

My eyes shift right then left, catching a couple of glances from Eric's coworkers whose attention we've seemed to capture. "Maybe later."

"All right." He places the dark cupcake and candle back in the box. "Can I at least buy you an early birthday latte?"

"Now?"

"Yeah, I've been here since seven. I could use a break."

The digits on my cell phone remind me there's no wiggle room in my schedule. Of course he's being all cute and available now. I let out a sigh and tuck the phone back into my prized Gucci briefcase, a gift to myself after I got my first big bonus last year. I've been trying to reconcile the fact that I may need to trade it for rent money. "Wish I could, but I have another interview." Lie.

His eyes widen. "Oh, yeah? What firm?"

"S.G. Croft." Liar, liar, pink panties on fire.

"Two major interviews in one day. Impressive. I'll walk you out."

"Thanks." I smile and slip back into my blazer, grateful for the extra time with him. With my Gucci and cupcake in tow, I follow him toward the elevator.

"For fuck's sake!" a man barks.

BANG! The raging executive's office door slams shut as we walk by.

"What's his problem?" I ask out of the side of my mouth.

"Who knows? That's Curtis Becker for ya. Shortest fuse on the planet." Eric hits the button to go down.

"*That's* Curtis Becker? The managing director?" I glance back at the hothead's closed door, wondering how guys like him end up with executive positions like that. Eric nods with a look that mirrors my confusion and we ride the elevator to the first floor.

"So what are you working on now?" I ask once we make it outside of the bustling lobby.

"We've got the Ezeus pitch on Friday."

"Seriously?"

Eric's been talking about this deal ever since he began working here. His smirk exudes confidence. I don't even remember the last time I looked as confident.

"Damn, I would love to get in on that."

The Ezeus IPO is the kind of deal that bankers fantasize about. It's rumored to be huge. Ezeus is the only operating system that rivals the top two. One of those nerd-to-billionaire business fairy tales. Monty Fuhrmann helped them get off the ground and they've been loyal clients ever since. No doubt they'll land a spot in the syndicate.

"So what's the plan?" I miss talking business.

He snickers. "Exactly what you think it is. This is Monty Fuhrmann. We'll take the lead, run the whole show, and make a shitload of money."

"You sure Fairbanks is gonna go for that after the last big IPO this firm took charge of?"

He shrugs. "Curtis Becker certainly thinks so."

What I would give to be in Becker's position. "Call me Friday and tell me all about it. I'm dying to know what happens."

"I will," he says, flashing his pearly teeth. "And don't worry. I have a feeling your luck's about to change."

From anyone else, the notion would've sounded trite, but from him, it sings of possibility. I want it to be true. Whether he's right or dead wrong, something has to change. Soon.

I hold up the little gift box. "Thanks for the cupcake."

"You're welcome. If I don't talk to you tomorrow, have a happy birthday, okay?" He pats my shoulder like I'm his buddy. "Now, go dazzle the executives at S.G. Croft."

The edges of my mouth pull back in a tight-lipped smile. I hate that I've lied to him. But it's better than explaining where I'm really going.

CHAPTER TWO

hurry down the busy street toward the subway. It's almost happy hour. A cocktail sounds perfect. But I can't. I pop in my AirPods to drown out the city. My "Feel Good" playlist booms against my eardrums. With the interview still in my head, I recall the moment Mr. Mustache told me how impressed he was with my knowledge of the firm and its dealings before he became mute. I hope it's enough to outshine the Miss-Mrs. mishap. Maybe I'm overthinking it? Then again, how many failed job interviews does one have to suffer through before the paranoia settles in? This vicious cycle of high hopes and deep plunges is ruthless. I'm starting to wonder if I have what it takes to play big. Maybe my dad's right. What if I'm not cut out for this place? What if I can't see myself clearly?

I swear sometimes I look back on my time at Howard Brothers Group and wonder if I made it all up. Was any of it real? Then, the nearly weightless white box in my hand reminds me that it was, because Eric is real. He's seen firsthand what I'm capable of and he thinks I'd be perfect for Monty Fuhrmann. But will Monty Fuhrmann think I'm perfect for them?

I suck in a deep breath and lift my chin. If they don't hire me, then maybe I'll apply for the analyst job instead. How can they say no to that? The idea of taking a step back just to be hired at the firm spoils in my gut like a bad street vendor hot dog. Gnawing at my lip, I consider my options. The taste of my Fierce Crimson lipstick turns metallic. I wipe the blood from my mouth. It's hard not to stress over every possible conclusion.

As I walk beneath the scaffolding toward the Wall Street station, I watch men in tailored Armani suits walk through the glass revolving doors of the various financial institutions that line the street. I bet none of them have ever had to even consider taking a step backward in their career just to preserve it. I should've known that choosing this life was going to be hard. My first clue was when my dad offered me a position at his firm that was subpar to the opening positions he offered my older brothers. It was as if he wanted to *discourage* me from being an investment banker. I wonder what he would've offered me if I'd been his third son. What would the world offer me if I were a man?

A loud crack thunders overhead and sparkling particles cascade around me. I duck, shielding my head with my free hand, and hurry forward a few feet.

What the hell?

Squinting my eyes, I turn back. A pair of construction workers yells obscenities at each other as they balance on ladders just below a partially lit deli sign. I increase the volume of my music and shake off the nerves. Inside the subway station, the stench of urine assaults my nose as I step onto the platform. Human, not animal.

Awesome . . .

It's almost comical how piss seems to be my life's theme lately. The universe pissing on my dreams, me pissed off at the world, not to mention scrubbing dried piss off toilets.

Yep, that's the big secret. I'm headed off to spend the next few hours cleaning some rich guy's apartment as a housekeeper for Amanda's Maid Service.

Never let another do Amanda's job.

That's their slogan.

Back in the eighties it was *Never let another woman do A-Man-da's job.* For someone who perpetuated the sexist stereotype for so many years, Amanda no longer cleans houses and she definitely doesn't need a man. That woman must be sitting on millions.

Sure, I could've been a bartender or server like the other dream-chasers do in this city. But I've never been good at mixing drinks, and I doubt I have the strength to balance a tray piled with hot plates or the patience to deal with customers snapping their fingers at me like I'm a house butler. Besides, it's so visible. The chances of waiting on an old business contact, or worse, a potential employer, are too high. This job generally gives me anonymity. I rarely clean the same place twice and the clients are never home. Plus, it's something I do well. I learned how to wash windows before I learned to read. My mother, somewhat of a Stepford wife, never made my two older brothers scrub anything except their own bodies. Instead, she groomed me to be her mini-maid. Who knew one day I'd make a mini-career out of it? Then again, the more I have to scrub the remnants off someone else's porcelain throne, the more it feels nauseatingly permanent.

The train arrives at my stop. I push my way out of the crowd and hike up to the sunlit street toward the client's apartment, four blocks away. Men sport biceps-hugging polos, and women show off their Pilates-toned legs in sundresses as they pass by. I slip off my blazer and check the weather app on my phone. Seventy-two degrees. I flip to Boca Raton weather. Eighty-nine degrees. Yikes, it's only early May. This day is too nice to be inside doing laundry and scouring bathtubs. Too bad I can't afford to skip this gig.

It hasn't quite been an hour since my interview, but I can't help checking my email.

Stay positive, Delia.

Who knows? Maybe there's an offer from HR asking if I can start tomorrow. Wouldn't that be a miracle? I hold my breath but not for long.

Nothing from Monty Fuhrmann.

Nothing from anyone.

A sigh escapes my lungs, and I change the playlist to something more somber. Only two more blocks to go. Good thing because these heels are starting to piss me off too.

The luxury apartment building casts a towering shadow while the doorman's gloves are blindingly white. He gives me a respectful nod as I step inside. Must be nice having someone there to open doors for you. I need three keys just to get inside my fourth-floor walk-up apartment. Then again, the hike gives me killer calves. The clack of my pinching pumps ricochets off the glittery granite walls as I walk along the marble floor. Every crystal dangling in the chandelier above the reception desk is pristine.

"Good afternoon, miss," the clerk says.

He knows I'm a *miss*.

I set last season's Versace sunglasses on the granite counter. "Hi, I'm from Amanda's Cleaning Service, here for apartment 29A."

He does a double take. "*You're* the cleaning lady?"

This guy has no idea how much I share his incredulity. Still, I hold my head high, clenching my jaw to the point of a toothache. "I prefer the term *cleaning professional*."

"My apologies," he says. "Most women I see going up to that apartment look more street professional and less Wall Street *professional*."

"I was a Wall Street professional and I'd like to be one again soon," I say, frowning.

His gaze drifts as he shakes his head. "I know the feeling. I used to run a gallery. Now I'm lucky if I make it to an art show."

"Sorry to hear that." And I am sorry. People like us come to New York to live out our dreams of grandeur. Has every person in the service field arrived there by default?

"Can I see your ID, please?" he asks. I hand him my New York driver's license, which I use more for drinking than driving. While he checks the card against his computer screen, my eyes wander back up to the glistening chandelier. Its light dims and amplifies like a slow pulse, struggling to regain its full glow.

"Elevators are on the left."

I return my attention to the man behind the desk as he slides a set of keys across the cold stone counter and motions down the hall. "Thanks. Good luck with the art gallery thing."

His dimples appear, but there seems to be little hope in his eyes. "Stay positive, right?"

I give him a thumbs-up with a matching smile, managing to delay my eye roll until only the elevator doors bear witness.

The twenty-ninth floor has only two apartment doors: 29A and 29B. Each must be enormous. I knock before entering the space, just in case. Light from the massive windows fills the airy apartment. I squint through the glare of the late-afternoon sun, taking in the view of the tall mirrored buildings; the Freedom Tower stands out above them all. With so much sky, this view is even better than Mr. Mustache's. Whoever lives here doesn't share my worries. I make my way into the kitchen, where it reeks like the breath of a drunk. The island bar top is littered with empty bottles of tequila. The rims of the margarita and shot glasses are garnished with smudged lipstick. Looks like Siren Red and Malibu Barbie Pink. Hmm, a brunette and a blonde. How nice.

I wipe my hand along the countertop. Tacky. Just like this filthy-rich display of excess.

"Must've been a wild night," I grumble, searching for somewhere else to place my Gucci briefcase. That sticky shit would definitely lower the resale value. The living room couch looks more like a hamper than an expensive piece of leather. A damp towel, boxer briefs, a guy's tank top. Bikini one, bikini two.

Who the hell is this guy?

Not knowing what other sticky shit might be lurking, I park my Gucci safely at the front door. I pull out an oversized shirt, leggings, and a pair of tennis shoes and change in the hall bathroom. Holding my breath, I lift the toilet seat. Luckily, no leftovers in the basin. Just dried pee splatters. Typical. You'd think an adult American male would have enough practice to make a clean shot.

Guess they can't all be marksmen. Then again, why would they be if they never have to clean it up?

Time to save the Gucci from eBay.

I slip in my earbuds and blast my dance mix. That's the one thing I like about this gig. I can cut a rug and vacuum it at the same time. Not to mention, shakin' off all the rejection by shakin' my thang is way better stress relief than drowning in cocktails. I bust out my best Beyoncé booty quake as I shake my way to the sofa, grabbing the stray garments and following the trail of dirty laundry into the bedroom. Bopping around with a mound of clothes piled high in my arms, I almost miss the familiar face in the carefully arranged photographs on the bookcase.

I gasp, letting the laundry fall at my feet.

It can't be. Can it?

I pull out one of the heavy frames for a closer look. That thick dark hair, that big toothy smile, and those coffee-brown eyes could only belong to Todd-freaking-Fairbanks, the founder and CEO of Ezeus. Either he has a twin that no one's ever heard of or I'm cleaning the tech millionaire's apartment.

Holy shit.

My hands tremble as I replace the photo exactly where I found it. I retrieve my phone from my pocket. Eric's never going to believe this. Wait! Shit. He knows nothing about Delia the maid.

I mean Cleaning Professional.

I tug out my wireless earbuds and listen for Fairbanks in case he snuck in. Nothing but the sound of my own breath. I scoop up the fallen clothes and tiptoe around on the pale maple flooring.

No sign of him. Or anyone else.

I exhale a sigh of relief and a little prayer that he doesn't return before I leave. I've dreamed of meeting Todd Fairbanks. Introducing myself as his housekeeper is not what I had in mind. When I close my eyes I can see it—me working for Monty Fuhrmann, dressed in an expensive tailored suit and shaking Todd Fairbanks's hand from across a conference room table, both of us congratulating ourselves on a successful deal. It's like a clear memory. Everything about it, from the fluorescent lights to the smell of freshly printed pitchbooks to the touch of a firm hand against my own. But his underwear, six inches beneath my nose, brings me back to reality.

After hours of dusting and scrubbing and loathing, I take in an exhausted breath. A mix of lemon-scented cleaner and bleach lingers in the air. I pack my earbuds neatly in their plastic case and tuck them into my briefcase. Wouldn't it be great if this were the last apartment I ever cleaned besides my own? I chew my lip as I open my email, hoping to find that the answer to that question is a resounding yes, yes, oh, hell yes! Just imagine, cleaning Todd Fairbanks's apartment on Wednesday then working on his company's IPO on Friday.

Still nothing from Monty Fuhrmann.

I pick up my briefcase and spot the little white cupcake box on the floor. It's as if it was hiding behind the leather bag, not wanting to admit that tomorrow I'll be another year older and worse off than I could've imagined at this point in my life. I grab the box and peek inside. My mouth waters at just the sight of the deep dark chocolate frosting swirl and specks of crumbled cake.

How did Eric remember my birthday, let alone my favorite

Brooklyn blackout cupcake? I spot the unlit birthday candle lying inside and blush at the idea of him singing "Happy Birthday" to me in front of his coworkers. I should've let him do it. Only a guy who likes a girl would do something like that, right? Maybe Eric's onto something and my luck is about to change. Maybe this is the year I'll get everything I want.

I pull at the door handle but then let it go. This is Todd Fairbanks's apartment. If I don't get the job at Monty Fuhrmann, this may be the closest I ever get to him. I shift my glance between the cupcake box and the gorgeous apartment.

Why not? I deserve a break.

I walk back into the kitchen, setting aside my phone to ready the cupcake. Pulling open drawer after kitchen drawer, I finally find a lighter.

Aha!

With a flick of the spark wheel, I light my little birthday candle, knowing exactly what to wish for. Not that birthday cake wishes ever come true. If they did, I would've married Lance Bass before I got my first period.

But seriously, why should I have to *wish* for what I want, anyway? Especially when I've done the work. I've shown up fierce. Haven't I proven myself? Is it too much to ask to get what I've earned? Deflated, I look out the window at what seems to be an arrangement of glittering stars. The cityscape of lit windows and buildings comes into focus. And if I don't get a real job soon, I might just throw myself off one of them.

Too dark, Delia. Get some perspective.

I shake away the thought and remind myself to be *positive*. This is New York after all. Anything can happen.

Melted wax bubbles over the edge of the candle as the wick burns in a mesmerizing flame. With a slow, deep inhale, I wish from the bottom of my heart that somehow I can get a job at Monty Fuhrmann tomorrow. Not just any job but a job I truly deserve. I force a gusty exhale and the lights go out.

Not just the candlelight. All the lights.

"Huh?"

I blink a few times and focus on the window. The entire city is just as dark as the apartment. Pitch. Black.

It's a blackout.

My palms grow sweaty and my heart begins to race as if I'm being suffocated by the city's shadow. I scramble to find the lighter, but instantaneously the room is bright again. The city's awake, barely skipped a beat.

Okay. Definitely time to call it a night.

I grab my cupcake and chuck the box in the garbage before heading out the door. I walk toward the elevator but then stop short. It could've been a fluke power outage, but who wants to risk getting stuck in an elevator, even a Class A model? Glancing around the hallway, I spot the entrance for the stairs. At least I won't be going *up* twenty-nine flights. My Gucci and I make it all the way down without incident and trek the well-lit journey down to the street. Heading uptown, pedestrians pass by, seemingly unconcerned about the momentary blackness. Probably all natives, such a steel-nerved bunch. I pass by the subway entrance. Don't want to get trapped in that tube either. The walk will do me good. Thank God I'm wearing sneakers.

What a weird day. It's like there are all these elements in my life that are the right ones, but for some reason, they're all misplaced. What would it take to sort them out? A bold gust of wind stirs the litter on the pavement and ripples through my T-shirt, sending a chill through my body. I pick up the pace and swipe my finger across the dark frosting. The sugary cream ignites a rich sensation on my tongue, instantly easing the tensions of the day. Maybe I just need more chocolate in my life.

I take the last bite as I approach my small apartment building. My keys jangle in my hand and I unlock the first door, and the second, then trudge the three flights of stairs up to my floor. The chatter of the evening news seeps through a neighboring door. Across the hall, laughter bellows from a live-audience sitcom. A dog yips and growls as I pass the unit next to mine. I slip the third and final key in the dated brass doorknob and step inside. My roommates, Regina and Frankie, are sprawled out on the living room rug. Accompanying them is a half-empty bottle of cheap red wine.

Perfect. I can use a glass.

CHAPTER THREE

H*ola, chica*," Frankie sings, lying on his stomach and turning the pages of *GQ*.

"Hey, guys." I step over his legs to the only clear space in the living room.

"You need to catch up," Regina says, propped up with a couple of pillows and texting singlehandedly. "There's a glass here with your name on it."

It's been almost three years since Regina and Frankie found this place. Regina told me about it one night when we were all out dancing. Well, more like shouted the details over the booming club beats—three bedrooms *with* closets, close to the subway, and totally affordable if she could find a third renter. Regina and I had been clubbing together since college, but as we embarked on our big-girl Manhattan jobs, we became true besties. She knew I was in a rough roommate situation and said that Frankie and I were her only friends that she would ever consider living with. For the longest time, I thought she and Frankie were siblings, sensing an unconditional love despite their incessant Spanglish bickering. Turns out, they're distant cousins who became best buds when Regina's family moved into the same Brooklyn apartment building when they were thirteen. So I figured any family of Regina's could be family of mine.

After scrounging the money together to get the place, we couldn't afford to go out dancing for a while. So we splurged on a few bottles of Two-Buck Chuck and drank them out of mismatched wineglasses on the living room floor. Since then it's become a regular ritual, and lately, the highlight of my week.

"After the day I've had, I'm gonna need a bigger glass," I say. My feet throb as I pull off my tennis shoes and let them fall to the worn wood floor. "I schlepped my ass all the way from Tribeca." I tug my ponytail loose and plop down on the small spot between them on our sangria rug. Can't remember if that's the original color or just a giant stain from actual sangria.

Frankie's eyes bulge. "You walked? As in too broke to afford the subway?" My lack of income makes Frankie nervous since neither he nor Regina can help cover my part of the rent. Even if they wanted to. Not that I would ever ask.

"No. As in avoiding getting stuck belowground."

They shoot me strange expressions.

"Because of the blackout . . ."

"Blackout? What blackout?" Regina asks. Not an ounce of recognition on either of their faces.

I pull my leg in, kneading my thumbs into the ball of my foot.

"It happened about forty-five minutes ago. I thought the entire city went dark for a minute."

"Not here." Regina's eyes return to the small screen in her hands.

"I doubt you would have noticed," I tease and Regina turns a deaf ear.

Frankie nudges me. "Hey, how was the interview today?"

"Same as all the others."

"Really?" Regina twists her mouth and glances up from her phone. "But you were so prepared."

Education, preparation, and hard work are *supposed* to get you where you want to go, but I'm beginning to think it's not really about my efforts. I grab the bottle of wine and inhale the fruity, dry aroma before taking a drink. Not bad for six bucks. "It gets worse."

"Aw, what happened?" Frankie pushes his magazine away and settles in next to me, draping his arm over my shoulder. I curl into his plushy side. The sterile smell of exam rooms lingers on his black scrubs.

"I'm gonna need more wine before I can talk about it." I clutch the bottle close to my chest.

Regina and Frankie exchange looks. "I'll open another bottle," Frankie says and heads to the kitchen.

"But you got to see Eric, right?" Regina asks.

The sound of his name is better than another slug of wine. I tuck my hair behind my ear, doing my best not to blush. "Yeah, I saw him."

Regina sits up, swats me on the shoulder, and shoots me *spill it* eyes. I pretend to read the alcohol content on the vineyard label while her laser stare burns into me.

I shrug. "What? There's nothing to tell."

"Really?" The corkscrew squeaks as Frankie yanks it from the bottleneck. "Nothing?"

Regina leans in, holding up her glass, and he tops it off.

"Maybe a little something."

They freeze, gawking at me like I've just told them we banged in a Monty Fuhrmann bathroom.

"It's probably nothing," I say, because it *is* probably nothing more than a friendly gift.

As if on the edge of her seat, Regina yells, "Out with it, woman!"

I take a nice long sip from the bottle to ease my Eric-jitters. "He bought me a cupcake."

They gasp.

"For my birthday."

Another gasp. "Oh my god." Regina's grinning like it's *her* birthday. "And then . . ."

"That was it." My gaze trails off, thinking back to the moment he looked into my eyes. "It was sweet."

"Yeah it was!" Regina says. "These days we're lucky if we get more than a happy birthday text. I think he likes you."

I shake my head, pulling myself down to reality. "I don't know. I mean, if he does, then why doesn't he just ask me out?"

"*You* like him and you haven't asked him out," Frankie says.

And I'm never going to.

Regina shoots me a smug smirk. "Exactly. It's not like you to hold back from what you want. I don't understand your hesitation."

"Because he's not just some guy. He's one of my best friends. I don't want to jeopardize that if he doesn't feel the same way."

Frankie slowly shakes his head. "It's a dating stalemate."

"Well, one of you guys needs to man up so you can get it on," Regina mutters into her wineglass. Some people get sympathy pains. She gets sympathy sexual frustration. My dry spell *is* beginning to border on revirginization.

"What kind of cupcake was it?" Frankie asks.

The best kind. "Brooklyn blackout from Three Little Birds Bakery."

Regina smirks. "He went all the way uptown just to get your favorite cupcake. And he remembered your birthday." She shares a look with Frankie. "Oh, yeah. You should ask him out."

"No," I say and press my bottle to my lips, wanting to chug the whole thing.

"Delia." Regina sits up straight, commanding my full attention. "If you're going to get out of this sex slump you've been in, you're gonna have to grow a pair!"

"I have a pair!" I cup my free hand around a breast. "So far they're not helping." In fact, lately they seem more like a liability.

She leans back on her pillows and shoves me with her perfectly pedicured toes. "I'm talking about growing a pair of balls. Have some damn confidence."

"Pff! I have confidence." I think back to Eric's sobering word. *Deflated.* Does everyone see that? My roommates? The man across the mahogany desk?

"Mm-hmm," she mutters through pursed lips.

I sink down, leaning against our narrow gray couch. "It doesn't matter anyway. Chances are I'll be leaving New York and I'll probably never see him again. Except on Instagram." The cold reality settles in. Maybe I should just admit that I tried and I failed. "Let it sting," my dad would say. And it does. Like a fucking swarm of hornets.

I throw back another swig. "Enough about me. How was work for those of you employed in your chosen fields?"

Frankie fills his glass to a modest six ounces. "Hmm, I got to assist in a stapedectomy today. It was really cool," says the third-year ENT resident.

"I sat in on a pitch for VP Barbecue," says the junior marketing executive.

My mopey mouth must be so dim compared to their self-satisfied smiles. "I got to wash Todd Fairbanks's dirty underwear today," I say with a mocking tone.

Regina springs up, splashing wine on her patterned leggings. "Are you serious?"

I tilt my bottle in the air.

"He is so cute. Can you hook me up? I could really use a lover right now." Frankie sends me a wink.

"A lover?" I let out a small chuckle.

He shrugs. "It's just a word I'm trying out. What do you think?"

"I don't think you're his type."

"Why not? I'm a lovable, smart doctor. Plus, with his cash, we could have a very satisfying shopping spree. I could dress him *and* undress him."

"Get out of that polo and into my bed," Regina chimes in.

"What I mean is, I don't think he's gay."

He makes a clicking noise through crooked lips and rolls his eyes. "Whatever. All the good ones are straight."

"What are you talking about? This is New York. All the good ones are gay." Regina flashes her purple-stained teeth and I imagine mine are beginning to have the same hue.

"I think it's kinda cool you got to go to his place, though," Frankie says.

"No, you don't understand. Monty Fuhrmann is pitching to Fairbanks this week. Eric's probably at the office right now working on it, making a real contribution. I should be part of it too. Instead, I'm cleaning the man's toilet. I mean, what the fuck!" The frustration of every closed door from the last four months culminates in my clenched fist. I slam it on the coffee table the way I should have hammered it on that man's desk. It does little to release my aggravation.

Regina and Frankie fall silent, watching me steadily.

I take a deep breath, hoping it'll fight back my impending tears. "Forget it. I'm getting ice cream." I head to the refrigerator in our poor excuse for a kitchen. That's one area where Florida has New York beat—real estate. For the price we pay for this apartment, we could rent a house that's five times the size and has a screened-in pool. But still, I'd rather be here.

"You're still in the running, Delia. It's not like Monty Fuhrmann said no, right?" Regina's tone is much gentler. Careful.

"They haven't said yes either."

"Well, when was the last time you checked your messages?" Frankie asks.

Knitting my brow, I slice my spoon through the heap of vanilla cream. "A while." I reach inside my Gucci briefcase for my cell.

It's not in its designated pocket.

I dig my hand in another pocket, pulling out my interview

dress and pumps, my research notes and resumes. Pocket after pocket and nothing. My cheeks blaze with prickling heat as the pit in my stomach grows to the size of my Gucci. "Shit. I must've left my phone at Fairbanks's place." I cover my face, groaning. Eric was right about my luck changing. It's worse.

"Ooh, I'll go get it for you," Frankie says. "Where does he live again?"

I give him a sideways look, almost tempted by his offer. "Nice try, but I doubt there's anyone there. The place was empty when I left."

"Here." Regina hands me her cell. "Just call it and see if someone picks up."

I take the phone and dial my number. A picture of Regina and me holding champagne flutes and wearing cone-shaped New Year's hats pops up on the screen. After a few rings, a man with a deep, rich voice answers. "Hello?"

It's him.

Todd-fucking-Fairbanks.

"Hi, this is Delia from Amanda's Cleaning Service. I accidentally left my phone." I shut my eyes tight, bracing myself for the blast of a displeased reaction.

"I figured. You can come back in the morning before eleven to pick it up. My assistant will be here to help you." I release one eye, then the other. The coast is clear. He doesn't sound bothered at all. Actually, he sounds . . . nice.

I bite my lip. "Great, and sorry about that."

"No problem. I think your phone is the only thing that's out of place in this apartment. You did a great job."

Well, at least someone appreciates my work today.

"Thanks. I'll be by in the morning." My finger quivers as I end the call.

Regina reaches for her phone. "Was that him?"

"Yep."

Her thumbs tap wildly on her device. "You just had a conversation with Todd Fairbanks on my phone. I need to tweet that."

"Gina, please don't. This whole thing is humiliating enough without you blasting it to the entire Twitterverse."

She frowns, setting her sidekick beside her hip. "Fine."

Frankie flips through the handful of notes that I tossed out from my Gucci: printed pages of bios, history, news articles, and everything else I could find on Monty Fuhrmann. He mutters something to himself in Spanish, then looks at me. "What's all this?"

"It's part of my prep. The more I know about the company and who runs it, the more talking points I have."

"She means the more brownie points she gets." Regina grins.

"Who's this Ian McKellen–lookin' dude?" Frankie asks, zeroing in on one of the sheets.

I give it a quick glance. "That's Liam Golan, the CEO. They call him the Rainmaker. Worth about eighty-two mil. Runs the company from the Zurich office, where he lives with his third wife and two Great Danes." Hmm, maybe I can try my luck in Switzerland.

Frankie doesn't seem as impressed, and gives me a concerned glare. "Stalk much?"

"I'm not a stalker. I'm thorough because I really want this job." How many other candidates are this well prepared?

Regina snatches my bowl and helps herself to a bite of ice cream. "So you can work next to your boyfriend again?"

My ears tingle at the sound of Eric being called my *boyfriend*. "No, because Monty Fuhrmann is the best in the biz. And I want to be the best." Working with Eric is just icing on the Brooklyn blackout cupcake. "Can we talk about something else?" Please!

"We can talk about why you don't want to celebrate your birthday tomorrow," she says.

I send her a biting stare. That's not what I meant by *talk about something else*. "I'm not really in a celebratory mood."

"I think it's time for Truth or Dare," Frankie suggests.

Now there's a good distraction.

It may be juvenile, but ever since we discovered the Truth or Dare app, it's become a staple in our cheap-wine-on-the-floor ritual.

"Who's first?" I ask.

"Me!" Frankie raises his hand. "Gina, truth or dare?"

"Dare!" she shouts. Someone's getting tipsy.

"I need the phone." He reaches for her cell. I crane my neck to see the screen as he opens the app and hits the "Dare" button.

"I don't know why but I love this one," he says.

"What? What's my dare?" Regina's wide eyes are a little glassy.

"Spell your name with your ass."

She claps and raises her arm, ready for the challenge. "DJ, drop that beat." With a few thumb taps on Frankie's phone, Regina's jam booms through our Bluetooth speaker. She shakes her hips in perfect rhythm. "You ready for the Regina?"

Frankie and I whoop, cheering her on. This one never turns down a chance to rock her rump.

"And it goes like—" The wannabe Fly Girl drops it low, brings it up slow, rolls it around, then pops it right like *hel-lo!* This dare is usually hilarious but Regina makes it look like a hot new move.

"Okay, JLo." I smirk. "You're getting an embarrassing dare next time."

Regina circles her booty in the final letter, finishing strong with a snap of her hip. "Whatever. You know you'd be makin' that *D* and the *E* and the *L* look just as good."

"But not the *I* and the *A*?"

She shrugs, making her way back to the floor. "Eh, can't win 'em all."

Ain't that the truth.

"Okay, Delia, truth or dare?"

I suck in a deep breath and release. "Dare."

She edges over to me on her hands and knees, wine sloshing around in her glass. Her face is so close to mine that I can smell remnants of merlot and vanilla bean on her breath. "I dare *you* to call Eric and ask him out right now."

"No way." I shake my head and jolt up like she's just dangled a scary spider in my face. I'd rather eat a spider right now than tell Eric how I feel. But I'd never say that aloud. Regina might dare me to.

"You have to. You said dare." She pulls me back down to the floor.

"Even if I was going to do that ridiculous dare, I don't have my phone, remember?"

Ha! Gotcha, Gina!

Her mouth puckers like she's not ready to accept no for an answer. "Use mine again." She grabs her phone from Frankie and shoves it in my face.

Uh-uh. I push it out of the way. "I don't have his number memorized. It's saved in my phone." In truth, I know his number by heart. I know everything about him by heart.

She gives me an incredulous look. I know she'd love nothing more than to see me call Eric and confess my love like an eighth-grade schoolgirl.

"Fine." Regina violently pokes her finger into my shoulder. "You got lucky this time, Reese. But as soon as you get your phone back, you're doing it."

I swallow hard and hope that she forgets about it by the time the sun comes up.

"Okay, Frankie. Truth or dare?" I ask.

"Dare," he says with a goofy smile and drooping eyes.

I search my brain for something fun, but can't think of anything good. "I need the app." I grab Regina's phone and select "Dare." A request pops up on the screen. "Ooh, this'll be fun."

"What?" Frankie grins before taking a sip from his glass.

I raise an eyebrow. "I get to text anyone in your contacts . . . from your phone."

"I hate this one." He groans and hands over his unlocked device. "Just don't get me fired."

Yeah, right. All we need is two roommates who can't pay their rent next month. "Don't worry. I'll go easy." I scroll through the list of contacts until I find someone that I *know* can take a joke. Someone who's joined us for a drunken Truth or Dare or two.

"Who are you texting?" Frankie bites the edge of his bottom lip.

"Your sister."

"What did you send?"

I hand his phone back. " 'I love you. And I need to borrow fifty bucks.' "

"She's gonna think it's real."

"Exactly, I could really use fifty bucks." I send him a playful wink even though it's no joke.

His expression softens as he turns to Regina. "Truth or dare?"

"Truth." She smirks playfully and I motion a yawn. Regina has very few secrets.

"Why did you *really* leave your job at MAD NY?" He glares at her as if he's prepared to challenge her answer.

She takes a slow sip, mirroring his stare. "I told you, I wanted to work for DF Bay."

Frankie doesn't blink. "Yeah, but nobody believes that."

MAD NY is the premier ad agency in the city, a dream job for any aspiring executive. It's pretty much the investment banking equivalent to Monty Fuhrmann.

Regina purses her full lips and shifts her eyes to the corner of the room. "Well, it's true."

Actually, it's not.

That's why no one understands it. Except for me. I know the real story. But it's top secret.

Regina shrugs. "All right, Delia. Truth or dare?"

I gulp down the last of my wine and set the empty bottle aside. My chest warms and my lips begin to tingle. A belly full of wine and a single cupcake leave me in a very honest mood. "Truth."

She takes a moment to focus her eyes on the phone and reads from the bright screen. "If you could change anything about yourself what would it be?"

I'd have a job, duh.

But what happens when that firm has another stint of layoffs? Then I'm back to square one. Back to being the woman all the firms pass up for a man.

"I'd have a dick."

"Huh?" Regina and Frankie look half-startled and half-confused.

"Yeah, I'd be a man."

Frankie holds his hand over his heart, seeming to hold his breath. "Are you coming out to us right now?"

"No." I shake my head. "But think about it. If I were a man, I'd have a job. A goddamn good job. I'd be ascending the corporate ladder and making boatloads of money. More than my female counterparts, by the way. And I wouldn't have to apologize for it. To anyone. I could have sex, so much sex, just rackin' up notches on my bedpost, and no one would call me a slut. I could be powerful and intimidating without being labeled a bitch. I could be the best and they would let me. I'd finally have their fucking respect."

My friends gawk, slack-jawed.

"Wow, Delia. I had no idea you had such penis envy." Regina shakes her head slowly.

Frankie wraps his arm around my shoulders and pulls me in. "She doesn't have penis envy. She's just depressed because she hasn't had a real job in months."

Regina rolls her eyes at him. "Yeah, because she doesn't wear a tie to the office."

"It makes no sense. If I were shit at my job then I'd understand, but I'm not. I'm really good at what I do. I can do it the same or better than anyone else, but they cast me aside because I'm a woman. It's not fair!" I squeeze my fists into tight balls of rage. My eyes begin puddling with tears. Unfortunately, the heat of my anger isn't hot enough to burn them away.

"Damn it! Why do I always cry when I'm pissed off?" I sob.

They sit on either side of me, patting my back and pouting their lips.

"Because you're a girl," Frankie says.

"Frankie!" Regina smacks the back of his head with one of her pillows. "Don't listen to him."

"You know what I mean. Being emotional isn't a bad thing." Frankie hands me a tissue and I snag it, wiping my wet cheeks. "But you're going to fuck up your contact lenses if you keep crying."

"You know what I think, Delia?" Regina says. "You're the Pink Power Ranger."

"What?" Pink Power Ranger?

She's drunk.

"Yeah, you're the Pink Power Ranger. You see, the Pink Ranger is just as powerful as the other Rangers, but no one takes her seriously because her uniform's pink. When really, she can kick everyone's ass."

"I'm sorry, but what does this have to do with a nineties kid show?" Frankie cuts in.

My tears come to a screeching halt. "She's right. I'm the Pink Power Ranger."

"Exactly, girl!" Regina snaps her fingers, letting her Brooklyn accent out the way she does when she's feeling righteous. "All you need is the right opportunity to slay the enemy and show that pink deserves respect."

I take a deep breath, wipe mascara from under my eyes, and ball my fists under my chin. "And what if I can't?"

Regina's brown eyes lock with mine. "What are you talking about? Not for nothin', haven't you gotten this far?" She's right.

I'm still here. I shouldn't throw in the towel yet. Anything could happen.

I muster a smile and nod.

"That's my girl! You know what you need?" She clicks away on her phone. "A shake-it-off!" A second later, the rapid taps of a drumbeat boom through the speakers. Ah shit, that's my jam. I lean into the rhythm, soaking up the kind of feminist anthem that would be the perfect companion to the Pink Power Ranger showing her enemies who's boss.

"Oh, yeah!" Frankie raises his glass and hops up. Regina joins him, bouncing her shoulders and pulling me to my feet. I roll my shoulders back, letting my problems roll away with them. My roommates sing along with lyrics that light a girl's soul on fire and a beat that makes me wanna march over to Monty Fuhrmann and take no prisoners. My tension releases with every shoulder shimmy and booty shake. I let the frustration fuel my intensity, and the more my pulse elevates, the more I can see myself in that moment. I feel the wine buzz tingle my skin as I shake my hips like there's no tomorrow.

"Get it, Queen D!" Frankie roots me on. We each dance with our own flavor at arm's reach in our tiny living space, the same way we do at a packed nightclub. We belt out the chorus—Regina and I take the high parts and Frankie takes it low. Literally, he's twerking on all fours. I throw my head back in a laugh, feeling so much freer than when I walked in the door. By the looks of it, I wasn't the only one who needed a shake-it-off. We all pop into our final poses on the last note of the song like we're a dance crew— the Wednesday Night Winos!

"Feel better?" Regina asks, catching her breath.

I wipe a little sweat from my forehead. "Hell yeah, I'm ready for anything now."

After another bottle and another hour laced with truths and dares and dance breaks, I stumble off to the bathroom and scrub the purple off my teeth. Struggling to steady my finger, I remove my last pair of contacts, which I've been wearing for two months to save a little cash. My vision is so bad that I can hardly make out the definition of my face. Better that I don't get a good look at myself in this state anyway. I shut off the light and make my way down the dark hallway to my room. Regina's and Frankie's doors are closed for the night. I crawl into bed and rustle my achy legs under the cool covers.

The ceiling looks as fuzzy as I feel, and I exhale slowly, my body still buzzing from the wine. I glance at the clock on my nightstand. Only thirty-seven minutes before it's officially my birthday.

My eyelids grow heavier than my thoughts. And the light goes dark.

CHAPTER FOUR

lift one eyelid just long enough to see that it's 6:32 a.m. My bladder begs me to get up but I ignore it, letting my lashes fall for
one last moment of sleep. I snake my arm out of the covers and
reach for my cell but only find my glasses. The frames pinch my
temples as I slide them on. They're not usually this tight, but I'm
not usually this hungover. Looking through the lenses is like peering through a glass bottle. I pull them off my face and stare up at
the ceiling. I can make out every indentation in its swirly texture.
In fact, everything is strangely clear in the soft shades of morning
light.

Shit. I thought I took my contacts out last night.

And my phone is curiously missing from its usual spot on the
nightstand.

Wait. Oh, yes, it spent the night at Todd Fairbanks's apartment. Lucky-ass phone. I, on the other hand, am clearly an un-

lucky hot mess. My sleepy consciousness begins to flood with flashes of last night's Truth or Dare dance party and wishing on a single candle.

Today's my birthday.

The thought of it blares in my head like an early-morning alarm—the kind of alarm you set to catch a five a.m. flight at JFK. *Hurry up! You don't want to be late!*

If it weren't for being without a salaried job with benefits for the past four months, I'd be right on time.

"Happy birthday, Delia," I mutter, an unrecognizable baritone vibrating my ears. I sound like shit. How much wine did I drink last night?

I take a deep morning inhale. The odor of oxidized grapes seems to be seeping through my pores. Gross.

I shut my sleepy eyes again, wishing the day away.

Come on, Delia. Remember positive? Remember confidence?

My eyes creep open. Okay, I'm gonna do it. I'm gonna drop this deflated bullshit and embrace my inner kick-ass Pink Power Ranger. Mainly because I really need to pee. I let out a yawn, flexing and tightening my muscles. Regina's right, this mind-over-matter thing might just work. I'm sensing an unusual strength this morning.

A sort of tingly sensation buzzes in my crotch. I reach under the sheets, grabbing at what now aches with a light pressure, and touch something . . . hard?

What the fuck? Did I take the wine bottle to bed with me?

My eyes fly open and I throw off the covers, staring down at my body. My tiny night tee clings to my torso like a second skin. And a rod inside my pink panties stands at attention.

Is that a . . . ?

No.

I gasp and hold my breath. This isn't my body.

I shoot out of bed like a blast from a Roman candle and hurry to the full-length mirror hanging on my closet door. A shriek rivaling that of a horror movie scream queen escapes my lungs. Except it sounds like a scream king. I cover my mouth with thick-knuckled fingers. My heartbeat ticks like a time bomb about to explode as I catch more glimpses of the figure in the mirror through rapid blinks.

Man, oh, man.

I lean toward the reflection and rub my hand over large pores and a George Michael–style five-o'clock shadow. Is this my face?

"Holy fuck!"

I shake my head and jerk back. No. This can't be. I crouch down, trying to conceal this *male* body in *my* tiny cotton tee and even tinier panties, but there's nowhere to hide. "No, no, no, no, no, no . . ." My breath turns quick and shallow.

I dash under the covers, gripping the edge of the sheet and shutting my eyes tight. "It's a dream. It's only a dream. I'll wake up any second. Wake up, Delia. WAKE THE FUCK UP!" I push the blankets off, but there's still a cock-sized bulge in my panties practically crowing cock-a-doodle-doo!

That is *not* the wake-up call I was hoping for.

"Ohmigod, ohmigod."

There must be some mistake.

Rushing to the bedroom door, I peek my head into the hall. The apartment is still and silent. I scurry to the bathroom, locking the door behind me. My giant hands tremble as I examine all the bottles on the sink. Does Frankie have some medical-grade magic potion that I used by accident?

No, that's crazy.

But so is waking up with a dick in place of my vagina. And my boobs! I press on my flat, hard chest. Where are my squishy boobs?

My bladder pleads with me, as if it's detected the toilet two feet away. Seat's up, suggestively saying, "Pee in me. You know you want to," while my bladder screams back, "I do, I do, I really do!"

But I can't!

Squeezing my groin, I pony around the plastic bottles that I tossed to the floor.

No. I don't want to. If I pee with a penis, then it's not some drunken dream. It's real.

"Ohmigod, what's happening to me?" I suck in a deep breath and hold it long enough to feel faint, then my stinging bladder jolts me to exhale.

Fuck it. But I'm not gonna look.

I keep my eyes fixed to the cabinet above the toilet. My petite panties cling to my hairy thighs and I tug at the penis, my penis, and aim at the bowl the best that I can. It shoots out like a water gun in the hands of a malicious kid, and I've missed the mark by, I dunno, a fucking mile.

"Shit!"

How is any of this actually happening right now?

Before I flood the bathroom, I halt the flow and flip the seat down. Squatting over, I aim my thing into the toilet. Oh my god! If I ever get my vagina back, I'll never complain about cleaning piss from a toilet again. I chew my lip, pissing from a penis like, like . . . like a fucking man! Why did I drink so much last night?

The pee squirts out, pausing in between like a pump. One. Two. Three.

Empty.

What the hell!

I yank the toilet paper off the roll and squeeze my eyes shut as I pat the tip dry. Do guys do this? The yellow water swirls around the basin as I lift my panties back up, but the fabric can't contain my package. I do my best to stuff the soft, sausage-like skin back in like I'm rearranging an overpacked suitcase. How did this fit before? Eww! I just touched a testicle hair. Bleh.

Suppressing my gag reflex, which has been known to trigger around dicks, I grab Regina's bathrobe from the door hook and put it on before pumping soap onto my hands. That's right. There's no reason to be a barbarian even if I am a man. I let my eyes wander to the mirror as I run my hands beneath the hot water. It's the strangest thing. Clearly this face isn't mine, but somehow, I still recognize myself in it.

My mind traces its steps back to last night sitting on the floor with Regina and Frankie—the merlot, the ice cream, Truth or Dare.

If I were a man, I'd get the fucking respect I deserve.

The words from my impassioned speech ring in my hungover brain. I stare at myself in the mirror, wide-eyed and spooked.

Did I do this to myself?

I take it back.

I take it all back.

How am I going to explain this to Regina and Frankie?

Oh, that's right. I can't because I'm stuck in this body with no fucking clue how I got here. Better snatch a pair of Frankie's scrubs from his bedroom floor and escape before they see me. But where will I go?

No cash. No ID. No phone.

No chance in hell.

Okay, Delia, think.

Maybe it's all in my head. It has to be. What if *I* see myself as a man, but everyone else sees me as, well . . . me? Only one way to find out. The door squeaks as I pull it open and peek my head out. Still silent, except for my pounding heart. Creeping down the hall to Regina's room, the extra sixty pounds weigh on me. I lift my toes, stepping lightly, like a ballerina. But my foot hits the creaky wood floor like the hoof of an elephant.

I push Regina's cracked door open with the tips of my beefy fingers. She's lying on her back, snoring like a stuffed-up pug, her long hair covering her eyes like a sleep mask. I reach her bedside and tug my lip with my teeth. It's like I've entered the lion's den. My heart is pounding in my ears like a stampede of terrified prey. This is it. Moment of truth.

I nudge her. "Psst! Regina. Wake up."

She grumbles and rolls over.

"Gina, wake up!" My rich voice escalates.

Regina flinches and looks up at me as if I'm a mangled-faced zombie. That answers that. Reaching for her baseball bat, she somersaults out of bed and positions herself like a wannabe Yankee, her white-knuckled grip around the base.

"Who the fuck are you?" She swings at me.

I dart in the opposite direction. "Regina, stop. It's me, Delia."

"Delia? You better not have hurt her. Delia! Are you okay?" she yells down the hall then points the bat at me like a fencing foil while I dodge her jabs. By the look on her face, I know she'll kill me. Mafia style. "Get out of my room, you rapist!"

"I'm not a rapist! It's me. I woke up like this and I need your help. Please!"

"A rapist and a psycho. I'm calling the police." Her stare holds me in chains as she rips her phone from the charging cable.

I'm screwed. Really fucking screwed.

My hands are frozen above my head. "Wait! Please don't call the police. You have to believe me. I need your help!" How can I expect her to believe it's me when I can barely believe it myself?

"Yes, I'm calling to report an intruder in my apartment." Regina doesn't flinch. Not even for a second. I knew she was a badass bitch, but damn!

"Regina, please. It's me! Delia!"

Go ahead, say it again. I'm sure she just didn't hear you the first two times.

She rattles off our address and my stomach tightens. I'm going to spend my first day with a dick behind bars!

I can't go down like that.

Think fast, Delia.

"I know about the affair with Dixon. Your boss. That's why you really left MAD NY," I blurt out.

She lets her phone drift from her ear. "How do you know that? I only told—"

"Me. Delia."

Regina bares her teeth, cheeks flushed and trembling. "I don't know who you are or how you know my personal shit, but you need to get the fuck out of here now!"

"Regina, please," I say. My arms are as weak as my spirit, and I lower them.

Her eyes widen as she points her bat toward the door. "Now!"

I recoil, turning away. This has to be a nightmare. I'm going to wake up as woman-me any second, tell Regina about it over our morning coffee, and we'll have a good laugh.

"Stop!" she demands. "Leave my robe, you sick bastard."

A gust of anguish and hopelessness sweeps through my body and my eyes begin to sting. I have no recourse. If I can't even get my best friend to believe me, then what chance do I have when the police arrive? With this face, I'll be the pink panty prisoner for sure. I squeeze my eyes shut one last time, urging myself to wake the fuck up from this hellish disaster. My fingers quiver as I let the bathrobe fall to the floor. I breathe out a deep, humiliating sigh and drag my feet forward.

Regina's bat slams against the hardwood and I freeze.

"Delia?" she says, her voice shaky.

I turn back. Her eyes trace my entire frame while the 911 dispatcher hollers through the phone. "Sorry, false alarm. It's my roommate," Regina says and hangs up. The phone slips from her fingers, tumbling near the baseball bat.

She moves closer, gaping, blinking . . . barely breathing.

"Regina?" I snap my fingers in front of her face.

"Oh my god."

"How did you know it was me?" I ask.

She pushes on my chest, spinning me around, then points to a spot above my ass. "Your bird tattoo."

"Huh?" I still have my tattoo? I whip my head around, but she grabs me by the shoulders to face her.

"That's not a Pinterest tattoo. It was custom designed by one of the graphic designers at my old firm for Delia. I mean you." Regina's eyes search mine as if she's looking through a window to see if anyone's home. "How is this even possible?"

I shake my head, feeling my knees buckle. "I don't know. Last night I went to bed and everything was normal. Then I woke up . . . like this."

"No. This is crazy." She pokes around my collarbone and narrows her eyes. "Who are you really? Did Delia put you up to this?"

"Regina, please! This isn't a fucking joke. Or, hell, maybe it is and the joke's on me. I just peed from a penis and it was a literal mess. And I have balls! Like, real balls. This is, like, some real-life Freaky Friday shit!"

Regina's face softens. "Delia's the only person I told about the affair."

"I am Delia, and I never told anyone. You have to believe me." I put my hands over my heart then ball my fists under my chin.

She gasps, covering her mouth. "Oh my god, I know what happened."

"You do? What?" Does she know how to reverse it too?

"Truth or Dare," she whispers.

Is she really asking me this right now? "Regina, this is serious! There's no time for a stupid game."

"No, last night you said if you could change anything about yourself you'd have a dick. And there." Her finger hovers an inch away from my member. "You have a dick!"

"I know what I said." I shield my overstuffed stuff with my hefty hands. "But that's absolutely ridiculous."

"And so is that bulge of yours." She cranes her neck, peeking around.

I step back. "Regina, please!"

"I'm just saying, how else can you explain it?"

"If I knew how to explain it, then I'd probably know how to fix it!" My voice rumbles along the walls.

She cocks her head back. "Guuurl, you sound scary."

I scrub my hands over my face and let out an irritated growl. I don't want to sound scary. I just want to sound like me. The real me.

"Okay, okay. I think I have an idea," she says.

I raise my brow. The next thing that comes out of her mouth better be brilliant.

"Truth or Dare," she says. "We can use the game to reverse this."

"Are you kidding me?" I may have morphed on the outside, but Regina's been transformed into an idiotic preteen. Is this the Twilight Zone? The Upside Down? Make No Damn Sense Land?

"No! Truth or dare?" Regina struggles to make eye contact and digs her nails into my arms, forcing me to look at her. "Truth or dare!" Between the two of us, she's the scary one.

"Truth," I say through gritted teeth.

"If you could change anything about yourself what would it be?"

"I'd have *my* body back." We wait for a moment, glancing around the room and at each other as if something magical is about to happen. "Did it work?"

She glances down at my crotch. "Nope. Maybe you have to go to sleep again?"

"Maybe we're both going nuts. I mean, what was in that wine last night? Or the ice cream? Or maybe it's this apartment. Do you think we have a mold problem that's making us hallucinate?"

Please, God, let it be that.

"I don't think so. Let's get Frankie. Maybe he can help." She picks her robe up off the floor and shoves it at me. I slide it back on. She loops her arm around mine, the same way she does when we shop sample sales on Saturday afternoons. Only now, her arm feels so tiny in mine and I'm significantly taller.

She looks up at me as we make our way to Frankie's room. "Fuck, I never thought I'd see you like this."

"And I never thought I'd have a wiener in my panties."

CHAPTER FIVE

Despite the commotion and the eastern sun glaring through his shadeless window, Frankie's sleeping like a baby. I envy the sweet oblivion on his face, body swaddled tightly in his blanket like he's just finished nursing. He's always told me that doctors can sleep anywhere. I guess they can sleep through anything too.

"Frankie, wake up!" Regina pesters his shoulder like a nagging mother.

His eyes shoot open as he gasps, flinching himself loose from the blanket. "Jesus, Gina. What?" He rubs his eyes, blinking a few times before focusing on us. Regina and an unfamiliar, slouching man in a woman's robe.

"We have a problem." She gestures to me as if the entire situation is obvious. I turn my mouth up into a timid smile and wave like a shy child. What are the chances he'll believe anything we're about to say?

Frankie glances between the two of us, snarling his lip the more he looks at me. "Who's this guy?"

"It's me. Delia." I clutch the worn terry cloth material and hold my breath. His reaction can't be worse than Regina's. Can it?

"Yeah, okay," Frankie scoffs and rolls his eyes. I guess that's better than meeting the end of a baseball bat. "For real, man, who are you?"

"Really, it's me."

He lets out a long sigh and pinches the bridge of his nose. "Okay, Gina and . . . strange guy in a robe. It's too early for pranks."

"It's not a prank!" Regina throws her hands in the air. "This *is* Delia! She woke up in this body and we don't know how to change her back." She spits this out in her Puerto Rican–Italian-Brooklyn accent, which I've dubbed her *cut the shit* voice. It's the equivalent of lighting a dynamite wick. Frankie and I know that when it starts we only have a few seconds to defuse the situation.

Our sleepy roommate seems to forget this fact as he rolls over, pulling the blanket over his head. "I'm not in the mood, guys. Shut my door when you leave."

If I gotta deal with this shit, so does he. Dude needs a wake-up call.

I march over, snatch the covers away, and yank him by his shirt, pulling him out of bed easily. "Damn it, Frankie! I am Delia! Now get up and help me!" My voice roars like a beast. Frankie's eyes widen as he looks into mine and a new sensation ripples through my veins. Power.

I let him go.

Frankie stumbles, catching himself on the wall behind him. "You're Delia?"

"Yes!" Regina and I shout.

He cranes his neck around my broad frame to look at her. "You know this is crazy, right? You really think this is Delia?"

"Trust me, boy. It's her."

My confrontational stance softens. "Seriously, Frankie, it's me."

With his arms folded over his chest, he gives me a suspicious once-over, stepping away. "I'm going to need proof."

"Show him, Delia." Regina nudges me.

My body locks up. "What? Why?"

"Delia, you don't have time to be coy. Just show him already." Her accent flares to life again. I nearly trip over my big, hairy feet as I turn around and lift the robe just enough to flash Frankie the bird on my lower back. His fingers graze my skin. I shy away, concealing my body with Regina's bathrobe again.

Regina shoves him. "Now do you believe us?"

"Woman, you need to keep your hands to yourself." Frankie aims a hostile finger at her and she backs off, mumbling something biting under her breath. He rolls his eyes then narrows his gaze at me, making a scratching noise as he rubs his chin. My hands find my own stubbly jaw and I rub against the grain. Now we're like two zydeco musicians scrubbing washboards. I used to think growing facial hair was my worst nightmare. Turns out growing a penis is.

I reach across my face to a clunky nose, running my finger down the long bridge to the spongy round tip, then up to what feels like furry caterpillars above my eyes.

Frankie circles me like Sherlock Holmes. "It's plausible, but that still doesn't prove that this guy is Delia. You gotta give me something else."

Of course he wants more proof. Any sane person would, let alone a doctor who's trained to question everything. But what more can I give him? It's not like I've got some juicy dirt on him like I do Regina.

Wait a second.

He's the one with dirt on me. My breath sticks to my lungs. Ugh, is this the best I can come up with? I scan my memory again.

Yep, it's all I got.

"Well?" he asks.

I swallow the lump in my throat. Sorry, Regina. "Remember when you caught me replacing the batteries in Regina's vibrator with the dead ones from mine?" This is a strange question regardless, but coming from the tenor of a man, it's even more bizarre. I don't know whether to laugh or cry hysterically.

"I knew it!" Regina snaps her fingers.

Frankie's jaw is practically on the floor, and his rapid sporadic blinking looks more like Morse code than shock. Stunned Spanish seems to spill out of him as he slowly covers his mouth and circles me again, this time like I'm the most magnificent sculpture he's ever encountered. "You really are Delia. How did this happen?" His eyes lock with mine. I can tell he not only believes me, but he recognizes me inside this unfamiliar form. Maybe the same way I did when I looked in the mirror.

I throw my hands in the air. "I don't know."

"Yes, you do. It was Truth or Dare." Regina swats my shoulder, but I barely notice.

"No, this is bigger than that. This . . ." He draws closer, assessing me with awed, Dr. Frankie-stein eyes. "This is a miracle. Divine intervention. Only God himself could do this." Frankie is technically a man of science but still fancies himself a devout Roman Catholic even though he only attends mass for Easter Vigil and Christmas.

"Are you serious? You think God did this?" Regina, on the other hand, renounced her strict Catholic upbringing, probably just to free up her Sundays for eggs Benedict and mimosas.

"You think Truth or Dare did this?" Frankie snaps back.

"You guys, stop! Look at me." When their eyes fix on me again, a woman in a masculine body dressed in a fluffy feminine robe, I instantly regret it. "What do I do now?"

Regina turns back to Frankie. "Maybe you should examine her."

"For what? A zipper that unfastens her male exterior?"

Regina finds his stethoscope on the dresser and tosses it to him. "I don't know! You're the doctor!"

He flares his nostrils and shoots her a cold look as he plugs the ends of the stethoscope in his ears. "Fine. Delia, take off your robe."

I wring the terry sash in my hands for a moment then tug it loose, pushing the warm fabric off my shoulders, letting it fall around my ankles. Regina stifles a laugh. I cross my arms over my broad chest. "This isn't funny."

"You're right." Regina gives my pink panties a hard stare. "This is quite a pickle."

Whether she's referring to the situation or my dick, she's absolutely right.

Dr. Frankie clears his throat and asks me to take a seat. I do so, dragging the sheet across my lap. "Deep breaths." Pressing the cold scope against my chest, he listens to each side then asks me to turn around. "I can't believe your whole body changed except for this tattoo."

Regina peeks over. "Crazy, right?"

"*That's* what's crazy about all this?" I twist my body, but I can't see the ink, my flexibility traded for bulk. Are there any other marks that stuck around? I scan my body as I inhale deeply for the doctor. "Look!" I say between breaths and point to my right shoulder. "This is my big freckle." Glancing at my bare knee, I spot my Alaska-shaped scar. "And this is from an accident on my ten-speed pink-and-white Huffy."

"Shhh." Frankie pulls one of the ear tips from his head momentarily. "I can't hear."

So I'm not completely different. Well, sitting with a sack squished between my legs—that's different. Not to mention uncomfortable. No wonder men are always adjusting themselves. I resist the urge and instead sit still, patiently waiting for Frankie's diagnosis.

"Hmm, well, the skin's the largest organ of the body, and heals the fastest, which pretty much makes it the most resilient, so it could make sense that it survived the change with the least amount of alterations. Your heartbeat's slightly elevated, but everything else sounds good. Have you noticed anything abnormal . . . besides the obvious?"

"Are you kidding? I'm just trying to wrap my head around the obvious." I sweep my hands in front of my body, a body that in some moments feels like mine and in others feels like a foreign invader. "I don't know." I shake my head. "It's difficult to explain. I feel like me, but at the same time, I don't."

Frankie squints in thought as if trying to decipher my dualistic puzzle.

"None of this makes sense. But there is one thing."

"What?"

"My vision is perfect. No glasses, no contacts." My deep voice reverberates in my throat, and I realize I keep waiting for it to go back to normal like the temporary effects of helium.

"Interesting . . ." Frankie pulls out both earpieces and swings his stethoscope over his shoulder.

"Does that mean something?"

He shrugs. "Honestly, your guess is as good as mine. This isn't exactly the kind of thing you read about in medical research." What would they call this in the medical journals? Divine Dick Syndrome?

He instructs me to lie down, then pokes and prods around my stomach, asking if anything hurts. It tickles, so I tense up. "Have you been working out?"

I lift my head and the three of us survey my new six-pack. "Not this hard."

"Nice upgrade." Regina flicks up her brows.

I sit up and catch a glimpse of myself in Frankie's dresser mirror. A chiseled jawline, deep-set eyes, and broad muscular shoulders, the kind that look great in a tank top. Hmm . . . on the hotness scale, Delia's a seven, but male Delia—he's a ten.

"Okay, I'm going to examine your genitals now," the doctor says.

"Want me to turn around?" Regina asks.

I glance up at her, thankful I'm not in this alone. "No, it's fine. We're all in this together now."

"Would you mind removing your . . . panties?" Frankie's cheeks glow a rosy hue. No private parts in the ENT field.

Regina spews a chuckle. "Now there's a sentence I never thought I'd hear Frankie say."

I draw a deep breath and rise from the bed, letting the sheet fall. Shit's about to get *real* real. With my eyes shut tight, I coerce my pink undies down my beefy thighs. My coiled snake is finally freed from its cage.

Ahh, that feels better.

I want to look.

No, I don't.

But I have to look.

My eyes open and I'm instantly drawn to it. Mesmerized by its magnificence. The length. The girth. The veins that ripple down tantalize me in a way I've never experienced as a woman. Elation fills my chest. Is it infatuation? No. It must be love.

Oh my god.

I really am a man.

"Ahh!" I cry, jarring myself out of the wiener trance. Is this why men are obsessed with their pricks?

"I haven't done anything yet." Frankie freezes, his face inches from my jimmy. For a second, I wonder if he's mesmerized by it too.

"Sorry." I shake off the warm and fuzzies about the new man in my life.

Control yourself, Delia!

Frankie feels around carefully. Surely, any second now, he'll be holding my testicles and asking me to turn my head and cough.

Wait. Something feels funny.

He removes his hands immediately like he's accidentally activated a bomb.

Regina barrels over laughing. "You gave Delia a chubby!"

"He did not!" That's what *that* feels like?

"Look." She points, but I don't have to look down to know my main vein is waking up. I can feel it. "Holy shit, are you hot for Frankie?"

"No!" I scramble to pull my underwear up. "No."

Regina can hardly stop laughing long enough to ask, "Then why are you aroused?"

"I'm not aroused. I don't know what happened." Using my hands as dick armor, I feel it relax beneath my fingers. I'm not turned on by Frankie. It was a fluke. A pure mishap. Like the rest of this shitty situation.

Frankie's face turns as pink as my panties. "It's okay. You've never had a penis and you're starting out with a full-grown monster. It's a lot to handle."

"So, what? It has a mind of its own?"

He shrugs. "Sometimes, yeah. Guys usually have it handled by their teens, but you're going to need a crash course in taming it."

"Taming it?" I hold my monster, all lax and bulgy. Girls are lucky. A woman can be hot and horny, on the verge of losing it, and you'd never know it just by looking at her. We don't have to tame anything. Or is it *they* don't have to tame anything? Oh, geez . . .

"Yes." He crosses his arms with the same intense look he got when he was studying for his medical boards.

"I don't want to tame anything. I just want my body back!"

"I know, Delia. But right now this is the body you're in." He shoots a quick glance below my waist then shakes his head. "How is *this* my morning?"

I ball my fists and settle them on my hips. "Oh, I'm sorry, Frankie. Are you having a bad day?"

"I'm just trying to help," he says with a glimmer of guilt on his face.

I release a sigh, knowing that I'm stuck like this. At least for now. I look down at my full-grown beast, all snuggled up in my cotton panties. "Okay, how do I . . . tame it?"

"Simple. The mind is very powerful." Frankie taps his temple. "It won't always seem like it, but your brain can overpower your body. But you have to distract it with something that's the opposite of sex. So, from now on, any time you feel an erection coming on just think about something serious like ASPCA commercials or golf course silence. Sometimes whistling helps."

"So I got to be a fuckin' snake charmer with this thing?"

"In a manner of speaking. You'll find what works for you. Personally, I think about washing dishes because soggy *conflei* floating in watery old milk grosses me out."

Hmm . . . What should I focus on if it happens again? Funerals? Tennis? Toilets? That's it! I'll think about scrubbing dried, crusty pee off a toilet seat. My memory flashes to my own morning piss. The toilet's not the only thing that needs a wipe-down. Being a man might prove harder than I could've imagined. Who knew the dick would be the hardest part? No pun intended.

"Okay, I can't take it anymore. You have to put these on. Your nuts are peeking out of the sides of your panties." Regina tosses me a pair of Frankie's scrub bottoms, and I slip into them. What a relief wearing pants. And these fit perfectly too.

"So what's the prognosis, doc?" she asks.

Frankie clears his throat. "From what I can tell, you're a perfectly healthy . . . person?"

"That's it?" Regina says. "So much for knowing a human biologist."

"I'm an ENT."

"So you don't have any idea how I can undo this?" I ask.

"Yeah, hormones and surgery. That's pretty much all modern medicine has to offer."

"I can google it." Regina raises a finger. "Frankie, hand me your phone."

He scoffs. "What? You think there's an app for this?"

"I think it's worth looking." She stomps over to his nightstand and snatches his device. As much as I doubt the internet's ability to solve this issue, I'll take what I can get. Regina clicks away on the phone, her mouth twisting more and more as she scrolls through. "Yeah, okay. I'm pretty sure this is an isolated case."

Isolated is the perfect word to describe how I feel right now.

"You should come to the hospital so we can run some tests—DNA, hormones, maybe an MRI," Frankie suggests.

Regina jumps in front of me with her arms sprawled out. "Uh-uh, no way, Frankie. She's our friend, not your science experiment!"

"It's not like you have a better idea, Miss Truth-or-Dare-Did-This!"

Their voices rise with every comeback and quickly escalate into loud, passionate Spanglish with wild hand gestures. Regina crosses Frankie's declared boundaries and he karate-chop blocks her hand when it gets too close to his face. The heat of anger and frustration wrestles inside my chest, but this time there're no tears threatening.

"Enough with the bullshit, you two!" I yell. They halt in a way I've never seen before. I could get used to commanding attention like this. "Can we please focus for a fucking second? What do I do *now*?"

"What can you do? You may be Delia on the inside, but on the outside, you didn't exist until today. Other than coming to the hospital with me, leaving the apartment could be dangerous."

He has a point. Who knows what kind of shenanigans I would find myself in if I went out? What can I really do in this city with no identity anyway?

"How can you be such a pessimist?" Regina asks Frankie then turns to me. "The fact that you didn't exist like this before today isn't a bad thing. It's an *opportunity*." She draws out the word with breathy speech like it's a brilliant affirmation.

I rub my temples with the bases of my palms. "An opportunity for what?" If anything, this is an opportunity to hide in the apartment and binge-watch Netflix.

She looks me square in the eyes and wraps her little hands around my biceps. "Delia, we don't know how this happened or how to fix it, but here you are. So own it! You can be anyone you want to be. You said yesterday that you wanted to be a man so you could get the job and respect you deserve. You've earned that. This is your chance. Go out there and use this body to take back what's yours!"

Her words seem to course through my veins, rushing alongside testosterone. I puff up my chest. What *can* I do in this city with no real identity?

Anything I fucking want to.

Regina's right. This isn't just an opportunity, it's *the* opportunity. I don't have to be Delia Reese, unemployed investment banker mopping floors. I can start fresh. Be anyone I choose. Do anything I please. Last night I declared that having a dick would solve my problems. Let's see if I'm right.

And I know exactly what I'm going to do.

But first, I need to be positive.

I nod. "I'm gonna go for it. I'm getting a job today. A job I deserve."

"All right!" She squeezes my biceps in excitement then sends me a wink. "Nice arms, by the way."

"Thanks." I return the wink.

Frankie folds his arms. "I don't know if this is a good idea."

"Relax, Frankie. I got this." And for the first time in months, I actually believe it. "But if I'm going to land a job today . . . I'll need to borrow your best suit." I march toward the closet. He's always sporting the latest trends when he's away from the hospital, allocating a good portion of his budget to fashion. It's why he has imported dress socks but no curtains for his window.

"Wait!" Frankie leaps between his beloved wardrobe and me. "My suits are tailored for me. What makes you think they'll fit you?"

Regina shifts glances between the two of us. "You're about the same height and she fits in your scrubs just fine." We inch closer.

"Well, hold on! Before you go picking through my closet, let's consider something."

"What?" I ask.

"Like, what's your plan? You're just going to roll up to one of those big firms and say, 'I'm a man. Give me a job'?"

Regina clicks her tongue. "C'mon, Frankie, growing a dick didn't make her stupid. Right, Delia?"

"I sure as hell hope not. But he's right. What am I going to do when I get there?" I pace back and plop down on the bed. Being able to see around problems is my specialty, or at least it used to be. We live in a post-9/11, post-every-moment-of-life-on-social-media world. I've got nothing, except a beast to tame.

"Just apply for a job," she says. "See if you get a call back."

Frankie glares at her, still guarding his closet. "How is she going to do that if she isn't even a real person?"

Regina gasps, balling her fists at her sides. "How can you say that? She is a real person!"

"That's not what I mean!"

Regina gets in his face and it spirals into yet another Spanglish screaming match. I slap my hand over my eyes and drag it down to my stubbled chin.

"For Christ's sake, stop fighting!" I roar then suck in a deep breath as they shut it. "I need to think and I can't do that with you two fussing like children."

They lower their heads. "Sorry."

"Okay. So I'm not technically a real person, and even if I create an identity, how long will I be able to keep it up? What if this is who I'll be forever?"

Frankie snaps his fingers. "Exactly!"

"You'll figure it out," Regina says. "What other choice do you have?"

It's true. Survival is a pretty powerful motivator. That's why I've been cleaning toilets. I had no choice then and I have fewer choices now. I'll have to put on Frankie's best three-piece suit over my birthday suit and hope for the best. Whatever the hell that is.

"I'm gonna need a name." I tap my finger on my mouth. Name, name, what's my name? "You guys got any ideas?" I look to them, their eyes already scanning the ceiling.

"How about Cristiano Ronaldo?" Frankie says, batting his eyelashes.

Regina and I shift disapproving glances to one another. I may not look like Delia, but I definitely don't look like Cristiano. "I'm not sure I can pull off sexy soccer player, but thanks anyway," I say.

"Hmm, what if we name you after someone really cool? Who's your favorite male singer?" Regina asks.

"I'm not calling myself Prince."

"What about a family name?" Frankie asks.

I tilt my head. A familiar family name isn't a half-bad idea. My father and my oldest brother share a name, which was also my great-grandfather's name. "Richard. Can I pull off Richard?"

"Oh, yeah," Regina says as if the name fits like a perfectly tailored suit. "We can even call you Dick!"

I drop my head in a chuckle. Figures I'd pick a name synonymous with Dick. "You know, I think I've got enough of that goin' on. Let's just stick with Richard."

"You're the boss. Now what about a last name?"

Might as well keep it in the family. "How about Allen? Like my other brother."

She nods. "Richard Allen. I like it."

"Me too," I say. "What do you think, Frankie?"

His shoulders drop. "It's not bad. I like Cristiano better."

Regina and I exchange devilish grins and move toward Frankie, the closet guard. She narrows her glare and flips her hand in an attempt to shoo him away. He stretches his arms wide across the sliding doors, a bead of sweat falling from his hairline.

"Two against one, Frankie. You really gonna stand in front of your suits all day?" I ask, flexing my muscles like Wolverine. After all, Regina says I have nice arms.

"Fine, but I don't like this." Frankie slides the closet door open and pulls out a tasteful, yet stylish gray Michael Kors. "Come pick out a shirt and tie."

I thumb through the array of fresh fabrics, looking for any basic-colored shirts or ties. It's all pink and orange, yellow and purple. There's hardly any color in my wardrobe. It's all black and gray, navy and tan. "What do you guys think?"

Regina pulls a purple shirt from a wooden hanger. "This one."

It could work. It's the most muted of all the shirts.

Frankie smiles, running his hand along every piece displayed on glossy wood hangers. "I love them all."

A particular pink one tucked between two other pastel shirts draws me in. The last time I wore something this bright was at a frat party. But this shirt is less drunk college chick and more Pink Power Ranger.

"I'll take that one." I select it with my finger. "It's pink, right? I'm not colorblind now, am I?"

"It's salmon." Frankie grabs a matching paisley tie and pocket square. "And you're not putting this on until you take a shower. I don't want you stinking up my clothes."

"Thanks." I wrap my arms around him, giving him a tight squeeze.

He pats my shoulder. "You're welcome, Delia."

I strut my big feet, my little top, and Frankie's scrub bottoms toward the door. "It's Richard now."

CHAPTER SIX

lock myself in the bathroom and let out a heavy breath of relief. My friends not only believe me, but they're being supportive. What would I do without them? I stare at my new mug in the mirror, tracing my cheekbones to my ears with my fingertips, then down my jawline. Trippy. As the reality settles in, my wide forehead throbs from my straight brows to the edges of my temples. I press my palms to the sides of my head and shut my eyes tight. Is my brain on the brink of bursting?

I take in a deep, careful breath and slowly let it go.

Stay positive, Delia. You're still alive. You're not in any *immediate* danger. And you haven't changed species.

The pressure begins to release and I blink my eyes open. Ah, that's better. Accepting this reality might not be so bad.

Okay, Delia, you're in a man's body now.

I can do this. I can act like a man. I have two older brothers, years of experience in a male-dominated field. All I have to do is pretend I'm listening when I'm not, act like I know everything except how to properly sort laundry, and give up looking for the mustard in the fridge after two seconds. I should be able to manage that.

Ugh, if only it were that simple.

The shower faucet feels so much smaller in my hand. The hollow thud of water pellets hitting the porcelain bathtub fills the room. Peeing with a penis was a pretty confronting moment for me, so lathering it up in the shower will probably be just as solidifying. Hmm, maybe I'll use Frankie's Swagger shower gel today. What the hell does swagger smell like, anyway? Such a weird name. I suck in another deep breath, a failed attempt to ease my knotted stomach. It's time. If I'm going to man up, I have to strip down first.

Undressing is frightening and freeing all at the same time. Not to mention fascinating. Me with these abs, these pecs, this pecker. I place my hands on my hips and nod as if approving the new renovation. Surprisingly, looking at the nude version of my male-self is not nearly as disturbing as I'd feared. It's still me in this body. Maybe if I think about it like wearing a costume, it won't be so bad. Even if this getup comes with its own mechanics.

My clear vision takes in the full reflection. I curl in my fists, raising my arms like Arnold Schwarzenegger circa Mr. Universe. It's unlike me to admire myself in the mirror but how can I not? Defined muscles curve around my arms and shoulders as I flex. Gritting my teeth and glaring into the mirror, I let a slight growl escape my lips.

Intimidating.

I like it.

I whip around, twisting my neck. "There's my tattoo."

Yep, totally misplaced on my brawny male body. My ass is sitting in the right place, though. I shake it like a hula dancer. Yesterday, my butt would have jiggled up and down, backward and forward. Today it hardly acknowledges that I'm moving. All right, I could get used to this. I smack the tight flesh, playing my buns like bongo drums, and twirl back around, almost tripping on the bathroom rug. Damn, my feet are ginormous. I lift one at a time, checking out the soles. Seriously, what size are they? Everything is bigger. And hairier—knuckles, nose, ears, knees, eyebrows. I feel like the fucking Hulk.

Steam rises over the clear, pebbled shower curtain. I step inside and let the hot water cascade on my skin. Nice and refreshing. No difference here. It's weird, though, running my fingers through such short wet hair. But I kind of like it; it feels lighter, and I don't have to use as much shampoo. Lathering up my loofah using Frankie's musky body wash, I run the sponge back and forth across my chest and down my arms, getting a feel for my new shape. Not too shabby, unlike my shag-carpeted legs. Ew! I pick up my razor and consider a close shave, but I can practically hear it say, "I don't think so, bro!"

I rinse the soap off my legs, then gaze down at the third one.

"Now, what am I going to do with you?"

My buddy moves slightly as if it's talking back. After everything that's happened, a talking penis can't be that far behind. I've always been curious as to why some, if not all, men talk about their dicks like they're a loyal sidekick. Culturally, we enjoy jokes about guys thinking with their little head instead of their big head. Now that I've spent the morning with one, I'm beginning to see that these things really do have minds of their own. No wonder guys name them. One of my ex-boyfriends called his Moby. Sometimes he'd call it Mobes for short. Hell, I called it Mobes a couple of times too. And now, staring down between my legs, I'm tempted to name my own Moby Dick. Nah, I can't feed its ego like that. It's already out of control.

"So what should I name you? Hmm, Little Dickie?" I ask in the same tone I used when training one of our childhood dogs.

It moves again. Okay, now I swear it's listening to me. And I'm pretty sure it likes the name. So it's settled.

"Ready for a scrub-down, Little Dickie?"

No response this time so I start slow, dabbing it gently with the sponge. So far so good. I should probably really get in there. I'm a cleaning professional after all. I maneuver around all the hanging skin, making sure not to miss a single spot. Sudsy bubbles release from the loofah as I squeeze it, then let the sponge go. My soapy hand is slick and slides easily up and down the shaft. Up and down. Feels kinda nice. Up and down. A tingling sensation shoots to the tip and the soft skin solidifies.

Whoa . . .

The rhythmic motion slowly pumps it up like one of those long carnival balloons. It grows longer and stiffer until it reaches its full potential. My rational Delia-mind is urging me to stop but my new friend likes it. It feels so . . . instinctual.

Geez. Really? I've hardly had this thing for an hour and I'm already playing with it.

Men.

I release my grip, and the hard-on stabilizes on its own. My hard-on. Little Dickie's not abiding by his name at the moment. The shower rinses the suds off my staff and I'm transfixed again. You'd think I'd never seen an erect penis. All memories of various boners forgotten at the sight of my own. What's happening to me? Just yesterday I was in here shaving my legs for the millionth time since I was twelve and now I'm doing this? My mind begins spinning for a split second but then curiosity reins it in. My buddy's enthusiasm isn't the least bit deflated. Resilient little fucker.

A fist bangs at the door, and I jump so far off-balance that I have to grip the tiled wall for support. "Shit."

"Hurry up!" Regina's voice roars. "I need a shower too! My skin smells like spoiled grapes after last night."

I glance down at my flagpole, and the wind's died. "Be out in a minute!" So if piss-stained-toilet-seat thoughts don't keep it tamed, Regina yelling at me is a good backup plan.

Noted.

I towel off like normal, but then ease up the terry cloth around my goodies, treating them as carefully as a fresh manicure. I spent so much time stroking myself in the shower that I completely ignored that squishy scrotum. Yeah, not exactly ready to own that one. It just dangles there like a sack of potatoes with nothing better to do than wait to pull the trigger and shoot. Ugh. I was right to ignore it.

I wrap the towel around my chest and squeegee the steamed mirror with my hand. Oops. No tits to cover anymore. Loosening the towel to my waist, I stare at my naked reflection. My gaze wanders south. The image invokes a memory of the man attached to Mobes. After showering, he would open up his towel and do the Twist, slap his thing around like it was a Chubby Checker dance party on speed. Another way to play with it, I suppose. He'd laugh hysterically. The first time he did it, I humored him with a chuckle. Every time after that, I'd cover my eyes and beg him to stop. It's not like I got out of the shower and jiggled my breasts around to amuse him, or myself. Then again, he probably would've enjoyed that. So weird. It can't be that fun. Can it?

Only one way to find out.

Holding the towel up around my back, I begin twisting my hips and my ding-a-ling smacks back and forth. Smack, smack, smack. My mouth turns up.

Hey, this *is* kind of fun.

I ramp it up a notch, this time thrusting my pelvis and circling my hips, watching my plaything make its own circles in the air. I chuckle. How is this so entertaining? Little Dickie's like my own little puppet. And if I wasn't so determined to get a job, I'd stay here all day seeing what else it can do.

Another forceful fist bangs at the door. "What are you doing in there?" Regina yells, and Frankie mutters something about giving me two more minutes.

"Nothing!" I quickly wrap my towel around my waist before opening the door. I think I'm starting to understand why my brothers spent so much time in the bathroom when they were teenagers. Our poor mother.

Steam floods into the cool hallway. "Finally!" Regina throws her hands in the air and slips past me, slamming the bathroom door shut.

"C'mon." Frankie waves for me at the end of the hallway. "Let's get you some underwear that doesn't make your crotch look like an overstuffed taco."

"Does that mean I shouldn't go commando?" I joke, but he doesn't seem to think it's funny.

"No one goes commando in my suit except for me, got it?"

I raise my hands like it's a stickup. "Got it."

We head back into his bedroom and he pulls out a dresser drawer, revealing neatly filed fabric arranged by color. So many man panties to choose from. Frankie grabs a pair of red-and-white-striped boxer briefs, then flings them in my direction. "Try these."

"Are these your candy striper underwear?" I tug on the elastic band. He rolls his eyes without cracking a smile. That guy could use some shower time.

I slip on the boxers and adjust myself some. They hold all my accessories in the right place. "I am *feelin'* these."

"Nothin' like underwear that fits, huh?" Frankie asks.

"No kidding. My nuts were suffocating earlier."

His forehead wrinkles. "I can't believe I have to lend you boxers because you grew testicles overnight."

"You and me both," I say, patting him on the shoulder. "But thanks. I don't know what I'd do without your underwear."

"We can add that to the list of shit we never thought we'd say. C'mon." He nods. "You're going to need a hairstyle to match my suit."

The next thing I know, Frankie's blow-drying my hair with a boar-bristle brush and running some kind of waxy pomade through it with his fingers. I watch as he swoops it to one side then smooths it out.

"What do you think?" he asks.

I turn my head side to side, checking each angle of my new 'do. "I like it. Is it good enough for Michael Kors?"

"It'll do." Frankie hands me his deodorant stick. "Here."

"I have my own deodorant." I pop off the cap and sniff the solid blue gel. "They say it's strong enough for a man."

He makes a clicking noise with his mouth. "Yeah, and made for a woman. Just put it on so you don't ruin my shirt, okay?"

"Fine." I snarl at Frankie and smooth the deodorant over my underarms. It practically glues the pit hairs to my skin. Gross. Furry legs are one thing, but this? I'll be shaving later tonight. Got to draw the line somewhere.

I cap the container and hand it back. "Satisfied?"

"Mostly."

"Good, because it's time to suit up!" I say and head back to Frankie's closet. A gravelly grumble vibrates in his throat.

After I tuck in the "salmon" shirt and Frankie helps with the paisley tie and pocket square, it's time for the reveal. I step in front of his full-length mirror and take it all in. There's something about a nice suit that makes a man look instantly sophisticated. The tailored fabric and bright colors add a touch of pizzazz. Not gonna lie. I look good. It doesn't hurt that I'm standing a little straighter, keeping my head a little higher. My big head, not my little head.

Regina pops back in the room, half-dressed in a pencil skirt, camisole, and messy topknot. "What did I miss?" She stops short at the sight of me. "Whoa! You look awesome. Manhood is very becoming on you, Delia." She gives me a crisp nod.

"Thanks, Gina. Can you believe how well this fits?" I dust off the sleeves and shrug. "What do you think, Frankie?"

He looks as if I polished off the last sleeve of his Thin Mints. "Michael Kors looks better on you than it does on me."

"That's not true," I say, even though it is. "Besides, it's all about persona. That white lab coat of yours . . . totally hot."

"You think so?" He tilts his head.

"Oh, yeah. Doctors are sexy," Regina adds with a playful shove.

"Thanks, guys."

"So now what?" Regina rests her hands on her hips, ready for a game plan.

"Now I need to update my resume," I say, with a firm finger in the air as I march toward the living room. I grab my laptop off the end table and settle on the couch, curling my legs in and simultaneously crushing my bits and balls. That's not gonna work. I adjust myself up and spread my knees apart some. Regina and Frankie huddle next to me as I pull up the document. *Delia Reese* is typed in bold font across the top. I delete one letter after the other and replace it with my new name, Richard Allen.

Richard Allen, Richard Allen. *Hi there, my name is Richard Allen.* I need to remember that.

My eyes sweep the page of my experience, education, and accomplishments. I know I'm a stellar candidate. That's why these last few months have been so frustrating. It's like as soon as I walk in the room, they can't get past the fact that I have ovaries. Well, Richard Allen doesn't have ovaries. Unless they're bro-varies now.

Here goes nothing.

The hum of the printer sounds from the corner of the room.

"Wait, that's it? You're only updating your name?" Regina asks.

"Yep, that's it."

Frankie raises his brow. "Aren't you worried about them calling your previous employer?"

"Nope."

"Why not?"

"First, when we get that far in the process, they'll ask for my supervisor's name and number. I can figure that out later, along with a million other details. Plus, when Howard Brothers had that merger, a quarter of the staff were let go or replaced. Even if someone randomly called, it would make sense that their records would be a little screwy."

"So in this scenario, the merger's a good thing," Regina considers as she walks to the inkjet and lifts the top copy while the printer spits out the rest.

I never once imagined that my layoff could be helpful. "Yep. Seems like it."

Regina examines the fresh ink then hands the page over to me. "Looks legit."

The name *Richard Allen* printed in black and white makes my stomach flip. A fresh suit, an updated resume, and an unexpected appendage. I'd say I'm fully equipped to take on Wall Street. "Goodbye, Amanda's Maid Service."

"Speaking of, want me to call them and say you're deathly ill or something?" Regina asks.

"Nah." I tuck the finished stack of resumes safely in my faux leather padfolio. "I'm not scheduled to clean until tomorrow. If I survive the day, I'll handle it then."

Usually, I'm the responsible one with all my ducks in a row. Not Regina. I still have my concerns, but there's something about waking up with balls in a world where we revere those who have them that's given me carte blanche. Permission is a positively powerful thing.

"So, what are you gonna do now?" Frankie asks. I get the sense he's hoping I'll wuss out and stay home where his suit will be safe.

"First, I'm going to get my phone back." I pull the strap of my Gucci over my shoulder. Thankfully my beloved briefcase is uni-sex and pairs perfectly with my outfit.

Regina's eyes light up. "At Fairbanks's place?"

"Yep." I step toward the door, breaking in the feel of Frankie's black matte shoes. These are way more comfortable than my best pair of pumps. My roommates follow, encroaching on my personal space. Not that I've had much of it this morning.

"Will you come by the hospital when you're done dropping off your resumes?" Frankie asks.

I shrug. "Maybe. I'll see where the day leads me."

"Check in with us later, okay?" Regina says.

"Sure thing." I turn the brass doorknob. The tarnished surface feels different in my new skin.

"Oh, and happy birthday!" My friends bid me goodbye like I'm their child and it's my first day of school. I step out into the hallway.

Look out, New York. Here I come.

CHAPTER SEVEN

The air seems different. Better. Even the sun seems brighter, illuminating the faces of every pedestrian that passes by. Is it just my imagination, or does everyone seem to have more pep in their step today? Yes, everything's a bit clearer.

A bit more positive.

I don't even crinkle my nose when I walk down into the subway. It's as if someone scrubbed away the usual stench. No more piss. The sliding doors of the subway train open and I hop on a moderately crowded car, immediately grabbing one of the center poles. All of the morning commuters have company—they're scrolling social media or cozying up with a chapter in a book and, of course, all the news nerds have their papers. Why didn't I pick up a paper on the way? Aside from Little Dickie, I've got nothing on me but the stack of resumes in my Gucci. Feet planted firmly, I steady myself as the train begins to move.

One after the other, faces begin to turn up from screens and pages. Why are they looking at me? Should I have gone with a more basic shirt and tie? Not that Frankie has anything like that. Oh, no. Am I changing back into myself again? No. My big, hairy-knuckled hand holds the pole tight. But what if it starts with my face and works its way down? I lower my chin, tracing my fingers along the stubble above my lip. Hmm, what are they looking at? I adjust my pink paisley necktie, trying not to stain the fine silk with the tiny beads of perspiration puddling in my palm.

In my college psych class, we learned about this psychological phenomenon called the Spotlight Effect. It's when you think you're getting more attention than you actually are. Every time I'm alone in a long line at the bank, for coffee, or at Chipotle, I get the sense that people are focusing in on me. This is that. Only way worse.

I stretch my neck, peeking at the other end of the train, and spot some vacant seats in the corner. Walking the city streets with everyone so focused on where they're headed and not who's around them is one thing, but I'm not sure I'm ready to be front and center with this new look. Zeroing in on an empty seat, I excuse myself past a few other commuters. One catches my eye. Her freckles may be hiding behind this morning's *Wall Street Journal*, but nothing disguises that familiar red hair.

"Shannon?" At the sound of my baritone, I slap my hand against my mouth.

Oops.

She lifts her green eyes from their hot-off-the-press focus. Not an ounce of recognition registers in them. "Do I know you?"

Heat creeps up my face and my chest tightens at the sight of my longtime college friend's wrinkled expression. The way I see it, I've got two choices.

Truth.

Or dare.

"Columbia, right?" I rub the back of my neck.

"Yeah." Lifting a single penciled-in brow, she searches my face then finally utters a sound like I've stumped her.

I clear my throat and attempt to tuck my hair behind my ear, but there's nothing to tuck!

Well, nothing up here anyway.

"You want to sit down?" Shannon gestures to the empty seat next to her.

"Sure." I take the seat, instinctually crossing my legs.

Squish.

This fucking ball sack.

Ugh. I cringe quietly to myself and untangle my legs.

The color in Shannon's eyes seems to shift from a dark apprehensive green to a sparkling curious seafoam, and I'm hit with a wave of her citrusy perfume. "What's your name?"

"De—" I start before correcting myself with, "Richard."

"DeRichard?" She lets out a little snicker. "Is that a joke?"

Oh, girl, you have no idea what a joke this is. "No, sorry. It's just Richard."

Her Millennial Pink lips curl into a coy smile. "Well, I'm sure I would have remembered you, Richard." My fiery-haired friend says the name slowly, like she's tasting the syllable with her tongue, finishing off with that ever-so-subtle lower lip tug.

Oh, no . . .

Here I am sitting thigh to thigh with the girl I used to do body shots with to impress douchey college boys and now she's flirting with me like I'm one of them. Come to think of it, aside from the stylish pocket square and matching tie, Richard is totally her type. My stomach knots, and I inch back as much as this seat will allow. "Well . . . I look *a lot* different than I did in college."

"How so? You lost fifty pounds or something?" she jokes.

"More like gained fifty pounds of muscle." And a barbell to boot.

"Well, whatever you're doing, keep doing it."

This might not be my real body but I'll take the compliment. "Thanks. You too. Your skin is glowing." I've got to get the name of her facialist.

"Thanks." Shannon touches her fingertips to her jaw, batting her lashes. "You know," she starts, scrutinizing me again, "I still can't place you. Did we have a class together?"

Same year. Same major. We had a lot of classes together. It's only been a handful of years but it feels like a lifetime ago. Do I even remember a class we had together? Then I see it in my mind—the first week of fall semester, Shannon's slightly sun-burned nose, my glossy new white MacBook, and a professor with patchy tufts of gray hair. I snap my fingers at the memory. "Yeah, remember Financial Reporting with that guy that looked like Fire Marshal Bill?"

"Oh, yeah! Dr. Lawrence." She bursts out with a big laugh and playfully shoves my shoulder, letting her hand linger for a few extra moments. "That's so funny. My friend and I used to call him Fire Marshal Bill. I thought we were the only ones."

We were. "Well, the resemblance was uncanny."

"It really was." Her gaze falls slowly to my mouth, then my chest.

Hey, my eyes are up here!

"So what'd you end up doing after college?" she asks.

"I was at Howard Brothers Group for a while—"

"No way!" She grins. "That's where my friend works. The Fire Marshal Bill friend. Do you know Delia Reese?"

Oh, shit.

My ears begin to burn. It's like I've been caught red-handed. "Um, yeah." I bounce my knee and stumble through a jittery laugh. The truth closes in as if to strangle me with the least-threatening-looking tie on the planet.

Should I tell her the truth? That I'm not Richard, I'm Delia with a dick, and I haven't worked at Howard Brothers Group for months now?

I glance around me, playing out the possibility in my mind.

No. That's a bad, bad idea. Besides, as much as I adore Shannon, she's not really a keep-your-secrets kinda girl.

I'm really going to need another backstory if I run into anyone else I know today.

Or better yet, just keep your mouth shut, Delia.

"Small world, huh?" she says.

So. Freaking. Small.

"So, where are you now?"

"Huh?" I manage with my dry mouth.

"You said you were at HBG for a while, then what?"

Amanda's Maid Service.

Nope. That didn't make the resume.

"Monty Fuhrmann," I say casually, trying it on for size. I think it fits. Even if it is a lie.

"Nice. I'm a trader at the stock exchange." She sits up straight with pride. And she should. She's one of a very small percentage of women who work on the exchange floor. That job never interested me. Too chaotic. But Shannon loves the energy, which she has an abundance of. I should know. Back in the day, she'd keep me out dancing all night just to burn it all off.

"You're a trader?" I ask. The last time I talked to her she was still a trading assistant. A promotion like that is a big deal. Get it, girl!

She leans away and purses her mouth. "What? You think I can't be a trader?"

I blink, shaking my head a little. "Huh? No, I didn't mean . . ."

She glares, watching me squirm. If I tell her I thought she was a trading assistant she'll hear *I'm stalking you* or *Women can't be traders*. What's a man to do in this situation?

Apologize?

That might be a first.

"I'm sorry," I say. "That came out wrong. I'm sure you're great at it."

"As a matter of fact, I am." Her chin lifts and it's clear my apology doesn't penetrate.

My throat is thick with guilt. She must think I'm a chauvinist asshole. But I'm not. I'm just like her. *Was* just like her. The train slows down, and I peek through the cloudy window at the station name. My stop could not have been more welcome. I rise to my feet. "Well, it was nice running into you."

She opens her paper again, giving it her full attention. "See you later, Richard."

Well, she might call me Richard, but she definitely thinks I'm a dick.

Remember, Delia, you're a man now. Or at least that's how the world sees you. I take a deep breath and shake off the run-in. My heartbeat picks up as I climb the steps to the street on the way to Todd Fairbanks's apartment. There's a very good chance I'll meet him today. I wonder what he'll think of Richard. My stomach buzzes at the thought.

Wait. That's not a buzz. It's a tingle. And that's not my stomach. Stopping in my tracks, my gaze falls to my pants. Uh-oh. Little Dickie's awake. I start up again, slowly at first. Meeting Fairbanks is exciting, but is it *this* exciting? Do I secretly want the rich slob to be my lover too?

No, my body's wires must be crossed. Any chance I can invoke the warranty and return it to the miracle store? Walking in this concrete jungle has never felt more dangerous than in this moment. What was I thinking leaving the apartment with a beast in my pants?

You're doing this, so get it together, Delia!

I let out a deep breath and imagine scrubbing dried-shit-colored vomit from a toilet. The closer I get to his building, the more vivid the toilet tales become. It's working. I think Little Dickie's calmed down.

Whew. I shake my head and roll my shoulders back, adjusting my suit before approaching. The doorman greets me with the same respectful nod. I pass the front desk and take the elevator up to Fairbanks's apartment. My heart pounds, hitting my chest harder with every ascending floor. I step onto the floor, wiping my damp palms on my pants as I approach 29A. My hairy-knuckled fist rises as I suck in my breath. Before I can knock, the door swings open.

A woman about my age with long, wavy brown hair and wide-frame glasses winces and steps back. She looks at me like I'm about to sell her a set of steak knives or tell her about the word of Jehovah. "Can I help you?"

"I'm De—DeRichard." Shit! What's so hard about Richard? *I'm Richard!*

"Excuse me?"

"I'm Richard!" I blurt out, extending my hand.

She disregards my gesture and narrows her eyes like I'm a weirdo, which is the understatement of the year.

I clear my throat. "Sorry, are you Todd Fairbanks's assistant?"

"Yes." She drags out the word in a leery tone.

"Great. I left—" Not you, Richard! "I mean, the cleaning professional left her phone here last night. She asked me to pick it up for her."

"Oh, right. I have it. Come on in." Her face relaxes some. "Are you her personal assistant or something?"

I step into Fairbanks's foyer. It smells so much better in here than yesterday when I arrived. Looks good too. "I don't think cleaning professionals have personal assistants."

"This is New York. Anything's possible. Now where did I put that phone?" She taps her finger against her Berry Fuchsia lips and knits her brow. "Wait here. I'll find it."

I stuff my hands in my pockets and rock on my heels. Footsteps patter on the wood floor in the other room. Not the same sound as the assistant's clunky bootheels.

"I'm heading to the Hamptons tomorrow," a deep voice resounds.

Wait.

Is that . . . ?

I step lightly, peeking in the other room. Todd Fairbanks, technology wiz extraordinaire, veers over to the corner of the living room near the window wall. I gasp, unable to take my eyes off the back of his thick-haired head.

"Early. I'm canceling the Monty Fuhrmann pitch." Fairbanks turns on his bare heel, and I jet back around the foyer wall. Did I hear that right? I engage my ears as best as I can, considering my heart is pounding against my eardrums.

"It's that guy Becker. I don't trust him to play nice with the other banks."

Oh my god. Ezeus has been doing business with Monty Fuhrmann for years. And now, he's actually going to snub them!

"Yeah, they're out. The last thing I need is some kind of scandal."

"Holy shit," I mouth to myself.

"I have another call with S.G. Croft at ten. I'm giving them the lead on this. I know they'll run this IPO aboveboard. Then I'll call Becker."

He's giving the job to S.G. Croft? That's Monty Fuhrmann's biggest competitor. Talk about insider information. I need to warn Eric.

Oh my god, Eric. How is this the first time I've thought of him all day? And—

"Here you go!" Todd's assistant appears out of nowhere with my phone in hand.

I flinch, then quickly recover. "Um, thanks," I say, reaching for the phone with an uneasy smile.

"Sure."

I crane my neck a bit toward the sound of Fairbanks's voice, but the conversation's shifted. Not to mention, his assistant is holding the door open and shooting me a droll look.

"Thanks again," I say, slipping out the door with Fairbanks's words swimming in my head. The door slams, startling me again. My fingers tremble as I unlock my almost dead phone to send Eric a quick text.

Make that an impossible text. How am I supposed to type on this tiny keyboard with these colossal thumbs? Finally, I get the message out. Thanks, autocorrect.

DELIA: I need to tell you something about the Ezeus pitch. Can you talk?

I stare at the phone. "Come on, come on."

My phone jingles, and an image of Eric at our favorite bar smiles back at me.

I swipe the screen and place the phone to my ear.

Wait a second! I can't talk to him with this tenor!

"Hello? Delia? Are you there?"

I cover my mouth and hang up as fast as I can. "Shit!"

That was stupid. What was I thinking? I type another message, my oversized ape hands shaking even more.

DELIA: Can't talk now, but soon.

What does that even mean? I know that's what he'll be thinking. There's got to be another way I can tell him what I've just heard. Email? No, paper trail probably isn't the best idea. Hmm, I *could* send a stranger in with the message.

Richard perhaps?

CHAPTER EIGHT

'm a block away from Monty Fuhrmann, contemplating how I'm going to get the message to Eric with this body in tow. He sent five texts before my phone died two blocks ago—four to coax out of me whatever it was I needed to tell him about the Ezeus pitch, and one to wish me a happy birthday. I swipe my tongue across my bottom lip, remembering the sweet taste of his dark chocolatey gift. I know Eric was never meant to be my boyfriend, and for the most part I've come to terms with that. But now, I'm this! What if yesterday was my last real moment with him? Will I have to come to terms with that too?

One thing at a time, Delia.

Focus.

Okay, I have about an hour to give Eric a heads-up before Fairbanks cans the firm. Why did I have to tell him it was about the pitch? I could've just said, *I need to tell you something*. I really need to remember to think things through before I act today. So stupid. Am I supposed to just show up as Delia's messenger boy? He'll think it's totally bizarre. No, I need something clever. And clever does not happen while there's this growing pain in the middle of my forehead. Ugh. I know this ache. It's the same one I get every time I attempt the latest fad cleanse or detox diet—no sugar, no alcohol, no coffee. *No bueno.*

The dreaded caffeine withdrawal.

Usually by now I've had *at least* two strong cups. There's a café not far from Monty Fuhrmann Tower. At least one of my problems has an easy solution. Let's see if I can get this straight. Some things have inexplicably changed—like my genitals, vision, and facial hair. And some things are very much the same—like my memories, my tattoo, my caffeine addiction—because why not? Makes. Total. Sense. I shake my head at the discrepancies of my existence. Like I said. One thing at a time.

I *need* coffee.

The robust aroma of Colombian beans hits me as I push the café door open, consoling my headache just a little. It's almost nine. There are six people in front of me, all immersed in their devices. They're totally oblivious to anything that's around them until they get up to the barista and rattle off their convoluted orders. Yesterday, that would've been me too. But today, my phone screen's black. I doubt there's anything trending that's more interesting than the fact that I woke up with a dick, anyway. Eric's probably sent me another five messages by now. The pressure of it all is creating a venti-sized pit in my stomach.

My leg fidgets as I pretend to wait patiently at the end of the line. I'm pretty sure the woman at the front just placed her eighth order. Damn coffee run. I glance around for a free outlet, spying several near the tables along the walls. I pull out my phone and press the button one more time in case it's playing possum.

Still dead.

A yuppie sitting alone keeps glancing up at me while she nurses her cappuccino. The Spotlight Effect alarm buzzes in my brain. Is everyone staring at me again? I check the backs of my hands.

Nope, still a dude.

The yuppie stops staring and I shrug it off. There are more pressing matters. Like, how am I going to make it past Monty Fuhrmann's security? What will I say if I make it upstairs? How will I handle seeing Eric when I'm not completely myself?

I can't think with the noise of the espresso machines, the folky-electronic music, and the microbusiness owners tapping on their laptops.

"What can I start for you?" the barista asks, trying to look pleasant despite the flock of demanding customers.

"Grande soy latte, please." Better yet—"Make it a double."

She pulls a paper cup from the stack with her black marker ready. "Your name?"

My name? I've got this.

"Richard!" My voice booms at the same moment the espresso machine takes a break. Now everyone really is staring at me. Gotta get used to this new baritone.

"Seven fifty, please," she says.

Geez. I wish I'd remembered to make coffee at the apartment like usual. Then again, these are special circumstances, so I'll do something I almost never allow.

Charge it on my credit card.

I mean, Delia's credit card.

My wallet is understated, but I can't imagine any guy using it. I keep it tucked away in my Gucci and pull out the plastic card. She swipes it without bothering to check the name and hands it back with a smirk. "Bye, Richard."

I scoot over next to a young woman waiting on her brew. With her flannel shirt, denim shorts with stockings, and dark-framed glasses, she's more hipster geek than Wall Street.

"Grande soy latte!" the barista calls from behind the counter. That's mine. Thank God!

The geeky girl reaches for it.

"Did you order a soy latte?" I ask, and she nods. "So did I." We stare at each other for a moment. Delia would just take the coffee and jet out of there, but now I'm Richard. With a dick. And after my interaction with Shannon, I don't want to be a dick. "You were here first. This one's yours."

"Thanks." She smiles. "This is kind of a meet-cute, don't you think?"

What the hell's a meet-cute? "Not sure what you mean."

The girl blushes, letting her lashes fall. "You know, a meet-cute," she gushes. "It's a writing mechanism, a charming moment when two characters meet. Like in a romantic comedy."

Romantic comedy? "Are you a writer or something?"

She bobs her head. "A playwright. I've been working on a production for a small theater company."

"Great, nice to meet you." I watch the workers behind the counter. Where is my coffee?

"You too." She smiles brightly, then covers her slightly crooked teeth with her hand before walking off.

"Double grande soy latte!" the barista calls out. That's right! I got a double. I grab the cup with the name *Richard* written in big letters. Now all the tables are full and I really need to charge my phone. I scope out the place again. The playwright has an empty chair and an outlet at her table.

I walk over and glance at the name scribbled on her cup. "Camille, is it?"

"Yeah." Her eyes soften and her lips part. I think she likes me.

"Would you mind if I sit and charge my phone for a bit?"

"Not at all." Her cheeks are rosier than her rose gold aluminum laptop.

Oh, yeah, she does. How adorable is that? I made a girl blush!

"Thanks." I settle in, making sure my phone is charging. Camille watches me and it's not the Spotlight Effect. I glance between her and her laptop. "Don't let me interrupt you."

She wraps her hands tightly around her coffee cup. "Oh, you're not. I'm just waiting for my computer to boot up."

I nod, with nothing to do but taste the steaming, foamy latte. Mmm, there's nothing like that first sip. Camille watches me steadily.

"So," I start. "What's your play about?"

"It's an urban adaptation of Shakespeare's *Twelfth Night*."

I shrug. "I don't think I know it."

Her eyes practically bulge out of their sockets. "Seriously?"

I nod without a word and before I know it, she's pitching the play. Camille's words are fast and difficult to follow. If I ever pitched a client that poorly, they'd walk out before I could finish my first run-on sentence. My phone springs back to life. Eight missed messages from Eric. I swipe my phone to check them, then

Camille's next words hit me like a smack in the face. "She's so convincing as her twin brother that no one can tell them apart when he shows up."

I put the phone down and hold my hand up. "Wait, back up. This play is about a woman who's pretending to be a man and everyone believes it?"

She takes a sip of her coffee. "Yes. Although . . . there's one character who's suspicious, but it doesn't really come into play."

I rub my hand along my chin. Ooh, scratchy. "It doesn't sound realistic to me. It's a Shakespeare play?" I don't know a ton about English literature, but I'd expect something a bit more believable from the legend.

"Well, she's charming and quick-witted. But Shakespeare taps into something deeper."

I narrow my eyes. "What's that?"

"People see what they want to see. No one wanted to suggest otherwise because the majority seemed to buy it."

"Do you think someone could get away with this in real life or is it just Shakespeare stuff?" I wave dismissively.

Camille flips her long hair off her shoulder. "I mean, sure, Shakespeare's comedies are a little on the zany side, but his plays are very indicative of human behavior and motivation. Now, obviously, a woman would need a very convincing disguise. But if you think about it, most of us wear disguises every day. And we get away with it. Every day."

"Good point." I sit back, ignoring another alert on my phone. I've been wearing the friend-who's-not-cleaning-for-rent disguise in front of Eric for months. And now I have the best disguise there is—a dick with no identity. I can be anyone. Anyone in a suit. "In your play, what does this woman want? Why is she pretending to be a man?"

She looks me dead in the eye. "Survival."

Survival, huh? I can relate to that.

"So what about you? Is it safe to assume you're an investment banker?" She holds her cup up to her mouth with both hands.

Shannon didn't bat an eyelash when I lied about working for Monty Fuhrmann. Maybe I should try it on again. This time in a bigger size. "Yeah, I'm a managing director over here at Monty Fuhrmann." I nod in the direction of the building.

Camille flutters her lashes. "That sounds really cool. You must do well."

I pick up my phone again. "Uh, yeah. Hang on." It's got enough battery life to last me about an hour, which is just enough. Eric's left two voice mails and Frankie's left one. "Listen, I've got to run. It was really nice meeting you." I stand, yanking the plug from the wall and stuffing it in my briefcase.

Her jaw hangs. "You don't want to finish your coffee here first?"

"Can't, sorry. I've got a lot of work to do. Good luck on your play."

She rises to her feet while I grab my latte. "Wait! Am I ever going to see you again?"

I turn to her, chewing my bottom lip. Meet-cute or not, I'm not who this poor girl thinks I am. But she's kinda sweet and was nice enough to let me sit at her table. Not to mention the brilliant idea she just gave me.

So I hit my mark and take a beat. "I guess we'll let fate decide."

I had to give her something. And who knows? Maybe one day she'll write her own Shakespearean-style comedy about the woman who actually woke up in a man's body.

CHAPTER NINE

The Monty Fuhrmann Tower is only a block away. Cold beads of sweat sit on my neck, and I'm worried Frankie's antiperspirant isn't strong enough for a man or a woman. I down the rest of my coffee, chewing on my bottom lip between sips. I've done so much recon on this firm that I know it like the back of my hand. The back of my female hand anyway. I run my potentially insane idea over in my mind with every step toward the building. I'll either be the hero that saves this deal or the nobody who failed. Considering the circumstances, I'll take those odds.

I push through the front doors and walk briskly along the dark marble floor, keeping my head up. The lobby's bustling with busy professionals, same as yesterday afternoon. I scoot close to the guy in front of me passing through security and lower my eyes. A large man dressed more like a hotel clerk than a traditional security guard holds his hand out in front of me. "Do you have a key-card, sir?"

I do my best not to look alarmed, and I'm tempted to tell him I forgot it. "No, I have an interview with Lauren in HR."

"You're going to need to sign in at the desk." He doesn't smile, but extends his arm out to the side, both pointing the way and barricading me.

"Thanks," I say through as friendly a smile as I can muster, and head to the long reception desk. Yesterday when I signed in, some-one came down to serve as my escort. Will they let me upstairs without one? Guess I'll find out.

Behind the desk sits the same tiny-framed woman as the day before. Her black hair falls just above her collarbone. Her eyes lock onto me, her smile growing wider the closer I get.

"Good morning," she says.

I flash her a toothy smile. "Good morning!"

"Just sign in here, please." She points at the clipboard sheet. "Who do you have business with today?"

I keep her gaze; maybe this new face of mine can get me up-stairs with no further questions. "The HR department."

"There's Serena," the young guy next to her says. They both sit up a little straighter and turn their attention to the front doors.

A woman dressed in a modern power suit walks through the tall glass entrance. I'd know that short signature bob anywhere. "Oh my god. Serena Walters!"

"You know her?" the woman behind the desk asks.

"Excuse me," I say and hurry over to my professional idol. This is the first time I've ever encountered her in passing. Who knows if it'll happen again?

"Ms. Walters!" I catch up to her, and she turns to me. "I'm sorry to bother you," I say, slightly panting.

"Can I help you?" Serena's a single mother who runs a very busy private equity firm. Despite that, and having twin toddlers, she doesn't have a single strand of hair out of place or a speck of lint on her navy suit. Much less kid spit.

"It's an honor to meet you. I'm De—Richard," I start, holding out my trembling hand, praying it will steady. "You're my hero."

She takes my hand and gives me a radiant smile with a crisp nod. "Thank you. I don't often get that reaction from men."

"Well, you're an inspiration." I do my best to dial back my starstruck gawk and cross my arms so she doesn't see how much I'm shaking. "How do you get it all done?"

Serena lifts her perfectly arched brow. "Can you walk and talk?" She begins to move toward security.

I straighten up and quickly follow. "Yes, ma'am."

"To answer your question, I just do it. I see what I want, and I go after it." She points a stiff hand toward the elevator as we pass through. The guard isn't stopping either of us.

I'm in!

"But how do you maneuver into being such a success in a male-dominated field?"

She stops in front of the doors and looks at me with a flattened lip. "Despite what you may think, women are equally as capable as men."

Oh, great, now I'm offending *the* Serena Walters.

"I know. Like I said, you're my hero. What I meant was, how do you get *them* to see you as equal?"

Serena lets out a little laugh. "Well, I definitely haven't heard *that* question from a man before." She pauses. "Here's the thing.

The key to success is the same no matter which industry you're in. It's about confidence. You have to walk in like you own the place. Because when you roar like a lion, they'll treat you like you're the king of the jungle."

"Or queen?"

She chuckles, and the steel doors open. "Yes, or queen. The lioness does most of the hunting, you know."

"That's true." I follow along behind her. I can't believe I'm in an elevator with one of the most powerful women in the industry.

"Fortieth, please," she requests and I comply.

She stands next to me, a very comfortable distance between us. "You work for Monty Fuhrmann?"

I rock back and forth on my heels and keep my eyes on the doors. "Yes . . . yes, I do."

The lift halts and the doors open to the upper lobby. "This is me," I say. "It was an honor to meet you, Ms. Walters." I extend my hand once again, but she reaches for something in her briefcase.

"You seem like the kind of man who would do well at my firm." She hands me a business card. "If you're ever looking for a change, give us a call. That's my assistant."

The card feels like gold in my hands. "Wow! Thank you." She nods goodbye, and I step out of the elevator.

Holy. Shit.

A surprise dick, a run-in with Todd Fairbanks, and a conversation with Serena Walters all before ten o'clock! Where else will this day take me? I turn the corner to a lightly populated foyer and find a seat on a stiff leather chair. No one seems to notice me. It's as if they think that I belong in this building. Because I do. But according to Serena, it's not enough to just belong; I have to walk in like I own the place. Take what I want.

I know that philosophy. Watching my dad interact with people, all people, was practically a crash course in taking charge. Having that attitude got me into my top-choice university. They put me on the wait list until I showed up and convinced them to admit me in the fall. At good-ole-boys Howard Brothers Group, I always talked my way onto the best cases, even if that meant accepting a smaller role. I just had to get myself in the door. I *knew* my abilities would take me the rest of the way. When did I lose that confidence? Why did I start accepting *no* for an answer?

I check the clock on my dying device. Not much time. If I'm going to intervene, I'll have to do something ballsy and do it now. I close my eyes for a moment, scanning through miscellaneous facts about the firm, all the tidbits Eric's shared with me about the Ezeus pitch, and everything Fairbanks alluded to on his call.

Got it!

I snap my fingers. The idea is alarmingly audacious but it might be the only thing that'll work. I glance down at my masculine suit and large leather shoes. My fingernails dig into my palms, desperate to hold on to this opportunity. It could be my only chance. And at this point, what do I really have to lose?

I take a deep breath and make my way back to the elevator. I press the button for the thirty-second floor and the cab climbs. With every floor, my spine straightens taller and my chin lifts higher. The doors open.

It's now or never.

I fill my lungs with another deep breath and keep my chest

puffed up as I make a beeline for the office of the man in charge. Ready or not, here I come.

His assistant stands, holding her hands up. "Excuse me. You can't go in there. Sir!"

I barge inside without a second thought.

Five men hover over a spread of printouts. Curtis Becker looks up with an ugly scowl from behind the oversized desk. The other four suits turn to me with tilted heads and raised eyebrows.

"Charlene, who is this?" Becker barks at his assistant.

She shrugs but doesn't move past the doorway. "Sorry, Mr. Becker. I tried to stop him."

"Yeah, I can see that." He huffs, throwing his hands in the air. "Call security!"

That didn't stop me before. Should I press my luck?

"I don't think you want to do that," I say, unbuttoning my jacket. Despite the tension in the room, my muscles are relaxed. All of my muscles.

"And why's that?"

I smirk, moving closer to Becker. His pinstriped posse steps back except for one, who remains standing firmly at his side. I place my Gucci in an empty chair, feeling Becker's eyes sizing me up.

He's shorter than his reputation.

I lower my eyes to meet his. "I'm from the Zurich office. Liam Golan sent me."

That's right, I'm invoking the Rainmaker.

The suit guys take another step back. Using the name Liam Golan in this building is like saying *Spielberg* in a production meeting or *Jesus* in church.

"Does anyone know what the hell he's talking about?" Becker looks to his minions. They're all stunned, like deer in headlights. "Why weren't we informed?" he asks, clearly unconvinced.

I point directly at Becker. "Never mind that now. Did Fairbanks call yet?"

He gives me a pinched expression and waves off his assistant, who's been hovering in the doorway. "What are you talking about?"

"Todd Fairbanks is going to call any minute now and cancel the pitch tomorrow. He's shutting us out."

A few of the guys gasp, but Becker doesn't flinch, he just clenches his jaw. "Is this some kind of joke?"

"Do you think Liam Golan jokes around with deals like this?"

Becker pushes his way around the desk and stomps toward me. "I don't know who you are or why Golan felt the need to send you, but you obviously don't know shit about this deal. The meeting tomorrow is merely a formality. Fairbanks and I have an understanding." He points his finger an inch from my pink paisley tie.

His phone rings and all their heads whip in its direction. He rushes back to his desk and answers on speakerphone. "What!"

"Mr. Becker, Mr. Fairbanks is on the line for you." Charlene's words tremble.

Curtis Becker's eyes shift my way, narrowing in suspicion. "Put him through." There's a pause before the line clicks in. "Todd, how are you?" Becker's voice drips of pleasantries.

"Not too bad, Curtis. How are you?" Fairbanks's voice blares on the speaker.

"Doing great! Looking forward to our meeting tomorrow."

"That's actually why I'm calling." He pauses. "It was a tough call but I've decided not to include Monty Fuhrmann in the IPO."

Becker stands slack-jawed and red-faced. No one in the room is breathing. No one but me. I step closer and sit on the corner of Becker's desk like it's mine. "Mr. Fairbanks, this is Richard Allen. I work over here with Curtis and the team. The firm sent me in from Zurich just to meet with you tomorrow."

"Well, I'm sorry you had to travel so far for nothing."

My heart is pounding, but my hands are still. "Maybe you don't have to be."

"Look, I really appreciate everything Monty Fuhrmann has done for me over the years, but I've made up my mind on this."

Becker takes a breath and leans in, but I shush him with my hand.

"Mr. Fairbanks, we know you better than you think we do. I believe I know why you've made this decision, and I understand it. Like you said, we've done a lot together over the years. Why don't you just come in tomorrow as planned and listen to what we have to offer? I know what you're expecting, and I think we'll surprise you."

The other guys have lost all color in their faces now, even Becker. Fairbanks lets out a long breath. "Fine."

Sighs of relief fill the room. I hope Fairbanks can't hear them.

"I'll come in for a half hour," he says.

Becker's brows are now raised clear up to the top of his wide forehead. "Great!" he squawks then clears his throat. "Great, Todd. We'll see you then."

"See you then, Richard." Fairbanks hangs up the line and Becker remains stunned, speechless.

I clap once and rise to my feet. "You see? That's why Liam sent me."

Ta-da!

Becker rubs his forehead like he's got a migraine. "I don't understand. How did you know that was going to happen?"

"It doesn't matter. What matters now is that we're still in the running."

"You heard him. He's done with us." The guy standing next to Becker finally speaks. Owen Campbell. I recognize him from his LinkedIn profile. Eric's informed me that he's the good cop to Becker's bad cop but just as guilty. "We're totally fucked!"

"If you were totally fucked, Golan would've sent me here to fire you, which, by the way, he gave me authority to do." Attagirl. "But we can still save this pitch."

"How?" Owen asks, throwing his hands in the air.

"By having some balls!" I grab my crotch.

What am I doing?

I release my grip. "And some integrity."

The five of them gawk at me. Did I throw them by grabbing my nuts or by using the word *integrity*?

Owen puckers his mouth. "Can you be more specific?"

"Yes." I smile. "But I'm going to need a workspace and an assistant. Let me review everything and I'll meet with you in an hour or so."

Becker narrows his eyes again. "What'd you say your name was?"

Now, own it this time, Delia. "Richard Allen."

Curtis Becker subtly scoffs and looks to his team for backup. But the pinstripes aren't saying a thing. Their mouths just hang open, to the point I expect to see drool forming at any moment. I look to Becker and tap my watchless wrist with my finger. He rolls his eyes and presses a button on his phone. Charlene answers with a polite greeting, but Becker bulldozes her. "I need you to prep Sutton's old office right away. It looks like our guest is going to stay awhile."

CHAPTER TEN

I t's been a long time since I've impressed myself, but damn! Did I seriously just pull that off?

Man, that felt good.

This is big. Huge!

I follow Charlene to the other end of the floor and watch her open the door to a corner office. "Here you are, Mr. Allen."

Mr. Allen. From the Zurich office. Liam Golan's guy.

Oh, no. I'm not any of those things. I'm just Delia Reese trapped in this *man* body. And a web of my lies. When I said I wanted to get a job today, I meant honestly. Well, as honestly as possible given the circumstances. Damn it, I didn't think this through at all.

At this point, it might be wiser to go and bark up another bank's tree. After all, Fairbanks is coming in tomorrow, so mission accomplished. Except . . . he's expecting to meet with Richard Allen from the Zurich office. He's expecting Monty Fuhrmann to surprise him with our pitch. A *new* pitch that won't happen if I leave.

The coffee-shop playwright's words echo in my mind—*people see what they want to see.* The guys in that room weren't convinced I was anyone who mattered until I rescued that meeting right in front of their eyes. Now they think I'm the guy with the answers, and they're giving me a corner office. If I can just keep up this charade until we close this deal tomorrow, then I'll figure out my next move.

"Mr. Allen, are you all right?" Charlene tilts her head with a hint of concern on her face.

"Yes, thank you, Charlene. I'll take it from here."

Sutton's old office is equipped with everything a banking executive's corner office typically includes, with the exception of personal touches like photos of a prized sailboat and trophy wife. A set of glossy golf clubs sits in the corner. Nice. I set my Gucci down and pick up the driver. Growing up in Florida with a father who did most of his business on the course, I learned a thing or two. Though I haven't been on the fairway for a long time. I'd be curious to see if this new body improves my game.

I position my wider-than-yesterday hips and slowly pull the driver back. A woman behind me clears her throat, throwing my swing completely off. I whip my head around.

"Can I help you?" I ask.

Her long black hair cloaks the shoulders of her matching suit. Her expression is bleak. There's nothing friendly or warm about her save for the bright aqua color of her glasses. She walks in, keeping her hands stationed at her sides. "I'm Nicole. I'll be filling in as your assistant."

I extend my hand. "I'm Richard Allen."

She takes it. Stronger than she looks. "I know. Is there anything I can help you with?" Her tone is flat and I get the sense she couldn't possibly care less about helping me.

"No, I'm just getting set up right now," I say, resting the club over my shoulder. "You wanna take a swing?" I gesture toward the golf bag.

She doesn't even hint at a smile. Not sure if she's judgmental or annoyed. Perhaps both. "No."

I exchange the driver for the putter. "Guess Sutton forgot his clubs."

She sighs and folds her arms. "I'm sure he has plenty."

"What happened to him?" I take my position and pretend to putt.

"He retired. Lives in a beachfront house in Southampton. He invited the whole firm there for a Memorial Day party last year. It was fun." Nicole's face seems to lighten some, but not enough to convince me that she's capable of having fun.

I think I heard about that party when I was at Howard Brothers. But they never invited us lower-level employees to their fancy festivities in the Hamptons. We had our own celebration for the long holiday weekend. I spent the night drinking and dancing with the guys from the office, including Eric. He was dating someone at the time. Fiona. Or, as he called her on occasion, *Foxy* Fiona.

Ugh. I hate that name now.

And I hated her too, for no reason other than she was with Eric and I wanted to be.

There was one moment that night, just outside the bar. We were alone having a smoke, something he and I only do when we're really drunk. That's what we tell each other, anyway. I had caught a little chill from the breeze and he cupped his hands around my slender arms, brushing them up and down to warm me. A moment later, his face was mere inches from mine. I was sure we would've kissed if it weren't for Charlie busting out of the bar, hooting and hollering like a damn frat boy.

When Eric and Foxy Fiona finally broke up a month later, I expected him to confess his love or at least ask me out. But he never did. That's when I knew I'd imagined his attraction. Now Eric's somewhere on this floor and it's only a matter of time before he sees me like this. But he won't see *me*. He'll have no idea who I am. Thank goodness, I guess. Ugh. It still sucks. I frown and drag the putter back to the bag.

"Everything okay?" Nicole asks.

I look up with a half smile. "Uh, yes, um, sorry. All good. Just a lot of work to do. Can you bring me the proposal along with all the literature and data on the Ezeus IPO?"

"Sure. I'll have Becker give you access to the shared drive."

Crap! I forgot about technology. No company email and no access. Hopefully they don't catch on before I figure out how to fix that.

"Thanks, but I'm a paper and pen kinda gir—guy. Can you just get me the printed copies?"

She raises her brow and nods. I'm pretty sure I catch a glimpse of her rolling her eyes before she leaves. I walk over to my own window wall. Make that two window walls. The shimmering skyscrapers of Manhattan cut through the bright blue sky, filling the space like oversized cityscape photographs. My father doesn't even have a view this stunning.

I stand tall and take it all in, nodding slowly. "So this is really happening."

Nicole returns carrying a banker's box nearly filled with files. "This is everything," she says, handing it over.

"That was fast," I say.

Nicole cocks her head. "Did you expect me to be slow?"

"No, I just wasn't expecting—"

"Mr. Allen, I'm very good at my job. So unless you have anything else for me to do, I'll leave you to yours."

This woman reminds me of myself. "No, I'm good. Thank you."

"You're welcome."

She leaves my office, the door slamming behind her.

At-ti-tude! But I get it. We're sick of being questioned.

I take a seat at the solid mahogany desk and unload the files one by one. The next forty-five minutes give me a much clearer picture of the situation. Now I know exactly how I'm going to position this to Becker and Campbell. I lean back in the chair and take in a deep breath. How in the world did I go from being a woman completely on the outside to being the man in charge of this whole thing? I can't begin to decide which change is more miraculous.

And to think, if I'd woken up as myself this morning, I still would have encountered Fairbanks's phone call but the outcome would be completely different. Eric would have gotten the news from me, then I'd just be waiting by my phone to hear what happened. Secondhand. Maybe that's why this is all happening, so that I'm no longer the person who waits to be called.

For once, I call the shots.

I open the office door and poke my head out. Nicole types so wildly fast it almost sounds fake. But I know she's legit.

"Nicole, I'm ready to see the team. Can you bring 'em in?"

Her gaze doesn't budge from her computer screen as her fingers move effortlessly around the ergonomic keyboard. "Yes, sir."

I duck back into my office then pop out again. Nicole is already summoning the squad.

"Is there something else?" she asks as she hangs up the phone.

"Yeah. What are your thoughts on all this?"

She scoffs. "The last time I spoke up with my opinion I was asked not to interfere in matters that are not my business."

"Who said that?" I ask, remembering my two cents being rejected on several occasions.

She folds her arms again. "Who do you think?"

I nod. "Well, I'm not him. Do *you* have an opinion about this?"

"I think Monty Fuhrmann is out on this one."

"How come?"

She glances around, then leans forward. "One of my roommates is an associate at S.G. Croft, and I know Todd Fairbanks has been talking with them for a while. Pretty sure he'll give them the lead. But isn't that why you're here?"

See what happens when you shut women up? You screw yourself. "Yes, and while I'm here, feel free to interfere, okay?"

Her expression softens the tiniest bit. "I'll keep that in mind."

Hardly five minutes later, Curtis Becker, Owen Campbell, and two others file into my office. Not a woman in the group.

Oh, wait . . . nope, that's Nicole.

I greet my good-ole-boys club with handshakes. Owen brings the other guys forward. "Richard, this is Darren and—"

"Eric," I say, standing face-to-face with my crush, a goofy grin covering mine.

Shit!

So Richard Allen's a psychic now? Might as well add that to the backstory. How am I going to talk my way out of this one?

Eric's forehead wrinkles in that really cute way where he's trying to keep a straight face but can't. "How'd you know my name?"

Um . . . because I'm totally in love with you.

I can't speak, or let go of his hand, or breathe. I try to swallow, but my tongue is as dry as sandpaper. Can he hear my heart roaring in my chest? Can they all hear it?

"Are you okay?" he asks.

My smile morphs into something more serious. "Yes, fine. Sorry, we should get started."

"But how . . ." Eric tries again as I let go and turn away.

"We've got a lot of work to do, gentlemen. Why don't we all sit down?" Pull it together, Delia. It's go time.

The four of them follow me to the conversational seating area in the corner of the office. My office.

"Who has a copy of the proposal?" I ask.

Eric hands me pages of printed material, flashing me a curious glance with those brilliant indigo eyes. His collared shirt with a subtle woven pattern matches the sky today. It's hard not to ogle him when he looks so damn good.

Focus!

I shake my head and sit on the narrow leather love seat, careful not to squish my two-piece.

And I'm not talking about the suit.

Becker and Owen sit across from me in the club chairs, while Eric and Darren seem to stand guard beside them. Everyone's quiet as I flip through the proposal again, glancing at the handwritten notes on my yellow pad. I can't focus. Something doesn't feel right down there. Or rather, it does. I feel a little poke coming through.

C'mon, Little Dickie. This isn't playtime.

I scoot over, leaning my elbows on my knees to shield the little beast. I glance up. They're still waiting.

Just don't look at Eric. It'll go down.

"Everything okay?" Owen asks.

"Yeah." But it's not. I may need to intervene. Manually. "Actually . . ." And I just go for it—like so many men before me. "That's better."

I look up. Becker grimaces and Owen checks his watch while their guards quickly correct their own expressions. My cheeks warm when I glance at Eric, and I smooth my hair around my ear. If he knew it was me, I never would've done it. They have no idea that it's my first day with a dick. And if they did know, they'd tell me I'm doing a damn fine job.

Becker rolls his eyes. "Jesus! Are you good now?"

"Yeah." I nod. "I've never gotten used to European underwear."

Becker smacks his face and runs his hand down to his chin. He really doesn't like me.

I clear my throat. "Now, let's talk about why you almost lost one of the biggest deals this firm has ever seen," I say, darting a hard stare at my little nemesis.

He folds his arms in and leans back like he's protecting his ego. "Fine."

"Here's the deal. Fairbanks thinks we're bullies. That we can't play nice with others, and that we're going to bulldoze this whole thing and repeat what happened the last time an IPO like this went south."

"Sure, mistakes have been made," Becker says in a huff, "but c'mon, this should be ours. Especially after the relationship we've built with Todd. We've learned from the past. And we know his company better than anyone. Fairbanks owes it to us. He practically promised me the spot."

"Well, that may be true, but that promise is off the table and we're not going to see any piece of the pie unless we tell him what he wants to hear."

"And what does he want to hear?"

"That we're in wherever he wants us. Wherever he *needs* us. We'll take on whatever role he wants, and play with whomever he wants us to play with."

"What!" Becker's face turns pissed-off pink.

"Look, I know it's not glamorous and we're not going to make nearly as much money as we'd hoped, but I think we need to show him our prudent, humble side."

He gives me a sour look. "This is Monty Fuhrmann. We don't have a prudent, humble side."

"Well, we do now." I slam their proposal on the glass coffee table between us. "How's it gonna look if Monty Fuhrmann isn't even a part of the syndicate for one of the most anticipated IPOs ever? You heard it from the horse's mouth. Let's not sabotage our second chance with a shitty offer."

Becker bolts up. "This is bullshit! I can't believe he'd do this. It must be that new legal counsel of his. I knew I didn't like her. The little bitch. This is her idea!"

"Hey, hey!" I yell. "Let's not forget who fucked up and put us in this position in the first place. What's the matter with you, calling his lawyer a little bitch?"

"I don't have time for this!" Becker stomps his feet and storms out of the office. Eric and Darren move aside, keeping their eyes down.

Owen springs to his feet. "Curtis!" But the little asshole is gone. He turns to me. "Sorry, all of this really blindsided us. I'll talk to him."

"Please do. Is he always this hotheaded?" I ask, remembering Eric's words—*shortest fuse on the planet.*

Owen shrugs. "Eh, he can be."

I gesture in the direction of the door. "Yeah, go talk to him. I'm going to rework this proposal and I'll send it over this afternoon."

Owen nods and leaves my office.

"Okay, gentlemen. Thank you both for your help. I'll let you know if I need anything from you," I say, extending my hand.

"He *is* always that hotheaded," Darren says as he shakes my hand then proceeds toward the door. Eric stays behind, eyes narrowed with his tongue peeking out of his mouth. There's that thinking face I love so much.

"Did you need something, Eric?" My tone is sweet. A little too sweet given the circumstances. I straighten up, smoothing my tie down my chest.

"Do we know each other from somewhere?"

I pretend to really look at him, like I'm trying to remember him. Though I could never forget his face, or his smell, or those ol' blue eyes, or . . . Delia, pay attention! I fake a cough and look away. "I don't think so. Why? Do I look familiar?"

"I'm just trying to figure out how you knew my name," he says.

"Because a . . ." I whirl my hands around in front of me—a failed attempt at summoning the best answer. "You're new, and I've heard great things about you."

"Really?"

I scratch my head. "Sure, sure."

"Wait. I do know you from somewhere." He taps his finger to his chin. "I just can't place it."

I shrug. "Maybe you've seen my doppelganger at the gym."

Eric lets out a chuckle. "Maybe." I love making him smile. It never gets old.

He turns to leave and my eyes follow him, getting caught on his sexy behind. Mmm.

Another poke comes through.

Uh-oh.

I hurry to shut the door behind him, pressing my back against it and taking shallow breaths. That was close. I look down at my little troublemaker, who's fully alert like he's just eaten an entire bag of Giggles candies. So not funny.

"You need to control yourself, man. Get it together!" I command in an angry whisper, then I lean my head back on the hard wooden door. This having-a-dick thing is gettin' real.

CHAPTER ELEVEN

Personal space and privacy are luxuries in New York. This new office is affording me both. I hit control-P on the keyboard and watch page after page of my new proposal stack up in the printer tray. My stomach grumbles such a gutsy growl it nearly rattles the corner office windows. It's lunchtime already?

Another ferocious rumble.

Time to feed the beast. I pull my phone from the charger and dial Regina.

"Hey," she answers. "You got your phone back. How's the new man in Manhattan?"

"Cute. But you wouldn't believe me if I told you."

"That bad, huh?"

"Are you kidding? This is the most incredible day of my life! Hold on, I'll conference in Frankie."

He answers. "Delia, is everything okay? Are you hurt? Are you coming to the hospital soon? How's my suit?"

"Everything's fine. Can you guys meet me for lunch?" I ask. My belly begs again. "In half an hour?"

"Sure, where?" Regina asks.

"Il Vezzo. My treat." It's one of the best Italian spots in the city.

"Il Vezzo? Can you afford that?" Frankie asks.

That remains to be seen. I chuckle. "Who cares? YOLO, right?"

"No one says that anymore." I can practically see Regina sneering.

"Oh, yeah? I blame the penis." I glance down at my pants. Since Eric left my office, Little Dickie's been behaving himself.

"What's going on?" Frankie asks. He sounds like he's been worried sick all morning. Maybe a nice glass of vino will calm him down.

"I'll tell you if you meet us for lunch."

"Fine," he says sharply.

"See you in thirty," Regina says before they both hang up.

Good. Il Vezzo will totally hit the spot.

"Nicole!" I call out and grab my things. When I look up from the desk, she's standing in front of me as if appearing from thin air. I don't want to make the mistake of commenting on how quick she is again. "How's your day going?"

She pauses, puzzled, like she's never been asked this before. "Fine, sir. How is your day?"

"It's been interesting, Nicole." She has no clue just *how* interesting. "Would you mind delivering these to Campbell's and

Becker's offices in one hour? It's the new pitch." I hand her two stapled packets.

"Sure." Before turning on her heel to leave, she nods with the tiniest of smiles. I'll take it!

"Nicole," I call. "One other thing. I need you to make a twelve thirty reservation for three at Il Vezzo. Tell them whatever you need to. Tell them you're Todd Fairbanks's assistant if you have to."

"You got it, boss."

Boss, huh? No one's ever called me that. Bossy, yes. But never boss.

I like it.

I pass Nicole's desk as she's confirming my reservation. Best assistant ever.

She clicks the button on her headset. "You're all set. Oh, and here's your keycard so you don't have to deal with security. Have a nice lunch, Mr. Allen."

I take the plastic keycard. "Thanks! And you can call me Richard."

"As long as I don't have to call you Dick." Nicole's attention returns to her screen and I chuckle. She's my kind of girl.

In the elevators, I start to get another biological alarm, but the fix isn't fun like Il Vezzo. In fact, it's terrifying. Too bad I can't ignore it. The doors open and I step out into the busy foyer, glancing around for the restroom signs, which seem to be invisible. Eric passes by, his eyes fixated on his phone, tapping his thumbs against the screen. My hunger pangs transform into knots at the sight of him.

"Hey, Eric," I call out, rushing to his side. "Is there a bathroom on this floor?"

"Yeah." He offers a polite smile and points over my left shoulder. Instead of looking, my eyes lock on him and I can't help but turn my mouth up and give him a look that says, *You're my favorite person in the world.*

Why is he so cute?

He cocks his head and zeroes in on my briefcase. "Is that Gucci?"

His question knocks the goofy look off my face. I think I did a better job hiding my crush when I was Delia. "Uh, yeah. You know your designers." I've never known Eric to be a labels guy.

He gives me a funny look. "That's so weird, my friend Delia has the exact same one."

My cheeks warm and my jaw goes slack. Is he talking about me? To me? If only I could tell him that this *is* Delia's Gucci. Then again, I could use his ignorance to my advantage. Would it be wrong to inquire about this Delia, uncensored?

With wobbly knees and a mouth as dry as a glass of sauvignon blanc, I'm ready to add this to the growing list of shit I'd never do B.D. (before dick). "Delia, is that your girlfriend?"

"No," Eric replies, shaking his head slightly with a hint of a smile.

Hmm, that wasn't as telling as I hoped. Let's see, he didn't scoff or grimace, so he's not repulsed by the idea. No blushing, just a small smile. Is he simply content with our relationship status? You'd think having a dick would make it easier to interpret men's mannerisms, but I'm none the wiser. And maybe it's for the best.

"Well, she's got great taste," I say. "Gotta go. Thanks for your help." I pat his shoulder and head off toward the bathroom.

The restroom signs come into view and I push my way through the door. It's empty so I snag the first stall, which is my preference. I once read that people commonly overlook the first stall and choose succeeding stalls instead. If that's true, then the first has had fewer strange booties on the seat. My pulse quickens as I undo my belt. Every time I unleash this beast, something crazy happens. Crazy to me anyway.

I pull down my borrowed striped underwear, half expecting the troublemaker to pop out and say, "Hey now!" But instead it's cuddled up to my fuzzy thigh, fast asleep. Not quite as climactic as I made it out to be. I examine the extremity for a moment. Despite my morning shower, I hardly know my own penis. I probably wouldn't even recognize it in a lineup. It wakes up a little and I drop it before it decides it wants to play.

Maybe later, Little Dickie.

I take a seat, pointing the thing into the bowl. A sigh escapes my lips as I let it flow. Peeing with a penis isn't that much different from peeing without one. A urethra's a urethra, I suppose. I pull a piece of paper from the roll and gently dab around the tip before tucking it away again. Snug as a bug in a rug. I think I'm getting the hang of this having-a-penis thing.

As I pull up my trousers, two others enter the bathroom chatting up a gripefest.

Two other women.

Oh, no.

I'm in the women's bathroom. I didn't even think about it.

Shit.

I peek through the cracks of the stall doors.

"I should just tell them, you know?" one of them says in a thick

Long Island accent, applying her lipstick in the mirror. "I'm a human being, not a fucking workhorse."

The other woman scoffs, whipping out her mascara wand. "I know, it's, like, when did the sixty-plus-hour workweek become the norm?"

Stay calm, Delia. They'll leave eventually. I look down and gasp. If they see the size of my feet and style of shoes they might assume the worst.

"Oh my god!" I mouth to myself. This could be bad. Very bad.

What am I going to do? For a moment I consider an attempt to stand on the toilet to hide my feet. Then again, I don't need to risk any commotion. I hold my breath, staying completely still. Finally, the women close themselves in the other stalls and the coast is clear. I skip the sink and make my way out unnoticed.

Whew!

My pulse begins to slow. I raise my dick-holding hands like a surgeon waiting for their digits to be dressed in latex gloves. Only mine are in need of a scrub-down. Another suit guy pushes his way out of the men's room at the other end of the hall.

He takes a second to adjust his crotch and sends me a curious chin nod. "Hey, how's it goin'?"

"Good," I say, my hands still playing doctor.

Should I just whip out the hand sani and head to lunch or be brave and wash my hands in the big boys' room? Ugh. These are my options? I check around for a gender-neutral bathroom, to no avail.

C'mon, Monty Fuhrmann, get with the program already!

For now, I guess I'll bite the bullet. I walk down the hall, glancing left then right, then push my way through the door with my shoulder. It doesn't look that much different from the ladies' room—except for the row of urinals.

And that smell. What is that?

I head over to the sink, past the urinals, and—

"Oh, hey again," Eric calls, standing in front of the porcelain-lined wall.

"Uh." I stop short, blinking, blushing, and barely breathing. The sound of his stream fills the space between us. I shield my view with my hand, sneaking a few little peeks. "Hey."

"Didn't you say you needed the bathroom?" he asks, gesturing to the urinal next to him.

"Oh, no. I'm good. Just need to wash my hands." I scurry over to the sink, my fingers shaking as I reach for the faucet. A thunderous flush bounces off the tiled walls.

Oh my god! Eric just peed in front of me. Talk about intimacy.

I pump some soap and start to lather up while Eric takes the sink next to me, keeping his eyes lowered. Good, because I can't possibly look him in the face right now. My cheeks must be pinker than my pocket square.

"Hey," he starts, "since you seem to be so in tune with what's happening at the New York office, would you happen to know if there are any spots coming available on our team?"

"I'm not really sure, why?"

"A friend of mine's looking for a new job. I think she'd be good for this place." He has to be asking for me. Aw, that's so sweet! He must really want me to stay. "Plus, it'd be great to have at least one woman on the team."

He's not wrong about that. "I'll look into it and get back to you."

"That'd be great, thanks." Eric flicks the water with his fingers and snatches a paper towel from the machine before heading out.

The moment the door closes, I let out a giant exhale, taking shallow breaths over the sink. I think our relationship status just updated from "Crush" to "It's Complicated."

CHAPTER TWELVE

hail a cab to West Third and Sullivan. My phone provides a nice
distraction. I bypass the missed birthday texts from my family—
no way I can deal with them right now—and scroll through my
email. Let's see—Daily Digest from Dealbreaker.com, upcoming
shows at the Village Room, and a reminder about my yearly pap
smear. Bummer. I was really looking forward to those cervical
clamps.

I click through every new message in my in-box. Still nothing
from Monty Fuhrmann about my interview yesterday. I guess it's
for the best since Delia-me can't exactly accept a new position at
the moment. But an offer would be nice.

Finally, I arrive at Il Vezzo. Inside the restaurant, crisp white
linens drape square tables and sterling utensils shine atop black
napkins. Elegantly framed black-and-white photographs adorn

the walls, telling stories of an Italian family's history. Fresh pasta delights my nose, and I smile with an easy sigh. This is the sort of lunch I've only dreamed about lately.

"Do you have a reservation?" the waify blond hostess asks.

"Yes, table for three under . . . Richard Allen."

She flashes a smile and runs her finger down a list. My eyes fall to the barely there gold necklace with a tiny *E* initial pendant. It's so cute. I've been wanting to get something like that. Maybe even an *E* for *Eric*. How cheesy is that?

The hostess clears her throat, jolting me out of my jewelry trance. She points to her face with a tight-lipped smile as if to say, *My eyes are up here.*

I shake my head. "Sorry, I was just admiring your necklace."

"I'm sure you were."

"No, really, I've been looking—"

"You're the first of your party to arrive. Would you like to be seated?"

"No, thank you. I'll wait," I say. "Again. Sorry."

She motions me to take a seat and directs the group behind me to their table. Note to self—don't look below the chin. That's usually how Eric is. I've never caught him admiring my necklaces or anything else. Any chance I mistook his gesture of respect for a lack of interest?

Regina and Frankie pass through the front door. She's beaming at me like she's been looking forward to this moment all day. He's . . . not.

"You recognized me?" I ask.

"No one can miss that pink shirt," Regina says.

Agreed. I look to Frankie. "You all right?"

"I'm fine. I'm just worried about you." Frankie pats my lapel with care.

I lay my hand over my heart. "Aw, you're worried about me?"

He wrinkles his brow. "Not you, the suit."

"MK is doing just fine," I say.

"MK? Uh-uh, you are not on a nickname basis with my suit."

Regina leans in. "I think he's still upset about your effortless six-pack."

Frankie clicks his tongue. "I heard that."

The hostess, who's essentially a floating head to me now, shoots me a look before leading us to a table near the window. I nudge Regina. "Whatever you do, don't stare at her necklace."

"Well, now I have to look."

The three of us take our seats and she hands each of us a thick linen menu. Regina smiles as she takes hers. "Beautiful necklace."

The hostess smiles and runs her finger along the shiny chain. "Thank you."

Regina flicks her brows at me, and I roll my eyes before checking out the entrée selections. Scaloppine Capriccio, Pollo alla Parmigiana, Tortellini alla Panna. Is there any beef on this menu? Feels like a meaty kind of day.

There! Filetto di Manzo alla Fiorentina.

I glance up. Regina's and Frankie's eyes are glued to my every move like I'm some kind of animal, caged for observation.

I sip my water. "What? Am I changing back?" I set the glass down and hover my hands over the table, checking for feminine, hairless knuckles.

"No. Do you think you *will* change back?" Regina asks.

"How am I supposed to know?"

"I don't know." She waves a defensive hand. "I thought you might feel it coming on."

"What? Like my period?" No more tampons? Now there's the silver lining.

Regina shrugs. "Yeah, I guess. Frankie, did you look into any of this?"

I wait for his signature scoff, but instead he shifts his gaze left then right and leans closer. "Yes, and I read an incredible article about a rare condition occurring in young girls in South America and Papua New Guinea. When they hit puberty, they grow penises. They call it *machihembras*—first a woman, then a man."

I put my hand over my chest. "Oh my god. Is that what I have? *Machi, machihe . . .*"

"*Machihembras,*" Frankie pronounces perfectly. "No. For them, it's more like delayed development. Plus, it's really just their genitals that change. You chiseled a new jawline and washboard abs overnight while growing half a foot taller. Those twelve-year-old *machihembras* would be so lucky." He points an erect finger in the air. "Anyway, I also learned that there are some species of fish that change sex based on mating necessities. But it doesn't happen overnight."

"So you think I might be some kind of evolved human?" And am I evolved enough to spontaneously change back?

Frankie deadpans, "No, I'm saying I don't have a fucking clue what happened to you."

"Well, that makes three of us." Regina rolls out her black cloth napkin.

"Thanks for looking into it," I say.

"I'll keep searching but you might have better luck praying to Jesus." He raises a hallelujah hand.

"You think this could all be a crazy dream?" It's certainly unbelievable enough to be one.

Regina shakes her head. "Nope. I saw a guy urinating on the street this morning, right on cue. Definitely not a dream."

Our waiter arrives sporting a skinny black tie and a white button-up that stretches around his toned biceps. He introduces himself as Martino and proceeds with the specials. Listening to his genuine accent totally confirms my choice to come here and blow some of the little money I have left.

Regina flutters her lashes as she places her order with perfect Italian pronunciation.

"Ah, your accent isa very good. You speak *italiano*?" he asks.

"*Sì*." She's almost fluent thanks to her maternal grandparents. Martino begins a conversation with her in Italian. By the way she tilts her head and toys with a piece of her hair, I know she wants the tall, dark, handsome foreigner for dessert. But watching her flirt with a handsome hunk only reminds me of one gorgeous guy . . .

"Hey, Del!" Regina snaps her fingers in front of my face and I flinch. "Your order?"

I shake my head. "Oh, yes, I'll have the Filetto di Manzo alla Fiorentina." I say the words slowly as if it's some new magical incantation I'm practicing. My Italian accent isa not very good.

"And how would you like that prepared, sir?" Martino asks.

Just as I'm about to respond with the usual medium well, I remember this date I went on a while back. The guy ordered his steak medium rare, and as he bit into the flesh, a drip of blood trickled from the side of his mouth. Something about it turned me on, like I knew he could throw down in the bedroom, which he did later. Since then, I've associated bloody meat with manly. And when in Rome.

"Medium rare," I say and my friends tilt their heads.

"Very good, sir," Martino says with a tone of respect. Sir, huh? He collects the stiff menus and Regina ogles him all the way to the kitchen.

I wave my hand in front of her face. "Yo, Gina!"

"He's so sexy." Her grin stretches from ear to ear.

"Yes, he is." Frankie nods, watching him disappear behind the swinging door.

"So I guess Martino's the man of the hour," I say.

Regina raises her brow. "Please, you're the man of the day, Delia."

I let out a slight chuckle. "Tell me about it. But I gotta say, this man stuff is tricky."

"What do you mean?"

"Like this morning, I ran into Shannon on the subway."

The two lean in with wide eyes. "You did? What happened?" Regina asks.

"I said hi because I wasn't thinking and now she thinks I'm a Wall Street dick she went to college with."

"So you didn't give yourself away?" Regina seems to be wrapping her head around it, just as I was on the subway.

"I came close, but no."

"You poor thing. That must've been so weird."

"Trust me. My day got a lot weirder."

Martino returns to our table with the antipasti and places the platter in the center.

"Thank you, Martino," Regina and Frankie say in unison with matching coy smiles.

These two.

"Martino," I start, "can you bring us a bottle of Sassicaia?"

He nods. "Excellent choice, sir."

"That sounds fancy. Sassy Kaya," Frankie says.

"It is."

Sassicaia was the wine my dad would bring home to share with my mom every time he closed a big deal. When my brothers and I were older, he'd let us enjoy a glass too. It's like Tuscany in a bottle. Going from drinking a five-dollar bottle of wine to a two-hundred-dollar bottle feels like a victory in itself.

"Does expensive-ass wine mean we're celebrating your birthday?" Regina says.

"Yes, among other things."

"Such as . . ." Frankie gestures for more information.

I take in a deep breath. This is the first time I'm saying this aloud. "I sorta became the head managing director of the Ezeus deal at Monty Fuhrmann."

Frankie laughs, popping a slice of prosciutto in his mouth. "No, you didn't."

"Yeah, I really did."

Frankie's bottom lip practically falls on the table; he's apparently too stunned to speak. Regina, on the other hand, is never at a loss for words, and lets her Brooklyn accent dance freely. "How in the hell did you manage that, Mr. Managing Director?"

"So, you know how you said I can be anyone I want?" I take a piece of cold artichoke and stuff it in my mouth, followed by prosciutto, salami, pepperoni.

"Yeah."

"Well," I start through my meat mouth, "I gave myself—" I try to swallow, but the food's stuck.

In my throat.

I slam my fist into my chest and cough, but it doesn't move.

"Oh my god," Frankie says, the color draining from his face, and before I know it, he's lifting me out of my chair, hugging my waist, and pressing hard against my abdomen. A piece of salami flies from my mouth onto the plate of fresh antipasti.

I gasp for air and grab my Little Dickie instinctually.

"You okay?" he asks, breathless.

By now the patrons and staff are all staring at me, standing here clutching my Adam's apple and my crotch. That Spotlight Effect isn't in my head anymore.

"I'm okay." I hunch down and take my seat, my face flaming hot.

"I'm a doctor. Everything's fine," Frankie announces. "She's, I mean, he's okay." He waves proudly and everyone cheers.

Ah, yes. Everyone loves a doctor.

I cough. "Thank you, Dr. Ramirez."

He boasts to his adoring fans for a few more moments before shooting me a cold expression. "Chew your food, you caveman."

"I will. I'm just hungry." I guzzle my water, soothing my throat.

He fans himself. "I swear, you're gonna give me a heart attack."

"Please, like you didn't love being the hero just now." I reach for the plate and see my half-chewed breath-stopper lying like a slug.

Gross.

Martino hurries over. "Are you all right? Can I get you something?"

"Another plate of antipasti, please." Regina bats her eyelashes.

"Right away." A smiling Martino takes the plate from the table and leans into Frankie, placing a gentle hand on his shoulder. "That was amazing," he says, hushed.

Not secret hushed, but sexy hushed.

Then he winks. Winks! My choking might be the best thing that's happened to Frankie in a long time. If he gets a date out of this, he owes me, and I think I'll take the suit. Regina's mouth is a wide hole in her face as she watches sparks fly between Frankie and Martino.

Talk about a love triangle.

I stifle a chuckle.

"What's so funny?" She swivels her neck.

"The last five minutes. It's kind of a dramatic lunch. Don't you think?"

The three of us shift glances between one another. Our smiles grow wider by the second before we bust out laughing. The kind of hysterical laughter that gets louder and faster until you're practically snorting. Once again, I can barely breathe and the restaurant's attention is focused on us.

"Regina's in love with the waiter and . . . he, he"—I can hardly speak—"has the hots for Frankie."

Regina giggles uncontrollably, holding her stomach. "So what? You almost died by salami. Frankie had to save you!"

Tears form at the corners of my eyes.

Frankie's wiping his eyes too. "And Delia has a dick!"

After that we really lose it. Laughing off the whole damn thing.

Finally, we contain the obnoxious pig noises from our table and suck in deep breaths. My cheeks actually hurt. "Where's the wine?" I glance around for Martino.

"Right here," he says, turning the corner, and he places three red wine glasses on the table before uncorking the bottle. "A taste for you, sir."

"Oh, yes, please," Frankie says, watching him pour the sampling with an air of admiration. "Thank you." Without hesitation, he imbibes the red blend then smacks his mouth. "Mmm."

"Good, sir?" Martino asks.

Frankie sends a flirty smile. "Delicious."

"*Splendido!*" Our waiter meticulously fills each glass before leaving the table.

I hand my napkin to Frankie. "Here, you're drooling."

With an eye roll he swats my offer away. "You better tuck that over my paisley tie."

I chuckle, lifting the red to my nose and inhaling the bittersweet aroma. My friends do the same. It's exactly how I remember it. Bold, like the new me.

Regina patiently sets her glass down. "Okay, let's back up. How did you get a managing director position in just a few hours? Is being a man really all it takes?"

"It definitely helps." I motion for them to come closer. "So here's what happened. When I was picking my phone up at Fairbanks's apartment, I overheard him talking about Monty Fuhrmann. Long story short, he was going to cancel their pitch tomorrow."

"That's the one Eric's working on, right?" she asks.

"Exactly. We'll get to him in a minute."

Regina briskly rubs her hands together. "Ohmigod, I can't wait!"

"Anyway, I couldn't exactly go to Eric with this because, well, you know." I wave my hand in front of my body. "So, I sorta told them that Liam Golan sent me from the Zurich office to save the pitch."

Frankie raises his brow. "Wait, that old dude you're obsessed with?"

"You mean the CEO I have extensive notes on, yes. I told them Fairbanks was going to call and he did, so they bought every word. And now I'm running the show."

They back away, speechless for a moment. "Maybe you're right and this is an elaborate dream." Regina nods as if she's in the middle of an existential crisis, and I urge her to sip her wine.

"Whatever's going on, I have to say that this is the most alive I've felt in a long time. I'm leaping before looking, and now I have a corner office overlooking Manhattan. It reminds me of when I first moved to the city and how fearless I was."

"Girl, I get that, but aren't you afraid of getting caught?" Regina is rarely the reasonable one, but that question's been haunting me all morning.

"I am. But at the same time, it's totally worth the risk. Like you said, it's an *opportunity*. And who knows? If I can hold out until tomorrow and close this pitch, maybe they won't care because I'll be a hero and they'll keep me on." I know it's a long shot, but I've gotten this far.

"Okay, Power Ranger," Regina mutters into her wineglass.

Frankie squirms a little in his seat, picking at his nails. "Is that considered insider trading?"

"No, it's not stock trading. He said it right in front of me. I'm just turning Monty Fuhrmann's lemons into my lemonade."

"If you say so," he says. "I just want you to know that I don't have bail money."

My shoulders fall and sweat beads beneath my palms. For a moment, I imagine being escorted from the Monty Fuhrmann Tower in cuffs, a dismal mug shot of a face I barely recognize, and black ink soaked into my fingertips. Wait a second. Are my fingerprints the same? If they are, that means they're already on file at the SEC. Hmm, maybe my identity isn't completely lost forever. Even if my vagina is.

Our waiter returns with a fresh plate of food, and Frankie shifts his attention, complete with a cheery smile. "*Grazie*, Martino."

I take one piece off the plate, chew it, then swallow it entirely before speaking.

There. Good boy.

Regina claps her hands. "I want to hear about Eric now."

Blood rushes to my cheeks the way it always does when someone brings him up. At least this time it's not rushing below my belt. "Well, we're working together again."

"Just like old times!" Regina's voice raises a few octaves.

I nod, unable to conceal the shy smile that follows. "Not exactly. I am sort of his boss now."

"Aw, look, she's blushing." Her voice softens.

"The ironic thing is that now that I'm regaining my confidence, all I want to do is tell him how I feel. But now I can't."

"Any chance he'd be down with the new D?" Frankie asks, pointing below his belt.

"I don't think so."

He raises his hand. "Don't knock it 'til you try it."

Regina and I snicker. If you can't laugh at your own misery, you're screwed.

"Do you guys think I should tell him about 'the change'?" My stomach swirls with jitters at the thought.

"The change?" Frankie firmly sets his glass on the white linen as the wine rocks back and forth in his glass. "We're not talking about menopause. We're talking about an overnight, miraculous anatomy transformation." He lowers his voice. "No, you should *not* tell him. Don't tell anyone until you can come up with a better story than 'I woke up like this.'"

I throw my hands up in surrender. "You're right. I just feel weird not telling him."

"Well, toughen up and get over it."

"Geez, Frankie, what's with all the tough love?" Regina asks. "That's my department."

"Sorry"—his tone eases—"it's been a stressful morning."

"No shit," Regina and I chime in together.

Martino appears, this time holding an oversized tray with our steaming meals. My stomach jumps at the scent. I can almost hear it shout, "Feed me!" as he lays the plate of tender beef in front of me. I wet my lips and stab a fork into the juicy slab, watching the crimson seep out. I take a deep breath before indulging in my first bite. "Oh, man. This is so good. You guys wanna try?"

They decline with a look, digging into their own dishes. Frankie lowers his fork. "Are you sure you can pay for this?"

"I'll figure it out." I chew carefully before swallowing my steak to continue. "And if there's anything I've learned today, it's that we should take advantage of the time we have when we have it. You know, carpe diem."

"Well, that's something, I guess," Frankie says as he glances up at Martino.

Regina stands, leaving her napkin on her chair. "I'll be right back."

I reach for the wine and sip slowly. My taste buds seem to be unaltered, because I love it just as much as before. Once Regina turns the corner, I lean over to Frankie. "I need to talk to you about something. Guy stuff."

"What guy stuff?" he asks.

"Well, besides the fact that my balls got a little sweaty when I had to walk a few blocks, I'm having another issue."

Frankie cringes. "Eww. I know we're both guys now, but please don't tell me about your sweaty balls during lunch."

"Sorry."

"You can keep the underwear, by the way." He gives me the kind of look your parents give you when you've done something stupid but forgivable. "So what is it?"

"My Little Dickie's been waking up. Sometimes with good reason, but other times not so much." I motion just beneath the table.

"Little Dickie? Did you just call it Little Dickie?"

I shrug. "Yeah, I named it in the shower today. Thought it might help. Haven't you named yours?"

"Maybe," he mutters into his glass.

"What do you call it? Oscar de la Renta?"

Frankie shakes his head. "Pepe."

Huh? "Did you say Pee-pee?"

"Pepe!" he snaps.

I giggle but he doesn't seem amused.

"Didn't you have a question about *your* Little Dickie?"

I glance around and whisper, "Random boners. Is that normal?"

"I wouldn't call it abnormal. But it can be inconvenient."

"How often does yours . . . report for duty in a day?" I doubt guys usually talk to other guys about this stuff, but I need to get guidance somewhere. I'm a late bloomer.

"Oh, at least half a dozen, maybe more."

"Really? What a nuisance."

Frankie gives me a good-ole-boys pat on the back. "Welcome to penishood, my friend."

"Thanks," I say, rolling my eyes. He takes a sip and ogles the waiter like he wants to devour him the way I'm devouring my medium-rare steak.

"You should ask him out. He could be your *lover*." I nudge him with my elbow while savoring another bite.

"You think so? He's not too hot for me?" Frankie is always a little self-conscious, but he has no reason to be.

"No way. Besides, he's totally into you. He wants you to ask him out." We look over at Martino, who's serving another table. He catches us and sends another smile Frankie's way.

"Did you see that?" I ask like a high school girl encouraging my BFF with her crush.

"Yeah, but I don't know. He'll probably just break my heart." Frankie is classically a dumpee instead of a dumper.

"Well, you'll never know if you don't ask him out. And if I can charge into Monty Fuhrmann and make them believe I'm some bigwig managing director from across the pond, then you can definitely get that guy's number. C'mon, have some cojones." I grab mine for the millionth time, completely disregarding that we're in a five-star freaking restaurant.

"Okay, I'll do it," he says, and I cheer him on.

Regina pops back from the ladies' room. "Do what?"

"Hook up with Martino later." I bounce my eyebrows in a suggestive manner. She doesn't seem pleased. Poor Gina. "Don't look so glum; we'll get you a guy."

"Actually, I've been thinking it would be pretty cool to get you a girl." She mimics my brow bounce.

"What do you mean? Like sex? With a woman?" My pulse quickens with every question.

"Yeah, aren't you a little bit curious?" The naughty glimmer in Regina's eyes tells me that if she were in my shoes, she'd do it in a New York minute.

Last night I did mention that if I were a man I could have more sex. But experiencing sex as a man with a woman? For a moment, I try to imagine what it would feel like to have something warm and wet enclose my—

"Nope." If I can't wrap my head around it, then I can't handle it wrapped around my . . . head. "I think I'm better off keepin' it in my pants."

CHAPTER THIRTEEN

Our plates are nearly cleaned and it's about time to head back to my new job. I set my black napkin on the table. "I need to pee."

"Me too," Frankie says and pushes his chair back.

I rise to my feet. "Is it cool for guys to go to the bathroom together?"

"It depends on who you ask. C'mon." He gives me a little shove.

I follow him into the men's room, but pass up the row of porcelain pee stations and head for the first empty stall. Frankie positions himself in front of one of the urinals. The scratching sound of his zipper stops me in my tracks. I shift my glance between him and my chosen toilet. I've always found the idea of urinals off-putting. Guys lined up, pissing and looking around at each other, talking about last night's football game or their hot Hooters waitress or maybe comparatively peeking at one another's goods. Come to think of it, I could've had a little look at Eric's earlier. I bet he has a nice one.

Maybe it wouldn't hurt to learn to pee standing up, since I have my own set of goods and all. Besides, it's just Frankie and me. I step over to the ceramic wall basin next to him and avoid looking at his Pepe, even though he's seen my Little Dickie.

"How does this thing work?" I ask, glancing around, expecting to see a metal drain at the bottom, like the kind in a locker room shower. Instead, it's a mini basin with a puddle of water—just like any other toilet.

Frankie keeps his eyes focused on the wall in front of him. "Easy. Carefully take your penis out, direct it at the bowl, and pee."

I step back and the urinal flushes automatically. The water sucks down the toilet-like drain in a spiral then refills.

Hands-free, huh? That's cool.

Taking a piss in front of a urinal has to be easier than dangling my dick over a toilet. I cringe at the memory of my morning spray-palooza.

"Here goes nothin'." I unzip my pants and try to pull the penis out of my boxers. "I can barely fit this thing through my fly. Am I supposed to undo my belt and pants? And why is this underwear hole so small?"

He laughs, wiping a tear at the corner of his eye.

"What if I pee all over myself?"

His amusement ceases. "You better not."

"Then help me!" I glare.

Frankie starts snickering again. "Look, it's really not that hard."

My hand's swallowed up by my pants' fly. "Easy for you to say; you've had one of these for decades."

"Okay, there's two ways you can do this, over the fence or through the gate." He demonstrates the motion with his hand.

"The doorway's a little too narrow for me, if you get my drift."

He shakes his head as if I'm too cocksure myself. "I've seen it, Queen D. It'll fit. But most guys go over the fence."

I unfasten my belt. "Hey, how do you know most guys go over the fence?"

"I just know," he says like he's got a secret. "Be careful that your pants don't go sliding down your legs. That shit's embarrassing." Luckily, these pants aren't oversized and hang nicely on my hips. "Then just whip it out over your boxers and give yourself some space. You don't want to squeeze your balls with the elastic."

Think I'm ready for blastoff. I thrust forward, leaning into the urinal. Please don't make a mess, Delia. Using my hand, I direct the flow. A slow smile lengthens across my face as I let go, watching the urine drain perfectly into the bowl. I'm doing it! I beam a proud grin at the wall in front of me.

It feels good to have some control over this thing.

I think L.D. likes it too.

"You're doing good!" Frankie says.

I turn to him and he's leaned forward, watching the whole thing. I stop peeing. "Dude!"

He shrugs. "What? I'm basically your doctor."

"I think I've got it from here," I say and start the flow again.

"Okay." Frankie zips up and walks off, the urinal flushing at his heels. He turns on the faucet at the sink.

"So which way do you go? Over the fence?" I ask.

"None of your business," he says, grabbing a hand towel, then leaves me to finish on my own, which I do, *very* well. Not a spot of pee on the floor, on the wall, or on Frankie's suit. As I scrub my hands at the sink, I flash a smile at the mirror. A little wine stained, but no debris. I take a closer look at my skin. Its tone has never been so even. What a relief not to be concerned with foundation flakes and smudged eyeliner in the middle of the day. I push the men's room door open, nearly smacking into Frankie and Martino and disrupting their close encounter.

Frankie gives me a glare that says, *Get out of here now!*

"Sorry!" I say, picking up the pace back to the table. Our leftover wine bottle is already corked. Regina stuffs it inside her oversized designer bag that cost as much as the average American's monthly mortgage payment. She's still paying it off on her credit card.

Frankie emerges, flaunting his phone. A new contact by the name of Martino has a home in his address book. "We're going out next week!"

"Good for you," Regina huffs.

I glance at the time above Martino's name. "Ooh, time flies when you're choking on salami."

"What?" She wrinkles her nose.

"I gotta go. My new colleagues will be getting my pitch by now."

CHAPTER FOURTEEN

Cabs are practically lined up outside of the restaurant, so I slide into one. "Monty Fuhrmann Tower, please," I tell the driver.

Damn, it feels good to say that.

He nods. "Yes, sir."

After a twenty-minute stop-and-go drive, we approach the tower. The sun reflects off the mirrored exterior, shining brighter than a new Rolex. My stomach flips and it all settles in again. Did I really wake up like this? Hijack a pitch at *the* Monty Fuhrmann?

All of it feels so real. But how can it be? What if Delia-me is lying in a hospital bed, comatose from too much wine and binge-dreaming this ridiculous series of events my subconscious has produced? At the same time, life has never been so energizing. And the results speak for themselves. I've accomplished more in the last five hours than I have over the past five months. Does the difference between yesterday and today simply come down to having a dick?

Well, whatever it is, I'm in it now.

I pay the driver and head inside, whipping my keycard out of my Gucci and breezing through security. Riding the elevator up thirty-two floors and walking past the bullpen to my office already feels like a familiar commute. Before I can take a seat, the door lashes open, crashing hard against the doorstop. Becker stomps toward me red-faced and raging. It's a tough call between which will explode first, his bulging bloodshot eyes or that pulsing vein down the middle of his forehead.

"Are you out of your fucking mind?" he screams, pointing his finger at me like a toy gun. "Reducing the fee? This makes us look like little bitches. What kind of business are we running here?"

I've been around hotheads like him all my professional life. I know exactly how to tamp down this fireball. "Hey! I'm getting really sick of you acting like an animal in my office." I get right in his face. My voice lowers to a threatening tone. "I know you don't like it, but you need to chill out or I'm gonna throw you out altogether. Now get out of my office." Having assertive authority in business, without being labeled a *little bitch*, is liberating.

"You sure your name's Richard? 'Cause I'd swear you were a Dick." He grits his teeth so hard his face trembles. "You better watch your back!" Becker drills out of my office like a tornado.

A twinge of doubt stabs my gut. What if he's right? What if I'm being too soft? Making too many concessions? If I were a man, would I approach it the same way?

Hold on, Delia. You're letting him get in your head. The real question is, if I were a man, would I doubt myself right now?

Doubt it.

I can't back down now. Not because of some baseless masculine pride but because this is the right call. It's what Fairbanks really wants. I told him we'd surprise him, and he's definitely not expecting this proposal. And since the tech mogul seems to have a slight disdain for Curtis Becker, I'm forced to make another shrewd move. Becker's really gonna go berserk.

I march over to Owen's office. A woman sits quietly at her desk just outside his door. I send her a smile. "Hi, I'm Richard Allen."

Her eyes light up as if I'm the first friendly face she's seen all day. "Oh, so you're Richard Allen." Her eyes trail down to my chest. "Nice shirt."

I smooth out my tie. "Thanks. And you are?"

She extends her hand and I take it. It feels so small in mine. "I'm Ashley, Owen Campbell's assistant. Everyone around here's talking about you, ya know?"

I tilt my head. "And what are they saying about me?" What would I say about the dramatic entrance of Richard Allen if I were in the bullpen right now?

"It depends on who you ask," she says playfully.

"I appreciate the info. Does Mr. Campbell have a moment for me?" I keep my eyes politely on her face. Even though I know she's wearing a cream suit I've been eyeing at Saks.

"Sure." She nods and I get the feeling she likes working for Campbell. Unlike Charlene, Becker's assistant. I'd rather clean more shit off Todd Fairbanks's toilet than work for him.

I knock on the doorframe. "Am I interrupting?"

Owen's office is noticeably smaller than Becker's and even mine. But there's something cheerier about it. Maybe it's the direction of the sunlight or the fact that he's actually wearing a smile. In either case, I'm warming up to him.

"Richard, come in." He motions me to sit. "What's going on?"

"I have a couple issues about tomorrow." I settle down where he's offered and search his face for some indication that he wants to overthrow me as much as Becker does.

He looks off with a sigh then returns his attention to me. "All right. What's the problem?"

"The thing is, I can close this deal tomorrow but I'm missing something vital."

Owen folds his arms over his chest. "Okay . . ."

"You and Becker have a personal connection with Fairbanks. I don't. I'm concerned about the three of us coming together on this."

Owen leans in as if he's about to let me in on a little secret. "Well, you're right to be concerned. Becker likes to be in control, as you can probably tell. But he and I are essentially partners. We have this sort of good-cop, bad-cop dynamic."

"Who's the bad cop?" I ask.

He lifts his eyebrow at my rhetorical remark. "Truth is, I was a little worried something like this was going to happen."

"Really? Why?" I ask.

He lowers his eyes as if trying to recall a memory. "Todd said something to me earlier this year that made me think something wasn't right. Maybe it was more of a gut feeling. But when he called, I knew I should've listened to my instinct. Anyhow, I think your proposal will work. It's smart. But Becker has his own ideas. I'm amazed he's let you move on this deal as much as he has."

Me too. But then I remember why they've really let me run the show. "It's not me. It's Golan."

"Right, Golan." Owen rubs his chin, pausing for a moment. "I have to be honest. I was surprised to hear that Liam Golan knew so much about this. How did he know Todd was going to cancel? It's . . . unusual."

I can't tell if he's suspicious that Golan might employ spies on the streets of New York, or if *Owen's* in cahoots with Becker. He did say they're partners.

Just stick to the story, Delia.

"It's not unusual at all. He pays closer attention to things like this than you realize. If this doesn't happen, it'll definitely damage our reputation. And we sure as hell don't need that."

"Makes sense," Owen agrees. "Let's meet later this afternoon and I'll give you some insight on Todd Fairbanks."

"Thank you," I say, a little taken aback by his offer. Just hope it's not a trap. Especially since his partner is so unpredictable.

"So what's the other issue?" he asks, tapping his pen on the desk.

I stand up and close the door to his office, puffing my chest a little before I speak. "I don't know if it's a good idea for Becker to be in the meeting with us tomorrow."

Owen drops his pen and his jaw. "You're kidding, right? He'll really go ballistic."

"Look, I'm not saying he can't work on this deal, but I've been informed Fairbanks has grown . . . leery of Becker. If he's not there, it'll give the impression of a cleaner slate. I'm also concerned Becker will run his mouth off and we'll lose our chance."

Owen nods, letting out a long sigh. "I see what you mean."

"So, you agree?"

"Yeah, but let me tell him. I think it'll be better coming from me."

That's too bad. I would've loved to see his face when he got the news. After all, I told him I'd throw him out. Then again, he warned me to watch my back. "He's not dangerous, is he?"

Owen waves off any concern. "Only to himself."

Not sure I buy that.

"One other thing. Why don't we have more women on the team? It's like a sausage party out there."

He lets out a small laugh like he knows it. "Yeah, I'm not crazy about it either."

"Then why don't you do something about it?" It's not like *you're* powerless.

Owen shrugs. "You know how it is. We don't get as many female applicants. A smaller hiring pool means fewer women on the team."

The ole "women aren't applying" excuse. With my lack of callbacks, I'm not convinced this is really the reason for the gender gap. "Well, as soon as we close this deal, I want to get some headhunters out there looking for some kick-ass female perspective. This is the twenty-first century. We've got some catching up to do."

CHAPTER FIFTEEN

I shut Owen's office door on my way out and breathe a sigh of relief. His support speaks volumes. Ashley flashes a smile as I walk toward her.

"Can you tell me where I can get a cup of coffee around here?" I ask.

"I can make you one," she says in a sweet tone.

"Thanks, but I wouldn't ask you to do that."

"I don't mind. Otherwise, there's an employee break lounge down that hall, on the left." She motions with her willowy arm.

"Thank you, Ashley." I nod. "I appreciate all your help today."

"You're welcome." Her eyes gleam with sincerity. A little bit of appreciation goes a long way. There were so many days at work when I felt like the job was going to kill me and no one seemed to acknowledge it. It's not like I was asking for an award or even a raise. All I wanted was a simple *thank you* or *we appreciate your hard work*. How fucking hard is that?

I walk the perimeter of the bullpen toward the hall, keeping my head high. Ashley said they're all talking about me. Well, they're all staring too. But this time it doesn't bother me. That's right, take a good look. I'm the badass who put Becker in his place and turned the Ezeus deal around.

When I walk into the break lounge, Eric and two other guys are conversing in a casual circle. My cheeks warm at the glint in his eyes beneath the fluorescent lights and I smooth my hair around my ear. Their laughter breaks as I approach, and my straight spine begins to stoop. Were they gossiping about me?

No, guys don't gossip.

Unless that's just a myth.

My crush takes a sip from his steaming cup as I brush past him to the coffee maker.

"Hey, Richard."

"Hey, Eric," I say, hoping my face cools soon. At least Little Dickie's down. Must've been that glass of wine at lunch. The other guys still haven't spoken a word. "Don't mind me." I grab a clean mug from the cabinet and load the one-cup device. The quiet brew of the machine dulls the sharp edge of the uncomfortable silence, but I can still hear every crinkle of the sweetener packages as I riffle through them. This is the longest coffee drip ever.

"This is Mike and Brian. They're associates," Eric offers in a friendly tone, pointing the guys out. It's not unlike him to show kindness to everyone—must be his Midwestern charm. I've always loved that about him, but in this moment, I appreciate it so much more. No one likes to be the outsider. And I should know. Even though I work in a male-dominated industry, I'm not a guy's girl. I don't drink beer. I didn't like any of those street-racing movies—can't even remember what they're called. And I don't fart in front of anyone. Ever. So sliding into an all-male water cooler conversation was never easy. I finally have a chance to be one of the guys.

"Hey, guys. I'm Richard." I give a dude(ish) chin nod and lean against the counter, folding my arms like I'm trying on Casual Guy. "So, what's going on?"

Hand tucked in or out?

Now I just look uncomfortable.

Mike narrows his eyes. "With . . . ?"

I shrug. "With whatever you guys were talking about."

They exchange glances.

"We were talking about Mike's girlfriend," Eric says, and Mike shoots him a look. "Yeah, she's pressuring him to get married."

"Ah, she wants you to put a ring on it," I tease, flashing my left hand back and forth and popping my hip. From Casual Guy to Beyoncé Backup Dancer. By the looks on their faces, I see I've become a whole other type of leper. I immediately knock it off and stuff my hands in my pockets.

That would have gone over so much better with a group of girls.

"Um, yeah . . ." Mike says.

Okay, Delia, less Queen B, more Jay-Z.

You can come back from this.

"That's what my girlfriend always says. 'When are you gonna put a ring on it? When are you gonna put a ring on it?'" The guys give me nothing as my palms go clammy. Without taking a second to think or breathe, I stumble on and reach for something, anything, a dude would say. "I'm like, whoa, slow your roll. It's not like I'm bugging her to put a ring on my dick."

Uh, what the fuck did I just say?

"Right . . ." Mike replies with a look that reflects my own confusion. "Anyway, I'm not ready to settle down and all that." Brian and Eric nod with affirming expressions as they raise their mugs to their mouths. I'm not ready to get married either, mostly because that's when everyone starts hounding you about when you're gonna start a family and get pregnant. But seeing Eric agree without a second thought makes me wonder if he's not the commitment type. Are any men in this city the commitment type?

"How come?" I ask and drip a single creamer pod into my hot mug, stirring slowly.

Mike narrows his eyes. "'Cause, *you* know," he says as if I should know. I don't, of course, but I want to. Maybe even have to. So I take what I believe to be an educated guess.

"Yeah. A playa's gotta play." I raise my hand and wait for fraternal daps of acceptance. But the guys look deadpan, leaving me hanging.

Guess again, Delia.

How am I in this body but no better off relating to guys than I was before? And why did I say that thing about putting a ring on my dick? Now they probably think I'm into cock rings. What the hell are cock rings for anyway?

Walking away isn't the worst option right now. But I refuse to leave on this awkward note.

I rock on my heels, hoping someone will say something, but

the room grows cringingly silent again. "So uh," I start. "Have you guys . . ." Blank. My mind is totally freaking blank.

C'mon, Delia, say something. What are *all* men into?

"Seen any good porn lately?" I blurt out like word-vomit and Brian nearly chokes on his brew.

Eric snorts a laugh. "What?"

Okay . . . so not that, but I can't backtrack now.

"Like on the internet." If I could capture their faces on camera it would make the perfect WTF GIF.

Eric leans in, lowering his voice. "We know what you're talking about. Do you always talk about porn with strangers?"

"Pff!" I send a dismissive wave. "Yeah, Swiss people are very open on the subject of porn. It's as common as discussing art films."

"Really?" Brian gives an intrigued expression and his full attention.

"Mm-hmm," I mutter. After this, I'm writing an apology letter to the good people of Switzerland.

Eric shrugs. "Well, have *you* seen any good porn lately?"

Staying in this room was a total mistake. They're just staring at me, awaiting my answer. Then again, they do seem genuinely interested in what I'm going to say. Could I have cracked the code?

Hmm . . . okay, porn. Have I seen any good porn lately? Since losing my job, I've been home alone a lot. All horned up. So I've been cleaning my browser history almost as much as I clean toilets. "Uh . . . sure. Yeah, I saw a good one last week."

"What site?" Mike asks.

I only know one porn website and it's got porn-for-women written all over it. "Uhh . . . I honestly can't remember."

"What was so good about it?" Brian smirks.

I scan my brain trying to remember any porn I've seen. They're all kind of the same. Girl blows guy. Guy does girl. The finale comes, because he does, and it's over. Hmm, there is one porno flick that sticks out in my mind. "They were in the kitchen," I say, but the guys don't seem to follow. "I like that stuff, you know, when my girlfriend surprises me in the kitchen. It's spontaneous . . ." I nod slowly, clearly unsure of myself.

"Any criticisms?" Eric baits. Is he indulging me or teasing?

How do I critique porn like an indie fest film? Come to think of it, I do have a consistent criticism with erotic cinema. No way in hell the women reach orgasm that fast and that often. But this probably isn't the audience to voice that gripe with. On the other hand, it might be the perfect one. Men need to know it's *not* that easy.

Now, what was wrong with the kitchen porn?

I got it!

"Yeah, they kept the faucet running the whole time."

"And . . . ?" Brian asks.

"And, nearly a billion people on the planet don't have access to clean drinking water and they just let it run. It's so wasteful." Turns out I'm not just the Pink Power Ranger, I'm a Planeteer too. Judging by their silence, it seems I'm the only one. I shrug, hoping my words roll off their shoulders too, then send a small smile Eric's way. He kindly returns it while Mike's and Brian's eyes meet in a sideways glance over the tops of their mugs.

Okay, last try. What's a dude-safe topic?

Women?

No, that's what got me into trouble in the first place.

Weekend getaways?

Like anyone here has time for that.

Sports!

Yes, men love sports. How did I not think of that earlier? Would've saved me the embarrassment of water-wasting porn talk. "Did you guys catch the game last night?"

"Which game?" Brian asks.

"Um . . ." I exhale. The only sport I know is golf, but you don't catch a golf *game* on TV. What sports season is it? Baseball? Basketball? Is there even a game on Wednesday nights? "I don't know. I don't keep up with American sports anymore. Just trying to make conversation."

The guys sip their coffee without a word. If I spontaneously changed bodies, maybe I can spontaneously disappear.

Mike clears his throat, then turns on his heel. "Well, we better get back to work." Brian follows. I watch them swagger out the door like the cool kids I desperately want to be in with while Eric takes a seat at a small table with his cup.

"You're not leaving with your friends?" I ask, pulling out the chair near his.

He pushes his mug around in a circle on the table. "They're my colleagues. Not my friends."

"Oh." He's by far the coolest of the bunch. The one I really want to be "in" with. Well, really, I want him to be in me . . . Not sure that would work now.

I frown. "I don't think I made a great impression on them."

He leans forward with a sympathetic look. "With all due respect, you're a little . . . different."

Now *that's* the understatement of the year. "You have no idea," I say under my breath.

"It's not a criticism. You're kinda funny."

"I am?"

He lets outs a little laugh. "Yeah, when you did that Put a Ring on It dance, it reminded me of my friend—that girl who has your same briefcase."

My face gets warm and tingly, and I press my lips together trying not to totally geek out. "Oh, yeah. Delia, right?" I lean on my elbows, resting my chin in my hands like a teenage girl gazing at her crush.

He looks taken aback. "Good memory." It's very easy to remember your own name. A lot easier than depicting your faux identity. "Yeah, she loves Beyoncé." What can I say, the man knows me. "I remember this one time back when we were all working late at HBG, I went by her desk to say good night. She had her earbuds in, dancing in her chair. I didn't want to startle her, so I let her be."

My cheeks have got to be salmon pink by now. I literally must've been dancing like no one was watching. Except Eric saw the whole thing go down! How embarrassing.

"That's funny," I say.

His gaze drifts away, and an endearing smile pulls at the corners of his adorable mouth. "It was really cute. But I've seen her out a few times. She's a really sexy dancer."

Sexy? Did he just call me *sexy*?

Let me check.

"Sexy?"

He chuckles, running his fingers through his hair, and I watch his face flush a cosmopolitan pink. "Yeah, especially when she lets her hair down. She's so hot. And the way she throws her head back in a laugh when something is really funny. I love when I can get her to laugh like that."

Ohmigod, ohmigod, ohmigod. He thinks I'm sexy. *Sexy*!

"She sounds . . ." I can't think of words. "Great." I glance at his earlobe, wanting to bite it. There's a lot more of him I'd like to nibble. The heat from my face draws down my neck, past my chest, and hits below my belt. L.D. begins to rise and grow like the elation in my chest. I shift in my seat, crossing my arms over my lap. My body seems to scream at me—*Let me out! He thinks we're hot!*

"She's . . ." His Sinatra gaze drifts again.

What? What's he going to say? Is she smart? Is she beautiful? Is she spank-bank material? Spit it out, Eric!

He grins. "The greatest girl I know."

My eyes fixate on his. I have no breath because he always takes it away. *I'm* the greatest girl he knows? He likes me—for real! Why hasn't he said that to me before? Any of it? There's got to be more to this story.

"Oh, so, uh . . ." Damn it, Delia, breathe! "Why isn't she your girlfriend?"

He shakes his head, leaning away from me, and the idea. "Good question. I'm not entirely sure she feels the same about me. Besides, she's having some job issues and might move away. I wouldn't want to make her life any more complicated than it already is."

Frankie was right. Eric and I have been in a dating stalemate. If only I could morph back into my old body, I'd tell him everything—that he's my favorite person to sit next to at the bar, that he makes my skin tingle when he's close by, that his laugh dispels all my worries, and that before I go to sleep at night, he's the last thing on my mind. I don't want to pretend anymore. I have to come clean—confess everything right now!

Who cares if I have a boner while I do it?

My heart is a pounding lump in my throat. I swallow hard. "Eric, I need to tell you something." My tone turns serious and my pulse is so loud in my ears I can barely hear my thoughts.

"What?" he asks, like he knows what I have to say is truly important.

Then, a voice in my head busts through and yells, "Are you fucking nuts? You can't tell him the truth. He'll have security take you out faster than a porn star's fake orgasm!"

Shit.

Why didn't I tell him how I felt when I had the chance? What if there are no more chances? What if it's too late? I swear, if I ever get my body back, I'm going to march right up to him and kiss him the way I've dreamed about since the day we met.

His brow begins to rise impatiently. I bite my lip, then let out a deep sigh. "If you don't tell her, you'll regret it for the rest of your life. Trust me. I know."

Eric nods. "I gotta say, after that player comment, I would not have expected to take your advice about women. But I think you might be right about this one." He pulls his phone from his pocket. "I'm gonna tell her. Right now." He stands and slowly walks toward the door, focused on the tiny screen.

My pulse quickens. "Now? As in *now* now?" I attempt to rise to my feet but my boner catches on the edge of the table. Fuck, that's inconvenient. How the hell do guys walk around with these things all day?

I ease back into the chair, digging in my pocket for my phone. The moment my fingers grab my device, it starts to vibrate. The phone, that is. Thank God it's already on silent. What would I say if he'd heard Delia's ringtone too? There's only so much I can blame on the Swiss.

After a moment, he's gone, and I hate that he can't tell me, Delia-me, right now. I glance down at the pitched tent in my pants. "You can go back to sleep. He's gone now," I whisper.

But it does nothing, just stays there—like a dog waiting at the back door to go out and play. I let out a frustrated sigh and close my eyes for a moment, while thoughts of little pubic hairs stuck to dried pee on toilet rims play in my mind. How does that even happen? Are men simultaneously shedding while they piss?

Gross.

I peek one eye open and glance down at my pants, hoping to see a valley instead of a peak. Wishful thinking. My body feels wide awake. "Go away." I press my Little Dickie down with my palm, but the stubborn thing remains undefeated. There's no time for this nonsense. I have to get back to work.

I clench my jaw and send my crotch a stern glare. "You listen to me, man. I'm the boss. And you will go down!"

"Are you talking to me?"

Startled, I whip my head in the direction of the deep voice and spot a stranger in a suit. Where did *he* come from? "No." I clear my throat, lowering my eyes. "I was talking to . . ." I'm not sure if it was my strict demand or the intrusion but ding, dong, the boner is dead.

CHAPTER SIXTEEN

On the way back through the bullpen, I hum a Sinatra song quietly to myself. Heart fluttering and feet floating, I replay Eric's words—I'm the greatest girl he knows. I want so badly to be that girl again one day.

When I spot Nicole staring intently at her computer screen, I shake off the Eric-high and get back to reality.

"Hey, Nicole. Any messages for me?"

Her stare shifts my way. "No. I haven't had a single call for you all day. Does anyone even know you're here?"

"What do you mean?" I take a step back.

"I mean, does anyone know where to reach you?" She purses her mouth and blinks impatiently.

"Of course." Everyone *here* knows how to reach me. "Just let me know if anything comes in."

She returns her attention to the screen. "I will."

"Keep up the good work," I say and quickly shut myself in my office. Ah, alone again. I kick back in my plushy executive chair and retrieve my phone. Alerts of a missed call and two texts from Eric pop up on the screen.

ERIC: Hey, can you talk?

ERIC: I don't know what you were going to tell me about the Ezeus pitch earlier but there are some new developments here. I'll give you the scoop if you meet me later for a birthday drink.

I gasp with excitement and nearly jump out of my seat. Is that his clever way of setting up a date with me tonight? I want to text him *Yes, yes, baby, yes!* But I can't. Delia is nowhere in sight.

Damn it, universe!

I've blown him off too many times today to not respond now. But what do I tell him? I need something that sounds legit.

Washing my hair?

No, that's too Kelly Kapowski.

Sitting the neighbor's dog?

Nah, he might ask to join me. He loves little pups.

Hmm . . . what's something substantial? Where would Delia be that's important enough to miss a drink with the man of her dreams?

Grandma's on her deathbed?

Yes! It's serious and detaining. No mixed signals when it comes to dead relatives. And it's easy to avoid talking about. Besides, she passed away about five years ago. I'm sure Grandma wouldn't mind, given the circumstances.

DELIA: I can't. I might be leaving for FL tonight. I just found out my grandma isn't doing well.

There. That should buy me some time.

ERIC: Really? I thought your grandma died a while ago.

When did I tell him about my poor deceased grandma? And since when did any man ever have a better memory than a woman? We must've had a thousand conversations over the years. He probably knows everything about me by now. Everything except the one thing I haven't had the guts to say.

DELIA: Yeah, she did. This is my other grandma.

Good save!

ERIC: Oh. I'm so sorry. I thought your other grandma lived in Ohio.

Seriously? How does he remember the most mundane details like which grandma is alive and where she lives? It has to be love, right?

DELIA: Yes, but she moved to Florida recently to be near my parents.

My heart pounds harder with every character I type. I hate lying about my poor granny who's alive and well in Ohio.

I'm totally going to hell for this.

ERIC: Keep me posted.

DELIA: Okay. I will. Thank you.

ERIC: Call me when you get back so we can meet up. I've got lots to tell you.

DELIA: Okay, catch up later.

I imagine myself flying back from Boca, meeting him outside the terminal at LaGuardia. He doesn't say anything. Instead, he takes me in his arms and kisses me like he's been waiting his whole life to put his lips on mine. Then, we go back to my place and he tears off my clothes, unable to keep his hands off me for as long as we both shall live.

Or some version of that.

I shake the image as it's replaced with one of my new form. What if Eric never sees Delia again? Am I destined to be Richard Allen forever? My five-star lunch churns in my gut while my head feels as fuzzy as my hairy thighs. Why does it have to be one or the other; the guy with a great job or the woman with a great boyfriend? Is that what this whole experience is about? That I can't have it all? Do I have to choose?

My mind wanders to that dark place where all my problems linger and scheme about how they're going to make my life hell. I swivel my chair around and gaze out the wide window. New York is alive with taxis, bikes, and pedestrians flowing like blood cells through the veins of the city. The world never stops spinning. Even if you want it to.

It also never stops serving shit sandwiches. So pass the mayo.

Knock, knock.

Nicole slips into my office, shutting the door behind her. "I finally have a message for you." Her expression screams that there's a problem, a problem she's glad she doesn't have to contend with. "Becker needs to see you immediately."

I bet he does. There's a good chance Owen's delivered the news that Becker is officially excused from the pitch.

My brows squish together. "Do you know what it's about?"

"He didn't say, but he called me himself and he was . . . *cordial*." Nicole grimaces at the word.

"Maybe he's coming around."

She crosses her arms. "Becker is never cordial. He's up to something."

"I'm beginning to get the sense he's always up to something." I rise to my feet and zip past her.

This ought to be good. When I make it down the hall, Charlene's standing guard in front of Becker's door. Guess I taught her a lesson this morning. "Hello, Mr. Allen. He's waiting for you in the conference room."

Changing the location of the meeting last minute. A classic throw-off-your-opponent tactic. I shrug like a boxer ready for a match. Float like a butterfly, sting like a bee, baby. Charlene waves for me to follow her two doors down. Glass walls separate the long room from the hallway, and the blinds have been drawn. She lets me in, keeping her eyes lowered as I step inside. The door slams against my back. Becker sits behind a shiny twenty-person confer-ence table. "There you are!" A devilish grin grows from his lips. "So nice of you to join me. Why don't you take a seat?"

With that look on his face and all this privacy, something tells me he might actually want to fight me. I ball a stiff fist with one hand and pull out a leather chair with the other. Might have to pull some Krav Maga on his ass. "What's this about, Curtis?" My voice is as steady and strong as my hands.

"Interesting question. That's exactly what I asked myself when you busted through my door this morning." Becker leers. "Now I've got a question for you, *Richard*, if that is your real name." Uh-oh. "Who do you work for? Because you sure as hell don't work for us."

Oh. Shit. I gulp back all the moisture in my mouth and my fist falls. I would too if I weren't already sitting.

"Golan's office has never heard of you. There's no record of you at any Monty Fuhrmann office." He shoots me a self-satisfied smirk. "You're a fraud."

I can't speak. I can't breathe. I can barely think.

Heat creeps up my cheeks and my heart pounds in my ears. Curtis Becker actually outsmarted me. There's no more bullshit in my tank, no more tricks up my sleeve to talk my way out of this debacle. This is it. I'm finished. His dubious smile turns blurry and the room spins. Ugh. There better be a garbage can nearby. I blink a few times and finally take in a breath.

"I knew that would finally shut you up."

I clench my jaw so tight that my molars might crack. "So now what?"

Becker leans forward. "Who do you work for? Really."

It's truth time. I let out a breath. "I don't work for anyone."

He narrows his eyes and I hate his guts even more. "Then how did you know that Fairbanks was going to call and cancel?"

If I thought the answer would help me, I'd tell him. I'd tell him the whole damn story. But it would only make this devastating situation worse. "What does it matter? I saved your ass."

Too bad I can't save mine.

"Maybe you did. Maybe you didn't. But either way, tomorrow *I'll* be sitting across from Todd Fairbanks, pitching *my* deal, and you'll be . . ." Becker leans back in his chair like he's the Godfather. "Well, that depends."

I swallow hard, and a fresh wave of fear spills over me. "On what?"

Becker pushes a manila folder across the table as swift as a bullet. "The way I see it, you've got two choices."

My hands tremble as I open the folder to what looks like an ironclad nondisclosure agreement. I wouldn't be surprised if it also bans me from ever working here in the future. It feels like the old Hollywood threat—*You'll never work in this town again!* Only now, it might actually be true. "You can sign this agreement. I'll let you leave here with what's *left* of your dignity. And you will never speak a word of this to anyone. Ever." He slides a pen over and I pick it up. It's weighted with silver and reads *Curtis Becker, Managing Director, Monty Fuhrmann New York.*

"What's the other option?"

Becker hints at a villainous laugh. "Jail." The man doesn't move, doesn't blink. "We'll press charges to the fullest extent of the law."

Jail!

"For what crime?"

"Fraud. And maybe we'll throw in conspiracy for fun."

Fraud? Conspiracy? Me? With their hotshot legal team, who knows how long they'll put me away? Uh-uh. I'll never survive in jail. Orange is so not my color.

I shut my eyes tight for a moment, knowing I have no recourse. Why does every damn door slam in my face? Why can I never win? I glance up at Becker, whose patience seems to be wearing thin. Flipping to the last page of the contract, I scribble the name *Richard Allen*.

Oh, man.

This. Hurts.

"Good," Becker says. "I'm glad we have an understanding."

I stand, wishing, praying even, that there was something I could say—anything to keep me here. But I just agreed in writing to not speak of this. Ever.

"Your stupid bag is waiting for you outside the door, and there's a guard nearby in case you try to pull any shit." After this conversation, I'm surprised there's not one here already. "You can go now."

I drag my feet to the door.

"Hey, Dick," Becker calls out, and I turn back. "Fuck you."

Yeah, I'm pretty much fucked.

My Gucci's leaning against the glass wall. I give it a quick check to make sure nothing's missing, then hurry to the elevator. As I pass the bullpen, all I can think is *dead man walking*. The elevator ride down feels like descending back into an inescapable hell. Out on the street, Monty Fuhrmann Tower looms. I don't think I've ever felt this small.

It's over. It's really over.

Released back into the wild.

CHAPTER SEVENTEEN

My cheeks burn as I move toward the subway. What was I thinking? That I could just *roar* like a lion and save the day? Pretend to be something I'm not, and they wouldn't figure it out? I'm sure as hell no Serena Walters. Damn it! I've completely lost my chance at my dream job and my dream guy. And I'll probably have to hawk my Gucci just to pay off lunch. My vision grows fuzzy again. For a moment, I'm not sure if the city is actually spinning or if it's just the effect of my twisted life getting completely out of control. I blink a few times, sharpening my focus, but keep my gaze lowered to my big feet dragging along in Frankie's shoes.

The subway station is just up the block, but the thought of being swallowed into a sea of people on the train makes me feel less than the nothing I already am. I step off the curb, hailing with my heavy arm at half-mast. Lit taxis pass by, one after the other. Just as I'm about to give up, one finally pulls in front of me. Its bright sign is currently the sunniest thing in my life. On the ride, my despair swells with each passing block. What am I gonna do when I get back to my apartment? Mope around all by myself? I already do that most of the time. I'm tired of that pathetic habit.

Staring out the window, I spot a familiar bar up ahead. Frankie and I meet there occasionally since the drinks are cheap and it's close to the hospital. "Stop the car," I groan, and the driver complies. With Frankie and Regina busy at their *real* jobs, a bartender might be the best company I can ask for. Not to mention, a shot is the perfect antidote to getting sacked. I leave a decent tip for the driver, as he was kind enough to leave me to my silence the entire way.

This block is on the dingy side and the red neon *BEER* sign in the window does nothing to class it up. I creak open the door. The bar's dim, but not in an ambient way, desolate, but not in an exclusive way, and a little seedy, not in a trendy way.

"You guys open?" I call out to the bartender, whose tattoo-covered arms are draped in her dyed raven hair. It's not like I've ever seen the place packed, but there are usually at least a handful of drinkers.

"Yeah, we're open," she snaps with the husky voice of a good singer or a bad smoker.

I slog across the sticky floor, taking my pick of one of the empty barstools and setting my Gucci on the stool next to me. I lean my elbows on the counter and drop my head. How bad would it be if I tucked it in my arms and bawled?

"Rough day?" the bartender asks with a halfhearted smile.

I can hardly look her in the eye, let alone muster a polite smile. "You could say that."

She blows her pink gum into a cute little bubble, then bites it dead between her teeth. "What can I get you?"

As much as I want alcohol circulating in my veins, nothing sounds good. Not even the bottle of Sassicaia I had earlier. A place like this would never carry expensive wine like that. I shrug, pouting my lip. "Pour me a shot of whatever'll take the edge off."

"Mm-hmm, comin' right up." She moves quickly, grabbing a clear liquor bottle from the top shelf, and keeping focused on her task. "What's your name?"

My name?

Fuck if I know anymore.

I might as well start over. Be someone new. There's a cartoon character inked across her shoulder. I call out the name, "Mickey," in a flat tone. Works for me.

Her smile grows and she gives in to a small chuckle. "I'm Jen."

"Nice to meet you." Now where is that drink?

"You too, Mickey." She slams a tiny glass in front of me and fills it to the brim. A pungent waft infiltrates my sinuses before I even pick it up.

"Whew!" My face contorts. "What *is* this?"

"Something to take the edge off," she mocks.

It looks like Patrón but it smells like petrol. She motions me to drink up. Lifting the cold glass to my lips, I shoot the liquor hard and fast. "Ack! Tastes like lighter fluid." I gag, making a sour face with my tongue. Now everything from my chest up stings as badly as my ego.

Jen shrugs. "You didn't specify on taste."

"That's true," I say, hacking my lungs clear.

She leans on the bar. "So what happened to you?"

I finally look her in the eye, catching a flicker of her glittery purple eye shadow in the light. "It's a really long story."

She glances at the empty bar to the right, then to the left. "I've got time."

I push the drained shot glass back and forth between my hands, contemplating getting another one. "You sure you want to know? Wouldn't you rather scroll Instagram or something?"

She smacks her gum like a diner waitress. "I'm all caught up on social media and I'm bored. So c'mon. Let's hear it."

Part of me is dying to talk to someone about it, while the other part of me would rather suffer in silence. If I say the words aloud then they're real. As real as my ding-dong dick and my dead-end career. I take in a deep breath and let out a long sigh. Suffering in silence won't get me back to Monty Fuhrmann. It won't get me anything. "I got fired from the best job I've ever had."

She looks at me deadpan. No surprise. No sympathy. "Oh, yeah? Why'd they fire you?"

I drop my eyes when I say, "I lied."

"Everyone lies." She brushes it off like a speck of fallen glitter on her shoulder.

"Yeah . . . but this was a pretty big lie." I stare down at the grimy counter and it finally hits me. All of it. From Delia to Richard, from hired to fired, from a distant chance at love to no chance in hell. And now I'm sitting here in a shitty bar admitting to a total stranger that I got fired for fraud.

"Do you wanna talk about it?" asks the wannabe therapist, folding her arms and leaning over the bar.

My stare hardly lifts off the bar. The shot of moonshine, or whatever, hits my brain just enough to relax my frown. "You wouldn't believe me if I told you."

She laughs at this. "You'd be surprised by some of the stories I hear around here. I doubt you could tell me anything crazier."

My eyes shoot wide open. "Oh, yes I could!" I shake my head slowly. She's got no clue. "My day's been full of the craziest shit that's ever happened to anyone." She rolls her eyes, and I notice the rosary dangling around her neck. "Well, next to a virgin miraculously giving birth."

She shoots me a *WTF* look. There's a chance she's *Like a Virgin* circa 1984, but she's probably Catholic. Are Catholics allowed to have tattoos? Frankie has one, but surely the Pope doesn't approve of covering your entire body.

"Sorry," I say.

She stares blankly at me for at least twenty seconds then finally shoots me an impatient glare. "Still waiting."

"Nah, I don't think so." I twist my face into a vetoing grimace.

She leans back against the bar shelf, seeming a little miffed. "Why not?"

"I don't know you."

"Which is exactly why you should tell me. I don't know or care about anything about you."

I believe that. And a girl like her working in a desolate place like this must be thirsty for some captivating conversation. "It's a two-way street, ya know? Tell me something about you first?"

"What do you want to know?" Her voice softens to a flirty pitch. Boy, do I have a way with women.

"What's the craziest thing that's ever happened to you?"

Her lips turn up and she gazes off as if trying to calculate the wildest event in her life. I brace myself for some drunken anecdote. "Let's see. I think the craziest thing that's ever happened to me was when I met Davis Gage at a record store about two years ago."

Davis Gage is one of those sexy funk-metal guitarists who found fame and a drug addiction with a band in the nineties, went to rehab, married a supermodel, divorced the supermodel, then went solo in the 2000s. Not my cup of tea, but some of my high school friends thought he was the hottest.

My mouth falls open. "That's the craziest? This is New York. I see celebs all the time." Okay, I don't see them *all* the time, but celebrities do run wild in this city. Case in point, I encountered Todd Fairbanks *and* Serena Walters. And that was just today.

"You didn't let me finish my story," she says.

"Okay, good. Because that was really lame."

"Anyway . . ." she starts with another eye roll, "I bumped into him in the vinyl section and we got to talking about new wave and punk rock. And then he took me for coffee next door. It was the most amazing hour and sixteen minutes of my whole life." Her now still and starry eyes profess just how bad she had it for the rock star.

"That's pretty cool. You had a meet-cute with Davis Gage." I think I'm using that phrase right.

She shoots me a funny look. "A meet-cute? What are you? A romance writer?"

Romance writer? Now there's a profession that appreciates women. "No, I'm an investment banker." My shoulders slump, matching my frown. "Or was."

"Wall Street guy, huh? That's a tough gig." Jen glances at my shirt and silk paisley tie, then back to my face, with a smirk on her own. "Don't worry. You'll get a new job soon. But maybe ditch the pink."

"See, you just said a mouthful there. Pink isn't the problem. Society is the problem. They treat pink like it's an inferior color but it's not. Pink is a great color. It's basically a prettier shade of red. And everyone loves red. Do you know what I mean, Jen? There's absolutely nothing wrong with pink." My skin prickles, and not in a tingly, intoxicated way. Frankly, I'm getting sick of having to always defend being a woman on Wall Street.

With a knit brow she says, "Right . . ." And she sounds exactly like that executive behind the mahogany desk at my interview yesterday.

"You know what I think? I think pink deserves respect and it's about fucking time it got some!"

Jen stands there slack-jawed and blinking. "I didn't realize pink was so underappreciated by the masses."

"Eh." I tilt my head in a shrug. "How could you've known? As far as you're concerned, I'm just some fancy finance guy with fabulous taste in ties." I really do love this tie.

"You want another shot? It sounds like you need another shot." She reaches for the clear liquor bottle.

"No, thanks. That gasoline you served me was good enough."

She lets out a small chuckle and sets the bottle down. "Let me know if you change your mind." What are the chances Jen regrets asking me to talk?

I nod. "You know, it's my birthday today too."

"Well, happy birthday."

"No." I wag a finger. "It's not a happy birthday. I thought it could be because my birthday wish came true. Have you ever had a birthday wish come true?"

"I always wish to win the lottery, so"—she opens her arms, gesturing to the bar—"no."

"Well, it's wild when it does."

"Is that the crazy thing that happened to you?"

"Yeah, you want to know what I wished for?"

"Oh, so *now* you want to tell me." She gives me a wry smile and I return a flattened expression. "Okay, seriously. What happened?" Jen leans on the bar, and this time I can smell the cigarette smoke lingering in her hair.

"Well, I've been facing a lot of rejection lately. And when that happens you have to look at the common denominator. In this case, me." I tap my heart with my fingertips. "So, given the data, one can assume that's where the problem lies. So I wanted to be someone different. And this morning, I woke up a different person. And I mean, *so different* that my closest friends couldn't even recognize me at first. So I think, hey, let me use this opportunity to test this theory. And I marched out into the unknown with a completely different persona and refreshed perspective. Ready to conquer the world! But the results? Not exactly legendary."

"I think you need to adjust your definition of crazy." I'm tempted to be more specific, but think better of it. "Or maybe you just need to go back to being yourself again."

I lower my head. If only it were that easy.

"You want to know why I never get my birthday wish?" Jen asks.

I hardly look up at her. "Because the odds are one in three hundred million."

"No, because I never get around to buying the tickets. It obviously isn't that important to me."

"So what's your point?" It's a hopeful thing, buying a lottery ticket. The odds are stacked against us but we still trade our cash for a chance at a dream. We think *positive*. We tell ourselves anything's possible. Getting to work at Monty Fuhrmann today was like winning the lottery. And like so many lottery winners, I've managed to squander my luck.

"I'm saying you have to play."

"I do. I play again and again and again. How much more do I have to play?"

"As many times as it takes for you to win."

These days it feels like I'm playing a losing game. "And what if I never win?"

"So maybe you don't." She hits me with a look as if to say, *Grow up. The world doesn't owe you shit.* I lower my head and let out a somber sigh. It's a tragic thought—doing all of this, not just today but all of it, for nothing. No payoff. Then her raspy voice softens. "But you'll never know if you give up."

There it is again. It's up to me. It's about me. The me inside this body. If I'm going to have any shot at winning, I need to fix this and figure out how to get my life back. "You're right. I can't sit here all day, drowning my sorrows."

"Well, actually you can. We're open until four."

"As tempting as that sounds, I think I'm gonna head out." I slap my hand on the bar and reach inside my Gucci for my credit card. "Thanks for the talk, Jen."

She waves her hand, refusing the plastic. "It's on the house."

"Really? Why?"

"Consider it a birthday present." Jen smiles then nods toward the door. "Go ahead. Do what you need to do."

CHAPTER EIGHTEEN

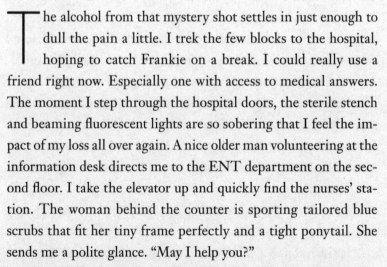

The alcohol from that mystery shot settles in just enough to dull the pain a little. I trek the few blocks to the hospital, hoping to catch Frankie on a break. I could really use a friend right now. Especially one with access to medical answers. The moment I step through the hospital doors, the sterile stench and beaming fluorescent lights are so sobering that I feel the impact of my loss all over again. A nice older man volunteering at the information desk directs me to the ENT department on the second floor. I take the elevator up and quickly find the nurses' station. The woman behind the counter is sporting tailored blue scrubs that fit her tiny frame perfectly and a tight ponytail. She sends me a polite glance. "May I help you?"

"Yes, I'm looking for Dr. Frank Ramirez," I say, peeking over the counter at the stacks of patient charts, scribbled notes on neon orange Post-its, and half-empty coffee cups littering the desk.

She picks up the phone receiver. "Your name and business with him?"

"Richard Allen," I say. "He's a friend of mine. Tell him it's urgent."

She nods and begins to dial, shifting her eyes suspiciously between the phone and me. I look down at her name tag—*Tara Hill, Registered Nurse*.

"Okay, I paged him," she says, hanging up.

"Thank you, Tara." I do my best to muster an appreciative smile.

"You're welcome."

Not sixty seconds later, Frankie rushes around the corner. His worried expression turns horrified when he lays eyes on me, and he picks up the pace. "Are you all right? What happened?" He grabs me by the shoulders, trying to meet my gaze. "Hey, what's going on?"

It's hard to look at him. Admitting this to Frankie is going to feel a lot worse than confiding in a bartender. The way I flashed my self-important arrogance at lunch makes me feel like an ass. My face starts to flush. "Is there somewhere we can talk?"

"Yeah, c'mon." He motions for me to follow him around the front desk, and we walk into a small, dimly lit office. Two computer stations squeeze in close together in an L shape, each with its own desk lamp and computer chair. He takes a seat at one and directs me to the other.

"Sorry I interrupted your day," I say, my head feeling as heavy as my heart.

"It's okay. I have a little bit of time. What happened?" Concern clouds his brown eyes.

I let out a long, sorrowful sigh and pick at my fingernails. "They found me out. Fired me."

He's silent, with a face that says, *Told you so*, but his words are, "That's rough."

"It gets worse."

He cocks his head to the side. "What do you mean?"

"Eric said he has feelings for me. For Delia. But I can't tell him like this." I motion to my miracle body.

Frankie covers his gaped mouth, his eyes glistening with empathy. "Oh, *chica*. I'm so sorry."

I lean forward, holding my head in my hands and rubbing my temples with my big thumbs. "Me too. Turns out, having a dick isn't all it's cracked up to be. That's why I came to see you. You told me we could do some tests. Maybe we can start trying to figure out why this happened to me. Find a way to reverse it."

Frankie twists his mouth. "I don't know if we *can* figure out how it happened. I can take your blood, do a hormone analysis, and send out a DNA test." He leans in, lowering his voice. "But . . . the more I think about it, the more I realize that it doesn't matter what the results are. You're in this new body. You have to deal with all the things that come with . . . well, havin' a dick."

My chest tightens with his words. "So you don't think I can be fixed?"

"You're not broken, Delia. I know it seems dire, but you're still a fully functioning human being." He puts a hand on my shoulder. "I don't know how this happened or how long it will last. But if you think about it, there is an upside. You can start over. And think of all the money you'll save not buying tampons." Frankie shares a friendly smile. "Things could be a lot worse."

"Yeah, but I don't want this. I just want to go back to my old self again." And I mean it.

"Well, maybe you will." It sounds hopeful in the same way a parent placates a child by saying, *We'll see.*

"How?" I ask, now knowing that the notion of magically changing back is as ridiculous as it happening in the first place. "Lightning never strikes twice in the same place. What if miracles are bound by the same laws?"

Frankie shrugs. "They might be. But just in case, we'll get drunk and play Truth or Dare tonight, you can say a little birthday wish, and tomorrow maybe you'll wake up as your old self again."

My thick eyebrows meet. "So . . . you think Gina was right? It was Truth or Dare?"

He rolls his eyes, making a clicking noise with his mouth. "I don't know what to think anymore. But I do know that until we solve this puzzle, you're going to have to figure out how to make the best of this . . . pickle."

"That's what I was trying to do—"

Frankie hushes me with an erect index finger. "I know, but at the same time, growing a big dick didn't destroy your brain cells or your sense. You knew there were major risks in what you were doing. It wasn't a small deceit. I don't even know how the hell you pulled it off."

"You think I have a big dick?" Maybe that's why I brought all that BDE today.

"Eh." He shrugs. "It's above average."

For now, I'll take it.

"It's like I've got two brains in my head. Yesterday, there's no way I'd have had the balls to pull a stunt like that. But this morning, with this body, the news from Fairbanks, and a pep talk from

Serena Walters"—I snap my fingers—"I had it all and I just fucking went for it. Go big or go home, ya know?"

"You should've gone home," he says with a patronizing expression. "And who's Serena Walters?"

"She's only my career idol." I shoot him a wide-eyed glare. "I'm sure you've heard me talk about her before."

"I can't keep up with all of the financial rock stars you're obsessed with. What did she say to you?"

"She told me her success is rooted in confidence and if you want respect, you have to demand it. So that's what I did and it worked . . . until it didn't."

"Yeah, but they didn't fire you for lack of confidence."

I shake my head. "No, but if I'd walked in and told them the truth, they either wouldn't have believed me or they'd have taken the information and left me out of it. I just wanted to be a part of it. Something important. Do something that I love. I don't know why that's so fucking hard. And I really don't know how I convinced myself that being a man would make it easier."

Frankie leans back and folds his arms over his chest. "I don't know either. In my experience, mo' dick, mo' problems."

I let out a half laugh, half whine. "I should've listened to you this morning. Why did you let me go out there? You should have placed me under a 5150."

He looks at me like I'm nuts. "How do you know about Section 5150?"

"I saw it on TV once."

"Well, first off, that's a California law." He covers a chuckle with his hand. "And the reason I didn't place you under involuntary confinement is because the more time I spent with you this morning, the more I could see that you're still you. You're still Delia. Doesn't mean I haven't been worried out of my mind, but I know you can handle this."

"Thanks." I let out a sigh, trying to wrap my head around the whole thing.

"So listen," he starts, "why don't you just go home, get some rest, write the day off as a wild adventure, and start fresh tomorrow? But I'd avoid going back to Monty Fuhrmann if I were you."

"Yeah, no kidding."

"There are plenty of other firms." Frankie sounds so freaking positive—he believes I can make something good come from all of this.

"Yeah, but . . ." I freeze, then grab my Gucci, pulling Serena's assistant's card out of the front pocket.

"What? What were you going to say?" Frankie pesters me.

I flash him the business card between my fingers. "I completely forgot that Serena Walters told me to call her assistant if I ever wanted to leave Monty Fuhrmann." It was just enough to push the corners of my mouth back up into a smile. "Maybe I'll get a second chance after all."

Frankie lays his hand on my shoulder. "Anything's possible." He pops out of his seat. "C'mon. I vant to draw your blood," he says in the voice of Dracula.

I shoot him an unimpressed look. "Please tell me you don't say it like that to all your patients."

His high cheekbones blush a rosy hue. "I don't, but I've always wanted to."

Frankie leads me out of the tiny office and down the brightly lit hallway. He peeks his head into one of the exam rooms before venturing inside.

"Take a seat," he says, pointing to a pleather patient chair covered with stiff tissue paper. I adjust myself on it, the parchment-like layer crinkling beneath me.

He slaps on a pair of purple latex gloves. "Take off my jacket."

"Huh?" I say with a confused stare.

Then he gives me one of those *get real* expressions. "You're wearing my suit, aren't you?"

"Oh, right." I slide the gray sports coat off my shoulders and unbutton the cuff of the starched salmon shirt, rolling up the sleeve in a careful fashion. He ties a bright orange rubber tourniquet above my elbow and presses against the few visible veins.

"So how did you find out Eric has feelings for you?" he asks.

I look ahead, feeling the tip of the needle touch my skin. "He told me, I mean Richard." The little prick stings the crease of my elbow. I look down, watching the blood fill the teeny tube. Real blood. My blood.

"What did he say?"

I let out a dreamy sigh. "Everything I wanted to hear. And more."

"I knew it." He smirks, keeping his focus.

Seconds later, the tube is full. Frankie tugs the little syringe from my arm and presses a fluffy cotton pad against the minuscule wound, taping it in place. "You okay?" he asks.

I stretch out my hand. "Yeah, I think I'm good. I'm gonna go home and get some rest like you said. Tomorrow, I'll call Serena Walters's assistant."

"Good. I'm glad you came by." Frankie smiles and jiggles the test tube in front of me like a tiny bell. "I'll order these stat and let you know when I get the results back."

I open my arms and bring him in for a hug. His body feels like mine, but in the moment, I imagine I'm my small Delia-self wrapped in the warmth of a big embrace. "Thanks, Frankie. I needed that."

He pats my back and pulls away. "Come on, I'll walk you out."

As we take the stairway down to the ground floor, Frankie's pager beeps impatiently.

He stops and grabs it from the waistband of his scrubs, silencing it in midbeep. "I gotta go to the ER."

"Ooh, that sounds cool. Can I come?" It's got to be more exciting than lounging around the apartment.

"It's not like TV. It's boring most of the time," he says, heading down the stairs again.

I follow close behind him. "Is that why you're not rushing to get over there?"

"Yeah, some kid probably stuck a bead in her ear. It happens a lot."

"Oh." That does sound lame.

We turn the corner to the emergency area. Empty gurneys line the walls on either side of the wide room. A few are shielded by blue-and-green-striped curtains. Frankie stops at the nurses' station, and I look ahead at the automatic doors leading outside.

I nudge Frankie with my elbow. "I think I'm gonna go."

The nurse hands him a chart before he turns to me. "Yep, a three-year-old stuck a pea up his nose. Told you it was boring."

I laugh. "That kid's smart. I bet his parents will never feed him peas again."

"You got that right."

"Anyway," I say, rocking on my heels. "Thanks again for your help today, letting me borrow your clothes and everything. It means a lot."

He pats my shoulder, examining me with his eyes. "I'm just glad you haven't ruined Michael Kors yet."

I glance over the sleek gray fabric, buttoning the jacket then dusting off the sleeves. Despite the disasters of the day, I haven't even spilled a drop of coffee on the suit. I turn for the exit just as a crowd of paramedics rushes in.

"Male, forty-eight, having chest pain, BP is one-ninety over one-fifteen," one of them calls out.

"He's having a heart attack!" shouts an oddly familiar voice.

Watching the horde bustling in, I zero in on the only person who's wearing a banker's suit.

No. Way.

Is that . . . ?

CHAPTER NINETEEN

O h my god, that's Owen Campbell!" I blurt out and rush
toward the commotion.

What's *he* doing here?

Frankie's footsteps are just behind mine. "Who?"

"One of the guys from Monty Fuhrmann." I'm merely a few
feet from the stretcher when Frankie yanks my arm back, warning
me to keep my distance.

I stand on my tiptoes, peering over the doctors' heads. Who's
having a heart attack?

A man stretched out on the gurney clutches an oxygen mask
to his face. The skin beneath his heavily receding hairline is pinker
than a Miami sunburn.

I shrug off Frankie's grip and turn back to face him. "Holy
shit . . . it's him," I mutter.

"It's who?" he asks, in the same low tone.

I glance back at the scene. Doctors rush their patient over to an enclosed room, their white lab coats catching air behind them like superhero capes. Owen stays on their heels until one of the nurses pushes her way in front of him, holding her hands out. "Sir, you need to stay here," she commands.

I return my attention to Frankie and grip his shoulders. "That's Curtis Becker. The guy who fired me."

Frankie stares at me as if he's trying to add it all up. "Who? The heart attack guy?"

"Yes." I release him from my grasp and wander closer to the commotion. The blinds in the room are nearly shut, and the only thing that's discernible is figures moving about. I tilt my ear toward the window, listening for words like *charge* and *clear*, but the voices are too muffled to make anything out.

Owen is just as entranced by the scene and doesn't seem to realize that I'm standing right next to him. With the color drained from his face, he looks utterly distraught. Poor guy. This day's been crazy for him too.

I tap him on the shoulder. He flinches, then squints as if he can't see straight. "Richard? What are you doing here?"

"Was that Becker on the stretcher?" I dart quick glances between him and the ER room.

"Yeah." With his eyes focused on the trauma room, he rises on his toes, craning his neck from side to side to no avail.

"What happened?"

Owen doesn't divert his attention. "We had a disagreement and he blew a gasket. The next thing I know, he's falling to his knees and gripping his chest."

"Is he going to be all right?" I ask, not really hiding the fact that I'm only mildly concerned. It's not like I want the guy dead—but he *is* at the top of my shit list today.

"I don't know." Owen stuffs his hands in his pockets, turning on his heel. "I should probably call the office and tell them to postpone the Fairbanks meeting."

I hurry after him. "No! You can't do that."

He pulls out his phone, cased in aluminum, and probably equipped with the Ezeus operating system. "You're in no position to tell me what I can and can't do. I know about you and your lies," he practically growls, baring his teeth.

I halt in my tracks, like a little lion cub put in its place. "Okay. You're right. I'm sorry. But listen, you have to trust me on this. If you cancel this meeting, you will *not* get another one."

"You really are a cocky son of a bitch, you know that?" He comes at me with a confrontational stance, his height rivaling mine.

He has no idea just how much cockier I am today.

Owen gets in my face. "How do you know so much about Todd Fairbanks, anyway?"

I take in a deep breath, but my airway seems to narrow. What can I say? That I've followed Ezeus since its early days? Kept up with every market development? Hung on every word from Eric about the IPO over the past few months? And not just because I always hang on his every word. It's more than that. I know what I heard. I know what Monty Fuhrmann has to do. And I know how to get it done.

A small, haughty laugh leaves his lips as Owen turns from me, pressing his phone to his ear.

Then, everything stops.

The ER goes silent. No one seems to be moving or even breathing except for me. I take another deep breath and shut my eyes. The day began with the shock of something new but also the promise of something different. Before my superiors broke me down, before society demanded that I be something I'm not, before I lost my voice, I was fearless.

"I was at Fairbanks's apartment this morning," I blurt out.

Owen whips his head in my direction, furrowing his brow. "I thought you said you didn't know him."

I glance back at Frankie, who gives me an encouraging chin nod.

"I don't." My voice grows stronger.

His glare shifts away. "I'll call you back," he says before hanging up. A bull-like breath blows through his flared nostrils. "You know, I was actually starting to like you until I found out that you're a complete fraud. How the hell do you expect me to believe anything you say?"

"Look, I know I wasn't completely honest about who I am, but I did know that Fairbanks was going to cancel—"

"And how did you know that?" he barks.

Ironically, in order for him to believe me, I have to bend the truth again. But just a little this time. "My roommate cleaned his place last night and left her phone. She asked me to pick it up for her this morning. When I showed up, I overheard him on a call telling someone he was planning to drop Monty Fuhrmann."

Owen's not buying it. He shakes his head like a disappointed coach. "You know, I really did think you were onto something. I told Becker that you may have been an imposter but you saved the meeting with Fairbanks and had some valid points. Then I suggested he sit out of the meeting, and he had a fucking heart attack!" He gets in my face again, jabbing his fingers into my chest. "Now what? I'm supposed to go into the meeting tomorrow and do this pitch myself based solely on what you supposedly overheard? I'd be an idiot to still listen to you."

"But you're not an idiot. The only reason you've listened to a thing I've said is because you know it's the right call. You told me yourself you thought something was up with Fairbanks." I roll my shoulders back, standing tall. "And you don't have to do the pitch alone. Let me come back and do it with you."

"Absolutely not." His hands slice the air between us like a referee.

"Why? You wouldn't even have a meeting tomorrow if I hadn't busted in there the way I did. And you wouldn't have a winning pitch either. Monty Fuhrmann stands to make millions because of me. I've earned that meeting." My words have the fervor of months of built-up frustration. If I can't go back to the way things were, then I at least want this. "And don't forget, *I'm* the one who spoke to him on the phone this morning. He's expecting me to be there." It's a dicey point, seeing as we both know I'm not Liam Golan's guy from Zurich. But it's the only card I have to play.

Owen throws his hands in the air. "He's expecting someone from our Zurich office, not some guy who showed up at his apartment. I couldn't let you in that room with him even if I wanted to. He'd recognize you from this morning. Did you even think of that?"

"He never saw my face. I don't even think he knew I was there. I swear." Now it's like I'm dangling from the edge of a cliff with a failing grip. Owen shakes his head and I know he's going to let me fall. I have to keep fighting. "This pitch is happening in sixteen hours and I'm the only one who knows it and the only one who knows why it's designed that way."

"What do you mean *why* it's designed that way?" He narrows his eyes with a threatening tone.

"I know what he's afraid of. I know what he's planning to do. Right out of the horse's mouth. Wouldn't you like to know what he said?" Out of the corner of my eye, I see Frankie slapping his hand to his mouth, covering either a nervous laugh or a gaping hole. My stare remains fixed on Owen. Hard to tell if he wants to relent or just punch me in the face.

"Humph." He bounces his hand, pointed at me like a gun. "I suppose the only way you'll tell me is if I bring you back."

Bingo!

"You didn't get to be a managing director at Monty Fuhrmann by accident. No one does. Wouldn't you do the same thing if you were in my shoes?"

His brow furrows so much that a crease appears down the middle of his forehead. "Who are you? Really?"

I sigh, keeping my eyes as steady and as honest as I can. "I'm Richard Allen. Just a guy who knows his shit and wants in the game."

He grits his teeth as if he's stifling the urge to scream at me. "I don't know anything else about you. You really think I can bring in some random guy to pitch one of the biggest IPOs we've ever been a part of?"

Frankie leans over, nudging my arm. "Show him your resume," he says out of the side of his mouth.

"Here." I pull a thick sheet of paper from my Gucci, hoping that it inspires some confidence.

Owen's scrutiny switches from Frankie to the resume. He

takes it from my hand, flashing curious glances at me between each section he reads. "So what? You have experience. Even *if* this is all true, it doesn't qualify you to sit at the table."

I stiffen my chin and fold my arms over my chest. "Maybe not, but what I did today does. My experience is real; that much should be obvious." Stepping closer, I look him firmly in the face. "This morning you told me you agreed with my strategy even though Becker didn't. If you don't close this deal tomorrow, you're not only losing Fairbanks. Others *will* notice." I take a breath, letting Owen feel the potential loss of millions for just a moment. "Becker's out. You're responsible for what happens now. So, what's it gonna be?"

CHAPTER TWENTY

He's quiet. But by the look on his face, I know he's mulling it over. The chances of him agreeing to my proposal are slim, slimmer than the stack of ones in my pocket. Taking a chance on me could be a major liability. I just hope he's willing to bet that I could be a huge asset. Because I will be.

"Fine. You can come back, but only as a consultant," he says with a firm stare. "And that doesn't mean you'll be in the meeting tomorrow. We'll see how the night goes."

It's not a hell yes, but it's a yes!

"Deal," I say before he can change his mind.

He nods toward the doors. "We better get to work."

I beam, feeling a surge of energy charge through my veins. What a rush! I'm back in the game, and on my own merit too. Happy birthday, Delia!

"Wait here," Owen says and jets off toward the nurses' station.

I rest my hands on my hips, catching my breath like I've just finished a fifty-yard dash. "Did you see that?"

Frankie doesn't seem to have any control over his floored expression. "That was amazing."

"Yes, it was." My adrenaline rush finally begins to slow while my heart is pounding so hard it's practically vibrating my paisley tie. "Okay, I have to get back to work. Don't wait up." I pat Frankie on the shoulder.

"Good luck," he says, taking a few steps backward before heading to his patient.

Owen says nothing as he approaches, just flashes his poker face. I follow him out of the hospital and begin heading up the street to catch a cab.

"Where are you going?" Owen calls out.

When I turn back, he's stationed in front of a black town car with tinted windows and a driver who's patiently holding the door open for him.

Back on the case *and* I get to ride in style!

I slide in next to Owen, making myself comfortable on the cushy leather.

The door slams shut. "This better work, Richard."

"It will." I'm no fortune-teller—obviously—but I *do* know this is the best chance Monty Fuhrmann's got.

The driver takes off and heads downtown. No jerking, bouncing, or stopping short. It might be the smoothest ride I've ever had on these streets . . . until it hits me: I signed a nondisclosure. And I didn't even read it.

Shit.

"There might be a tiny issue," I say.

He glares at me. "What?"

"Becker had me sign an NDA earlier and I didn't exactly have a chance for my lawyer to look it over." What exactly *did* I sign?

"I know. Becker brought it to our private meeting. Lucky for you, he didn't have a chance to send it back to our legal department before having a heart attack. It's still on my desk." Whew! That is lucky. Owen picks up on my sense of relief. "Doesn't mean I won't send it to them myself." His stern glare drifts away and he's silent for a few moments. I'm almost positive he's debating whether or not to tell the driver to pull over and let me out.

"I'll determine that later," he says, finally.

I straighten my tie and my attitude. That NDA will never see the light of day.

As we pull up to the tower, I know I've upped the ante. My stomach flips and my fingers tremble with excitement as I release my seat belt.

It's time to walk the walk.

Owen and I pass through security with ease and take the elevator up. The moment I step through the steel doors, my pulse steadies and it's like business as usual.

I follow the boss down the hall, glancing at the lock screen on my phone. It's almost seven. The floor isn't as lively as it was earlier, but there are still a handful of associates working away in their cubicles. As we approach Owen's office, Ashley is noticeably absent.

"Where's your assistant?" I ask.

"She leaves every day at five to pick up her daughter from day care." That's decent of him. He grabs a copy of the pitchbook, taking a seat on the sofa in the corner of his office. I spot the NDA on his desk and plop down on the chair across from him, wondering if he's going to look at me at all during this discussion.

His eyes stay focused on the pitchbook. "So why don't you tell me how this all started? And what, exactly, did you hear from Fairbanks?"

"Like I said, I went to his apartment this morning to pick up my roommate's phone."

"Wait." He looks at me, but with a suspicious glare. "Why did your roommate send you? Why not just pick it up herself?"

"How is that relevant?" I ask.

He crosses his arms over his chest, leaning back on the sofa. Earning his trust might be an uphill battle. "I'll ask the questions." Well, now who's the bad cop?

Let's see. If I had woken up as my Delia-self this morning, why would I have sent someone else to pick up my phone? "I assume it's because she's been cleaning apartments until she can land a finance job again. She hasn't met Fairbanks and probably didn't want to risk introducing herself as his cleaning professional."

His stony expression doesn't change and his office now feels as cold as an interrogation room. "Then what happened? Take me through it step by step, exactly how you remember it."

"Okay. His assistant invited me in while she went to fetch the phone. While I was waiting, I heard Fairbanks's voice coming from the other room. He said he was planning to cancel the meeting with Monty Fuhrmann because he doesn't think we can play nice with the other banks."

"We?" Owen's brow shoots up.

"The firm, I mean. I'm in this business, obviously, and I knew exactly what he was talking about. He specifically mentioned

Becker, and that he was concerned about a scandal. It's understandable after the IPO fiasco your team was responsible for."

He leans forward, resting his elbows on his knees while his intense stare stays fixed on me. "We'd never make the same mistake twice."

I return his bad-cop glare, stating in a stern voice, "Well, apparently Todd Fairbanks isn't willing to make that bet." I guess I'm not the only one trying to earn back trust.

Owen drops his tough-guy act and lowers his eyes.

"Another thing," I say, and Owen looks up again. "He said he was going to give S.G. Croft the lead."

"What?" He looks like he's about to shoot out of his chair like it's a cannon.

"He was going to call them after he canceled with Becker. There's a good chance it's already done. Which means that if we want in, we have to show him we'll do it his way. Play by his rules."

"And not bulldoze the deal," Owen says with a sigh.

I nod slowly. "Pretty much."

"Yeah, your plan makes a lot more sense now." Owen gazes off for a moment, seeming to take it all in. "What are the odds that you, of all people, would be eavesdropping on *that* conversation?"

"Trust me. Stranger things have happened. Consider it our lucky day."

"Well, it's definitely your lucky day." He shakes his head, rubbing his face in his hands. "I can't believe I'm saying this, but I think I'm going to let you do the meeting with me tomorrow."

My skepticism kicks in. "You are?"

He nods without a word, and I know he's trying to convince himself of his own decision.

"Thank you, sir," I say, finding it difficult to control the goofy grin covering my face.

There's a knock on the doorframe. Owen looks up and I follow, praying it's not Becker back from the hospital for another round.

"You wanted to see me?" Darren asks, doing a double take at the sight of me. I check my hands again.

Hairy knuckles are intact.

"Yeah." Owen gestures at the chair I'm sitting in. "Richard, why don't you head over to the conference room? We'll meet you there soon."

"Sure." I slap my thighs and rise to my feet.

"Hey, what are you doing here?" Darren wrinkles his brow as he walks in to take my seat. "They said you got called back to Switzerland."

Owen clears his throat. "When Curtis went down, we called him back. It's a good thing his plane hadn't left yet."

I press my lips together to hold in a chuckle and glance back to Owen, whose eyes flash me a quick threat, swearing me to secrecy.

Darren's expression turns crestfallen. "Oh, well . . . welcome back."

"Thanks. It's good to be back," I say, wondering why the long face. Doesn't he know I'm here for the rescue mission?

"Okay, we'll see you in a few."

I mime a salute to my new captain and walk out of his office. The door shuts behind me, and a swell of insecurity collects at the bottom of my gut as I bite my lip. What are they talking about? I consider pressing my ear against the door but think better of it. Besides, I've done enough eavesdropping for one day.

On the way to the conference room, I take a detour to my old stomping grounds. I spy Nicole's aqua glasses before I can make out the rest of her face. It's good to see her. Almost comforting.

"Hey, Mr. Allen. I thought Becker sent you back to Switzerland." She flashes her version of a smile.

"He tried, but he failed." I rest my hand on her desk and feel a slight pang of guilt for lying to her, especially since she was honest with me about her friend who works at S.G. Croft.

Her eyes return to the computer screen. "I knew Becker was going to have a heart attack sooner or later."

"Yeah, that guy needs a vacation."

She shrugs, unsympathetic. "Mm-hmm, I bet he was pretty pissed when he found out you weren't from the Zurich office after all."

My jaw practically dangles. Did I hear her right? "How'd you know about that?"

She shoots me a caustic stare, pursing her mouth. "Please, I figured it out within twenty minutes."

My cheeks flush and for a moment I want to puke. "You did?"

"Yep," she says, enunciating the word like she's blotting her lipstick.

I can't say I'm surprised she figured it out. Maybe she isn't my ally after all. "Did you turn me in?"

Nicole looks at me as if it's the dumbest thing I've said yet. "Are you kidding? Do you have any idea how much fun I've had watching these jerk-offs take hours to discover what I did in minutes?" Her mouth creeps up into a genuine smirk.

"You should be a detective."

She raises a thin eyebrow above the rim of her aqua glasses. "How do you know I'm not?" Nicole maintains a look more severe than the charges I would face for defrauding the firm. My chest tightens and for a second I think *I* might have a heart attack. Her straight face cracks into a giant laugh, so much so that I look around for hidden cameras. Or backup police. "Ha! I'm not a cop." She pushes up her glasses to wipe her eyes. "But you should've seen your face!"

Whew! I can't take any more jail threats, but I let myself laugh. Just a little. "You got me, Nicole."

Her laugh slows enough for her to catch her breath, and she pulls her purse out of a drawer. "I hope you plan to stick around. This place has gotten a lot more interesting since you showed up." Not as interesting as my life's been since my dick showed up. She walks around her desk, a residual smile on her face, then struts toward the elevator. "Good night, Richard."

As soon as the elevator doors close, I peek inside my old office, or rather Sutton's old office. No one's around.

No harm in going inside.

This could be the last time I'm alone in an office like this for a while. I pass up the abandoned set of golf clubs for the wide window view. The salmon-tinted sunset gives the city a warm glow as if it's satisfied with the day's events, and I find myself feeling a little more satisfied too.

I just wish I were here as regular Delia.

I grab a yellow pad and silver pen from Sutton's old desk and make my way to the conference room. Twenty empty chairs surround the glossy table. I run my hands along the tops, letting the smooth leather slide beneath my hand. I stop at the seventh chair, the one Curtis Becker sat in when he told me I was caught. Pulling the chair out to take a seat feels like a small victory, although there's a long way to go.

"What's up, Richard!" Eric's voice resounds through the doorway before he does. His smirk is cuter than ever.

My palms and face grow hotter by the second. "Hey, Eric. What are you doing here?"

He pulls out a chair near mine and slouches into it, resting his interlocked hands on his chest. "Owen caught us on the way to happy hour and asked if I could stay."

"I'm sorry," I say, secretly wishing I could go to the bar with him. I guess if Delia wasn't visiting her "dying" grandma, we'd be having drinks tonight. Maybe even coffee in the morning . . .

"It's okay." His eyes droop a little and I can tell he's starting to crash from that cup of coffee in the break room. I'd probably be crashing too if my adrenaline wasn't pumping a mile a minute through my veins. "It's not your fault Becker had a heart attack."

That's debatable.

"Good, you're both here." Owen makes his entrance into the conference room, Darren behind him like a shadow. Eric and I look alive, awaiting his instructions. A sour pout weighs on Darren's bottom lip as he takes a seat.

With his hands on his hips, Owen's glowering at me like I'm still on thin ice. "These guys are going to prep you on everything there is to know about Ezeus, past and present. When you're done in here, you and I will go over tomorrow's pitch."

"Sounds like a plan." There's a part of me that hopes this will take all night. The thought of being with Eric for the next few hours is almost as exciting as pitching to Fairbanks tomorrow. I glance down at Little Dickie. But not too exciting.

Eric and Darren are so on top of the data, there isn't a detail left out. Fortunately, it's easy for me to catch up, since Eric's been sharing bits with me for months. The volley between Eric and me is so natural that we often don't even need to use words. I've missed this. It's just like old times at Howard Brothers Group, working around a conference table with our team. Darren, one of the sharper guys I've met today, even asks at one point if we've worked together before. We say no but Eric acknowledges that it definitely feels like we have. But it doesn't take a few hours; it's taken a little over one.

"Any other questions?" Darren asks.

I flip through the yellow pad, checking my notes before I let them go. "Nope, I think I got it. You two are free to head to the bar."

Darren sends a sideways glance to Eric, who notices but doesn't seem to be bothered by it.

Eric smiles. "You can meet us when you're done. We're going to Pearl 20."

Pearl 20 is known for hosting cocktails with trendy investment professionals after the market closes. It gets busy again around nine, for those of us who get stuck at the office past happy hour. A couple of drinks to calm my nerves before I head home to bed sounds pretty good, especially if Eric's there.

"Thanks, maybe I'll stop by." I stand, buttoning my jacket, and the guys begin to head out. "I really appreciate your help today." I offer Darren a handshake. His is limp and tired. On the other hand, Eric's is firm and friendly. When he lets go, my skin tingles all the way to my . . . uh-oh. I grab my yellow pad to shield my first in command, recalling rueful moments with dirty toilets just in case. But there's no poke coming through.

Just call me beast tamer!

I head back to Owen's office. All the cubicles are empty and the entire floor is quiet except for the faint hum of a vacuum cleaner on the far side. I bang my knuckles on his open door. The overhead lights have dimmed to a warm glow and a brushed nickel table lamp illuminates his workspace.

"How you doin', boss?" I ask with a little smirk.

He doesn't look up. "Did you learn anything at your meeting other than your place here?"

I flatten my lips and clear my throat before taking a seat in front of his desk. "Yeah, you've got a great team. The guys helped a lot. All I need to know now is how you want to play this."

He lifts only his eyes from his desk, like I haven't earned his complete attention, and his serious expression has yet to relax. "I think it's best to just have the two of us. I'm running the meeting, of course. Having you there is going to show that we have some new, young blood on the team. Here"—he hands me a sheet of paper—"this is what *you* will present. Nothing more, nothing less."

I take a moment to review what he's given me. All things considered, it's not a bad break. From what I can tell, tomorrow is going to be more about impressing Owen Campbell than Todd Fairbanks. He can dazzle the client, and who knows, maybe I'll learn something. "I got it. You can count on me."

"Can I?" he asks, head up this time.

"Yes," I say, directly. No sweaty palms, no trembling hands or mouth. No doubt I'll nail this tomorrow.

He returns his attention to the work on his desk. "Okay. Good. I'll see you at eight a.m. sharp."

I stand, folding my assignment into a neat square before stuffing it into my Gucci. "You got it, boss."

He doesn't respond and it's almost like he doesn't know I'm still here. Or doesn't care. I better go.

"Owen," I say, just before I make it to the doorway.

He looks up.

"What happens to me after the meeting tomorrow?"

"Let's just get through the pitch. Then we'll talk." That doesn't sound any different from *We'll let you know*. I nod as I slowly turn and walk out. "Richard," he calls, and I look back. "If we close it tomorrow, then I'll make sure you have a job at the firm."

All right, Delia, stay positive!

"Well, in that case, I'm looking forward to working for you."

Owen's expression relents into a half smile. "Good night, Richard."

CHAPTER TWENTY-ONE

A warm breeze wafts through my short hair as I step off the curb and gaze up toward the top of Monty Fuhrmann Tower, trying to pick out the conference room window on the thirty-second floor. Only thirteen more hours before I sit at the table with Todd-freaking-Fairbanks. The sky has turned black, but the streets of Manhattan are brighter than ever. A perfect city for insomniacs, a club I'm sure I'll be joining tonight.

A melodic chime sings from inside my Gucci. I pull out my phone; the screen's lit with a picture of Regina pouting with the pair of Chanel stilettos she couldn't afford.

"Hey," I answer.

"Girl, I've been texting you. Where have you been?" Regina grills me like a fretful mother.

"I just left the office. Why? What's wrong?"

"You tell me. Frankie said you got fired and maybe rehired,

and then you gave a man a heart attack. Is that true?" I can't tell if she's more concerned about me or more pissed that she had to hear the latest scoop secondhand, and fragmented at best.

I roll my eyes. "I'm fine, and I didn't give anyone a heart attack." Well, not exactly.

"Whatever," she says, and I almost hear her head swivel. "Are you headed home?"

"No. Pearl 20. Eric invited me out for a drink." If only I could twirl my Delia-hair around my finger as I float over to the bar.

"Just the two of you?"

"No." And my feet ground again. I kick them along Broad Street. "There's a bunch of guys from the office with him."

"I should come with you." The sound of a nail file sanding down fingernails creeps through the phone.

"I don't need a chaperone."

"And I don't need to spend another night at home. I'll be there in forty minutes." And with that she hangs up. I consider calling her back, but I'd need a lot more than twenty percent battery life to dissuade her.

Inside Pearl 20, long pendulum lights reflect off the polished dark wood bar. There are just enough people to fill the place, but not enough for it to be considered packed by New York City standards. I spot Eric and some of the other guys standing around a high-top table. Their ties hang loose as they sip their short cocktails and chat above the bar music. He takes a sip of his old-fashioned. It's his go-to drink. There's something sexy about the way he barely touches the glass to his mouth then lightly licks his top lip when he's done.

"Hey," I call to Eric, totally ignoring the rest of the guys.

"You made it." He smiles. "Grab a drink, then come join us."

"Okay." I nod and head over to the bar. A beautiful woman pushes off the counter, sliding off her barstool. I glance down past her sleek, tanned legs to her rose-colored strappy stilettos.

"Cute shoes," I say as I take her seat.

The woman smiles and sends me a wink. "Thanks."

"What can I get you?" a bartender in a black button-down asks, watching her walk away. I don't think he's staring at her heels.

A pink drink sounds good. "Cosmopolitan, please." The man behind the bar quickly delivers my cocktail with a lemon twist. Back at the high-top table, most of the guys have deserted it but the break room posse remains.

"You remember Brian and Mike from earlier," Eric says, pointing to the guys.

"Yeah, what's up?" I send a chin nod before sipping from my martini glass. The sweet and slightly sour citrus delights my tongue like it was any other night at the bar after work. They both shoot me strange looks, and my cheeks grow warmer with every second that they don't speak. I guess there's not much to discuss past desperate girlfriends and water-efficient kitchen porn. What are the chances they'll walk away to avoid another oddball conversation and leave me alone with Eric?

Mike twists his face into an inquisitive look. "Rumors have gotten around. You really think you can close Fairbanks tomorrow?"

"Without a doubt, man," I say, believing every word.

Eric leans in, gesturing for us to follow. "I heard that if it wasn't for Richard, the meeting would have been canceled." That's no rumor, but I keep that to myself.

I tilt my glass, meeting his gaze for a moment. "Just doing my job."

"Well, you may have saved the deal, so I propose a toast." Eric lifts his glass and all eyes turn to him. "To Richard!"

"To Richard!" the guys shout, drawing attention from the other patrons. I relish in their brief tribute, but the only person's approval I care about is Eric's.

Darren wanders over, pushing his way in between Eric and Mike. "What's going on over here?" he asks.

"We were just toasting our savior from Switzerland," Brian says.

"Oh, right . . ." He doesn't seem amused and downs his short drink the way a parched gardener guzzles water on a hot summer day, then shakes the ice in his glass. "I'm going to need another one of these."

The moment he leaves the table, Brian points to a group of eligible ladies in their black and navy skirts with blouses opened just enough to let the "girls" breathe. He and Mike make their way over while Eric and I stay back, nursing our drinks quietly. My crush, who's been crushing on me—well, old me—doesn't seem as eager as the other guys on the team. Throughout the bar they're wearing pleased smiles, picking up women, and making connections.

"You're not joining the others?" I nod to the nearby metropolitan mating ritual taking place.

He shrugs, stirring his drink. "Nah, the girl I want isn't over there."

No, but she is right here. "You mean Delia?"

"Yeah, I was going to tell her everything tonight, like we talked about. But she's leaving for Florida. That's where her family lives. Her grandma isn't well."

Oh, man . . . *she* already left.

"I don't know why I thought coming out tonight would make me feel better. It doesn't." He frowns and pushes his drink aside.

He's actually really cute when he's moping over me. And at the same time, I hate seeing him like this. I give him a playful shove, wishing I could just take his hand for once. We didn't have this much physical contact when I was a woman. Who knew me having a dick could help bring us closer? "Cheer up. She's not the one dying. Maybe she'll come back."

He slouches down, staring into his drink again. "What if she doesn't? What if I missed my chance?"

Standing here listening to him talk about me is so bittersweet. I never thought I'd be one of those girls who would take the man over the job, but in this moment, I would give anything to be my old self again. I'd do anything to stay in the city with him. Even clean every apartment in Manhattan. I've gained fifty pounds of muscle, but my heart is ten tons heavier with regret. How can I have lost him before even knowing I could've had him?

Fucking figures.

"It's my own fault. I could've told her a million times!" He raises his voice in a frustrated roar and my heart soars at the sound.

"I know the feeling," I say, almost grazing his hand with my fingertips. But they don't look like my fingers. What I would give to see my real hands again.

"You do?" Finally his gorgeous blue eyes meet mine.

"Of course. Yeah, there's this, um . . . girl I used to work with.

She was my favorite person, but I didn't think the feeling was mutual so I never did anything about it. I keep thinking how things may have turned out differently if I'd had the guts to say something back then."

"I guess men can be really stupid sometimes."

I lift my glass to his. "Hear, hear."

Eric takes a drink of his old-fashioned. I could stare at him for hours. He's so damn cute. I just hope I don't have goo-goo eyes right now. Then again, I've done a pretty good job of keeping those to myself over the years.

He pulls his phone from his pocket and thumbs the screen a few times. "This is her." His bright screen is lit even more by a photo of the two of us, the real us, smiling during a night out almost a year ago. I can't believe he still has it. It feels like a lifetime ago now. I look terrible. It was the end of the night and most of my makeup had worn off. Plus, I wasn't getting a lot of sleep back then. Why couldn't he have used a filter?

"She's cute," I say, which is exactly how I think of myself. Cute.

"She's beautiful," he corrects, tenderly getting lost in the screen.

Beautiful? I don't know if anyone but my mother has called me beautiful before. Oh my god, I have to figure out a way to change back. I shut my eyes tight, wishing, hoping, and solo Truth or Daring that I can be Delia again. When I open them, I half expect to be back to my old self, in my own bed, waking up from an outrageous dream. But I'm still in this bar. Still Richard with a dick. My cheeks burn and I ball my fist. For the first time since I woke up this morning, I feel sharp tears prickle my eyes.

This sucks!

"You okay?" he asks.

I suck in a deep breath and blink back whatever tears have surfaced. "Yeah, I'm just a little tired."

Get it together, Delia!

I take a long sip of my pink drink, the alcohol soothing me some. Might not be a bad idea to change the subject, talk about guy stuff, but I don't want him to stop talking about, well, me. Especially when this may be my only chance to hear it. "So if she comes back, what are you going to say?"

"I'm not going to tell *you*. It's personal." He forces a smile the way he does when he doesn't want to talk about something. With one last gulp, he finishes his drink. Maybe a few more of those and he'll spill it.

"C'mon, man. It's not like I'm gonna tell her. Besides, don't you want to say it out loud to someone? Just a little bit?" I hold my thumb and index finger up with the tiniest space in between.

"Maybe a little." Eric looks hesitant, but I motion him to continue.

Exhaling a long breath, he keeps his eyes lowered. "I'd say, Delia . . ." I focus in on him, desperate to memorize every word he says so I can play it over and over in my head like my favorite song. "Don't move to Florida." My heart plummets into my stomach, beating so loudly I have to struggle to hear Eric's words. He pauses, turning his thoughtful, dreamy gaze my way, then says, "I'm crazy about you."

I can't breathe.

It's worse than when I choked on the salami at lunch. I want so badly to kiss him, tell him I'm crazy about him too. I feel faint. Have I been holding my breath this whole time?

"Hey," he says, giving me a strange look. "You sure you're not jet-lagged?"

I exhale and shake my head. "Yeah, I'm fine." I gasp for a non-fresh breath of bar air. A flicker of light catches my eye, and I look up at the smoky crystal chandelier hanging over the center of the room.

"So what do you think?" Eric brings my attention back. "Too corny?" He lowers his eyes, a little unsure of himself.

"No. It's perfect." My heart flutters when I say it, because if Eric never gets to say those words to Delia, at least he'll know that someone appreciated them.

He gives an accomplished nod and at the same time, a familiar scent lingers in my breathing space. Regina's Versace perfume.

"Eric! Oh my gosh! What are you doing here?" She's so believable even I forgot she knew we'd be here. I wait for her to acknowledge my presence but it's as if I've disappeared.

"Hey, Gina. What are you doing on this side of town?" he asks.

She sets her designer bag on the table. "Oh, I was at a client dinner down the way and thought I'd come in here and meet some cute Wall Street boys. Know any?" Her attention whips right over to me, flashing me her parted-lips sexy stare. She sends me a devilish wink.

Eric runs his fingers through his soft hair. "Gina, this is Richard. Richard, Gina—she's Delia's roommate."

"Hi there," I say, as Gina and I play up the whole ruse.

He turns his attention back to my best girlfriend. "How is she, by the way?"

"Yeah, I heard her grandmother's not doing well." I give Gina the old *you get my drift* stare.

"Let's just say she's had a rough day," Regina offers.

I pout my lip. "Aw, poor Delia."

Eric's head hangs over his empty glass, and Regina and I shoot each other telling glances.

"Richard, would you be a doll and buy a girl a drink?" Regina asks. Her smile's so big I can see all of her teeth. That's her *pretty, pretty please* smile. Why is she trying to get rid of me?

"Sure . . . What can I get you?"

"I'll have what you're having."

I narrow my eyes, wishing we could communicate telepathically. "Comin' right up."

Darren's standing by the bar, waiting for his next drink. "Heyyy, Richard," he says, patting my shoulder as I approach. He's got one of those big stupid grins like he's been shooting doubles all night.

"What's goin' on?"

He leans his elbows on the bar. "Just, ya know, decompressing. It's been a helluva day with you showing up and everything. Twice."

My mouth turns into an exaggerated O. "Oh, yeah, sorry, man. Duty calls." The bartender hands him his short rum and Coke, and I request a cocktail for Regina.

"Eh, it's okay." He takes a long drink. "You know, I was supposed to be in the pitch tomorrow with you guys."

My brow raises. "Really?"

He nods. "Yeah, been really looking forward to it. But with the new developments, I've been benched. The only way I'll be in that meeting is if you get hit by a bus."

Too bad for him this city is pretty safe for pedestrians. For a moment, I feel bad about his misfortune. Then I remember it isn't my call. "You want me to talk to Owen for you?"

He shakes his head with a clownish frown. "Nah, don't bother. I got an offer from another firm. I was on the fence about it, but after today, I'm gonna take it."

"Wow. Congratulations." I guess someone scooped him up.

Darren lifts his drink in the air. "Good luck tomorrow."

"Thanks." I lean against the counter and watch him walk off, bouncing a little with every step. He's definitely feeling that rum. It's a shame for Monty Fuhrmann to lose him. But hey, in the spirit of staying positive, more opportunity for me.

A woman pops in next to me, and I almost don't recognize her in the muted light. But when her cell phone illuminates the freckles on her face, I know exactly who she is.

"Shannon?"

I don't see the girl for months and now she's everywhere. Did Regina invite her?

She looks up and it takes her a second before her eyes light up with recognition. "Well, look who it is. Twice in one day. You're not stalking me, are you?" Her tone isn't as friendly as at our first run-in.

"No, I'm just having drinks with some people from work. You?" I ask, glancing around for Regina.

"Same. Just blowing off some steam."

"Hard day at the office?"

She gulps back the rest of her drink and glares at me. "Why? Because my job's too hard for me?"

Damn, she is *not* a fan of Richard right now. "Is this about what I said earlier?"

"Nah." She waves a dismissive hand. "I just love when men I hardly know question my ability to do my job."

"You're right." I raise my hands in surrender. "I'm sure you get a lot of unnecessary shit, and it isn't fair. But I really wasn't trying to imply anything. I'm sorry that it came out that way."

Her harsh expression softens a little as she circles the tiny black straw in her glass. "So then it's a programmed, Pavlovian response? Just one of those stereotypical things that seeps into our subconscious and rears its ugly head at the worst moment?"

"I don't know." I'd never thought about it that way. Maybe the sexism in our industry is more of a conditioned response than a deliberate one. Not that it makes it any better.

"Sometimes I think the Wall Street game is played in two different arenas. One for guys like you and one for women like me."

It's funny, even though Shannon and I are friends and both work in the financial industry, we've never really had any meaningful conversations about the daily uphill battles we face as women. In either arena, we have to be tough. This Wall Street world is like an exclusive club that we're lucky, or unlucky, enough to join. So why should we have the added hassle of proving that we're not inferior? We just want to kick some ass and make some money like everyone else.

"You know," I start, "I had a conversation with Serena Walters once."

Her eyes light up. "Seriously? I love her."

"So do I. She basically told me that if you want something you have to take it. It's all about confidence. If you have that, nothing can stop you."

Shannon's demeanor changes and she holds her head high. "Confidence, huh?"

I nod. "Yeah. The thing is, this business is tough no matter who you are. But don't let some man or job or stereotypical stigma stamp out your flame."

The bartender slides Shannon's fresh drink over. "Wise words from Serena Walters. And you."

I hold up my glass. "To Serena Walters."

Shannon clinks hers with mine, then gazes at me while we sip. "Well, I can appreciate a man who respects powerful women."

I know that look. She's sent it over to many men across the bar before. A laugh bubbles up in my mouth so I pop it with a tight-lipped smile. It seems that all is forgiven.

When her gaze doesn't relent, I pull my attention away, glancing over at Regina and Eric.

Wait. I don't see him.

Where'd he go?

"I gotta get back. See you around." I grab the cocktails and hurry over as fast as I can without spilling the vodka cranberry mix.

"Where's Eric?" I ask. My panicked pulse quickens.

"Headed home, I think. Said he was calling it a night. I tried to stall him but . . ."

"Damn!" My phone vibrates in my pocket and I pull it out. *Eric Walker* displays across our adorable bar selfie.

Regina peeks at it, tugging her bottom lip with her teeth the way she does when she feels sympathetic. "He misses you."

The ache is soothed for a moment by the warmth of those words. "What did he say?"

"He asked me to ask Delia to call him as soon as she can. He said he hopes she's not headed to Boca forever."

I hammer my fist on the table. "Damn it! This isn't fair!"

Regina flinches. "Damn, don't break the table. I get it, girl.

And while I don't have your exact . . . eh . . . situation, I know what it's like to want someone that you just can't have." Her lashes fall and she stares into her pink martini. It doesn't show often, but I know her secret love affair with her boss wasn't just about sex for her. It left a deep wound that has yet to heal. She begins to let out a sigh but then halts it as she peers past my shoulder. "Hold up. Is that Shannon over there?"

I don't need to look to know it's her. "Yeah, maybe we should—"

"Uh-oh. I think she spotted us."

"Is she coming over here?" By the look on Regina's face, Shannon's comin' in hot.

"Yep, this night's about to get interesting," she says through an inflated smile as the click of Shannon's heels draws closer. "Oh my god, Shannon! What's up, girl?" Regina holds out her arms and our fiery-haired friend plows right into them.

"I'm *so* glad I ran into you here. It's been *for-e-ver*! And Richard! I didn't know you knew Gina too." She tosses her hair over her shoulder, then returns her attention to Regina. "Is Delia with you?"

"No, she's headed out of town." Regina flashes me an uneasy look.

"Damn, I have got to catch up with that girl." Shannon settles in and sets her drink on the table. Looks like she's here to stay.

Oh, boy.

While my friends catch up, Brian moseys back over to our table, eyes locked on Regina like she's the answer to his JLo dreams. "Hey, Richard. Is this your girlfriend?" He flashes his left hand and pops his hip, mimicking the dance from the break room.

I snort a laugh. Brian might be making fun of me but his *put a ring on it* wave is pretty spot-on. "No, this is my friend Regina, and this is Shannon."

"I'm Brian." He offers his hand and his full attention to Regina while Shannon rolls her eyes and pulls out her phone.

Regina encourages his flirtatious behavior with a cute giggle. "I like your little dance."

"Yeah, Richard showed it to us earlier."

"Really?" Regina says playfully, and I know she's making a mental note to ask me about it later. "Well, Richard does love to dance."

"Oh, yeah?" Shannon's brows shoot up. "So do I!" My friend scoots a tad closer. Even though she's got no shot with me, which she would appreciate if she knew the whole truth, I think her interest is kinda sweet.

"So how do you all know each other?" Brian asks.

Regina and I trade slightly panicked *what's our story?* glances when Shannon offers, "College."

Good answer.

Brian seems satisfied with it. Probably because he's less interested in my connection with these two beautiful women and more interested in making his own with one of them. He cozies in next to Regina and compliments her smile in a way that's sweet, not slimy. I doubt the poor guy has a chance with her. He's too blond and Waspy looking. So not her type.

"Okay, speaking of college, I've got an idea." Shannon holds her hands up, and I'm almost sure spirit fingers will be making an appearance. The three of us freeze, awaiting what's next. "My friend just texted me from Solei. They're playing some throwback Thursday jams, and it's a party. We should go. I haven't been out dancing all week."

"I'm in," Brian says.

I shoot my roommate a wide-eyed look—*Regina, if you can tele-pathically hear me, I know you don't want to go home but I should probably get the hell out of here.* "I dunno, guys. I have an early day tomorrow."

"C'mon, it's on our side of town and it's your birthday. Don't you want to celebrate your special day?" I'm pretty sure my message was received and she's just ignoring it.

Shannon's face lights up. "It's your birthday?! Then you absolutely have to come out."

Regina leans in, nudging my arm. "Seriously, it's been the craziest day ever. What do you say? I know you could use a shake-it-off."

CHAPTER TWENTY-TWO

Before I know it the four of us are filing into an UberX headed for Solei, a club in the East Village. Just as I'm about to slide in next to Shannon, Brian taps my shoulder.

"Is it cool if I sit in the back?" he asks man-to-man. It's not just the back seat, he wants to slide into Regina's DMs too. I'd be surprised if he walks away from this night with anything more than a polite hug. But who am I to stand in the way of the mating game?

"Sure, *bro*," I reply like one of the boys. And with my blessing, he's off to the races. The car pulls out, and Brian drives a conversation with Regina, playing it cool with casual questions like it's their first date. Shannon, sandwiched between them, slouches in her seat and scrolls her phone. In the same way a yawn is contagious, I pull out my own device. A missed call from Eric and . . . a missed voice mail? My finger trembles against the screen while a stilted breath barely escapes my lungs.

"Hey, Delia. It's me," he starts with a dreamy tone. "I know you're in the middle of something important, and I've been blowin' up your phone, but I just wanted to say . . ." My heart pitter-patters with anticipation as I smooth the hair around my ear. His laugh breaks the silence, making my stomach somersault. "You never let me sing 'Happy Birthday' to you yesterday, and it's getting late, so . . . Happy birthday to you," he croons in a rich vibrato, Sinatra-style. "Happy birthday to you. Happy birthday, dear Delia. Happy birthday too-oo you." Oh, yeah. This takes the cake. If he'd been singing onstage, I would've tossed him my panties. My grin is so big you'd think I've got a winning lotto ticket in my pocket.

Best. Birthday gift. Ever.

"Anyway," he continues, "I hope your grandma gets better. And when you can, we'll go out and celebrate your special day. See you soon."

Ohmigod! That was the most amazing message I've ever gotten in my life! I may be in a man's body but in this moment I'm a sixteen-year-old girl in love. If I don't tell someone, I'll burst! I look back, the good news written all over my face, but Regina's immersed in conversation with Brian, who obviously wants to skip the candles and go for that cake. And it's not even his birthday.

Shannon spots my smile and leans forward with her legs on either side of the console. "What are you so happy about?"

"I just got a really nice birthday message from someone."

"Who? Your girlfriend?"

"No. Just someone I like." It's damn near impossible not to gush right now.

"Gotcha." She reaches into her bag and pulls out a packet of cinnamon gum—her favorite. Her lips wrap around the tip of the stick as she slides it into her mouth, holding my gaze.

Is she trying to wake up Little Dickie?

Nah. It's probably harmless. I know this girl—after a couple cocktails she'd flirt with my eighty-two-year-old grandpa.

"How many drinks have you had?" I ask in the same concerned way I always do at this point in the night.

"Just enough to start making bad decisions." That's what I was afraid of. She twirls a finger around her shimmery copper strands as she leans back, letting her skirt ride up her thighs. "You might have to keep an eye on me."

Yeah, no shit. She usually needs a babysitter once alcohol is involved. Just as I'm regretting my decision to stay out, I catch a glimpse of Shannon at an angle I haven't seen before.

Whoa.

She's pulling a Britney.

I stare a second too long before averting my eyes. Less than twenty-four hours without one and it's like I forgot what it looks like. With a small chuckle, I shake my head. Oh, Shannon . . .

My thoughts drift away to a night when Eric and I met some friends for happy hour after work. He wasn't dating anyone at the time, and I was convinced that it was the perfect night to make a move. He'd been drinking. I'd been drinking. But even with all the liquid courage, I still couldn't do it. So I excused myself to the ladies' room and called Shannon, who seemed to get any guy she ever wanted, for advice. "Take off your panties," she suggested, claiming that anytime she was DTF, she would lose her thong and the guys would be all over her. Especially the one she wanted. Said it had something to do with allowing more pheromones to release.

I told her I didn't think it worked that way, but she assured me it did. Every time.

So I locked myself in the stall, slipped off my underwear, and stuffed it in my purse. By the time I'd taken ten steps back into the crowd, something had shifted. I was turnt up and turned on. But when I returned to our corner of the bar, Eric had cozied up with some rando with fake tits and real sex appeal. From the way she unapologetically pressed her breasts into him, I knew she wasn't wearing any panties. I didn't tell anyone I was leaving. I just disappeared. Needless to say, it was a breezy walk home. Knowing what I know now, I shouldn't have conceded defeat so easily.

"We're here!" Shannon shouts as the car slows to a stop.

"Holy shit," I say, scanning the line of fifty people at the door. "We'll be here all night just trying to get in."

She pokes her head between the front seats and whispers in my ear, "Don't worry." Ooh, tickles. "I know the bouncer." No surprise there.

While I step out on the sidewalk to wait for the others, my head turns upward at the misty blanket of city lights clouding the night sky. Even if I can't see it, I know just beyond the veil is an abyss holding the moon, the stars, and . . . what? What's out there? What changed me? Will it ever change me back?

"C'mon, let's go inside." Shannon waves us to follow her, swaying her hips with the click of her heels. The bouncer, who looks like a retired UFC fighter, spots her approaching and unfastens the black velvet rope. The muscleman leans into Shannon's ear and she giggles, squeezing his swollen biceps in response. There's no welcome wagon for the boys. He just shoots us the stank-eye. Definitely not used to getting *that* look at the door.

Inside, Solei is the complete opposite of Pearl 20. The walls boom with EDM as guys in trendy jeans and girls in designer stilettos gyrate against each other on the dance floor. It's like every twentysomething in the East Village is here tonight.

"Should we grab a drink first?" Shannon shouts over the club beats, pointing ahead.

"Sure!" I shout back.

She takes my hand like it's the most natural thing in the world, guiding me deeper into the colorful flock of modern-day club kids while Regina and Brian follow close behind. As girlfriends, we've held hands a million times squeezing our way through nightlife crowds. But her fingers feel strangely small in mine now. Kinda trippy.

At the bar, Shannon manages to wedge herself between a couple of guys and hails the bartender like a taxi. "Can we get some drinks over here?" Between the two mixologists, neither seems to notice her.

Brian pushes his way through and waves a fan of cash. It does nothing to capture their attention. "Well, shit."

"I got this." Regina slinks in front of Brian, fluttering her lashes before she hops up, practically sliding her chest on the bar. With two fingers in her mouth, she blows out a piercing whistle amidst the deafening music. Somehow, it cuts through and one of the bartenders appears, eager for our order. "What can I get you?"

"You see this guy behind me?" She points my way. "It's his birthday. So let's get a round of birthday cake shots, and do a little something special for him, would ya?"

"Comin' up."

While we wait for our round, Shannon bops her butt back and

forth then playfully bumps me with her hip. So I tap it back with my hands in the air. "Heyyy!" I sing and catch Brian in a little snicker. But once he sees the girls make me a booty shake sandwich, all of a sudden he's rockin' away like he's Justin Timberlake.

"Oh, okay, okay!" Regina chants, sliding to his left. Who knew? The guy's got rhythm. I hope I still have mine.

"Here you go." The bartender sets a round of shots on the bar. "That'll be sixty-five fifty." A little birthday candle, just like the one I blew out yesterday, sits in the center shot glass with nothing but a bed of white whipped cream holding it upright. Isn't that cute?

"This round's on me." Brian hands over a wad of cash. Gotta love a free drink.

The barman lights the candle with a quick flick, and Regina carefully hands it over while Brian passes around the other drinks. For a moment, I get lost in the tiny dancing flame. The sound of Eric singing "Happy Birthday" resounds in my mind as I reflect back on sitting at Fairbanks's kitchen island. Never in a million years would I have imagined that this was how I'd start the next year of my life. And perhaps even the rest of my life.

"Wait! I'm here!" a familiar friendly voice calls behind me.

"Is that Frankie?" Shannon asks, and I look back.

Regina grins, waving at him to join us. "Yay! You got in!"

Frankie huddles in next to me sporting a black and white rose-printed shirt buttoned up to his Adam's apple and smelling like a fresh spritz of Dior. The gang's all here!

"Hey, what are you doing here?" I shout over the music.

"You're not the only one who needs a shake-it-off. Now make a wish."

"And make it a good one," Regina says with a wink. Who knows if I'll be lucky enough to have another birthday wish come true. But I close my eyes and dream of trading in this fine Michael Kors for my real birthday suit.

I just want my body back.

With lungs full of hopeful air, I blow out my cheeks and the flame disappears. Enthusiastic cheers and clinking glasses follow. Even Frankie mimes a shot. "Happy birthday!" We shoot back the liquid and Brian cringes. "Oh, God, that tastes like a drunk cupcake."

Turns out a drunk cupcake isn't as tasty as a Brooklyn blackout, but it gets the job done. Shannon comes at me with her thumb and gently wipes the edge of my lip. "You have a little whipped cream." The temptress holds my gaze, and I want so badly to tell her it's her friend Delia in here.

"All right!" Regina shouts, slamming her empty glass on the bar top. "Let's hit the dance floor!"

Shannon yanks me by the lapel, and for a moment, I'm sure she's gonna slip me some tongue. "C'mon. I'll introduce you to my friends." Releasing her grip, she grabs my hand again.

Whew! False alarm.

We make our way through the mass, letting the music carry us closer to the dance floor. Shannon cranes her neck from side to side then waves ahead. "There they are!" I peer over the crowd looking for a single familiar face and spot none. Out on the floor, her peeps circle around her like she's the It Girl. "You guys," she shouts, "this is my friend Richard!"

"What's up, Richard!" a few of them say in drunken laughter.

"Hey!" I wave, but feel myself curl inward and glance around for my friends. Regina's busting out booty moves and backin' up her dump truck. With a big-ass smile, Brian waves it into position. He shoots me a nod as if to say, *Look at this juicy thang!* Regina's not the only bootylicious babe. Frankie's making his ass clap and taking up more space than anyone else.

The DJ starts up one of those popular radio tunes that's been badly remixed into something barely recognizable.

"Whoo! I love this song!" Shannon whoops.

Right on cue, the rest of us let out a high-pitched "Whoooooo!" and I throw my head back in a laugh. Whoos are contagious to women. And apparently, even women in male bodies. All you need is one whoo to set off the entire place. Pretty soon lady-whoos are bouncing around the dance floor.

As the music flows through the speakers, I feel the birthday shot circulating through my body, heightening my senses and dulling my inhibitions. I move to the music in classic Delia fashion but it doesn't exactly feel the same with the restrictive sports coat and my Gucci slung across my body. I loosen my tie and sway my shoulders as if testing out the fabric's flexibility. My girl Shannon swivels her hips, running her hands down her body. If Eric thinks I'm a sexy dancer, he can thank Shannon for showing me the moves. The freckled vixen whips around, slapping her locks in my face, then pops her butt into my crotch. The friction sends a signal to you-know-who.

"Whoa, okay," I say, though she can't hear me. I can barely hear myself.

I don't think so, you little troublemaker.

My thing throbs for a couple of beats as if it's saying, *Yo! Nobody puts Little Dickie in a corner!*

I retreat half a step back and use my briefcase as a barrier between me and her buh-dunka-dunk. The last thing any single woman in this city wants is mixed signals. We're just here to shake it off.

A familiar rhythm overlies the last, morphing into an oldie but goodie. Ahh, yeah! With a smile swiped across my face I holler, "Oh, shit. This is my song!" Regina and Frankie know it too and close in on me as I unbutton my salmon shirt at the neck.

Regina gives me that go-time look. "Oh! Whatchu got, Queen D?"

The music penetrates my body, pulsing through my veins. Shoulders bouncing, head rocking, hips swaying, hands in the air like it's a par-tay. Queen D's in the house, y'all! Feelin' myself, I pop it like it's hot.

Pop, goes my booty. Pop, pop.

"Whoo! There you go!" Shannon plays along. Who knows what it looks like, but it sure as hell feels good.

Regina undulates in a full-on body roll with the beat, and Frankie and I emulate her moves until we're perfectly in sync. Even though I'm restricted with this suit and the jewels between my thighs, I feel as free as I did as an eighteen-year-old, shaking my ass at the Miami clubs in miniskirts and midriff tops. Nothing matters except me and this song.

Now this is a shake-it-off!

When the song breaks, someone pushes past Shannon, sending her right into my chest. I catch her in my arms and she grabs on to my biceps, squeezing it with her skinny fingers. "You okay?"

"I'm fine!" she says, hardly able to focus. She can't be *that* tipsy.

"Did you eat anything tonight?"

"Nope." She snickers and shakes her head. "You wanna get out of here?"

Uh-oh, I know what that means.

"Nah, let's stay and dance," I shout over the music. "I'll get you some water."

"See." She points at me, clicking her tongue. "I knew you'd keep an eye on me. You get me some water. I'm going to the ladies'." With that, she pushes herself out of my arms and heads into the sea of clubbers.

I catch Regina's eye and she shimmies over. "Hey, can you check on Shannon in the bathroom?"

Regina cringes. "Aw man, is she sick? Why is she always pushing her limits? Then we're the ones stuck spending half the night holding her hair back. That's why we stopped going out with her. We're not twenty-two anymore."

"I think she's fine. But can you go in there just in case?"

She folds her arms and rolls her eyes. "Fine."

"Thank you."

By now the line at the bar is twice as long as it was when we got here. Shannon's water's gonna be a minute. I'm bopping my head while I wait my turn when Regina taps my shoulder.

"You're right. She's not sick drunk, she's sext tipsy."

"Did you say sext tipsy?"

"Yeah, your girl's in there sending out booty calls."

Typical. She may not drink and drive but she shouldn't drink and text either.

"Well, I better get her out of here before one of the guys she's texting shows up and she regrets it in the morning."

"What?" she whines. "But it's your birthday."

"Trust me, I've had plenty of fun today." Enough excitement to last me until next year.

Frankie makes his way over. "What's happening?"

"Delia's gonna make sure Shannon gets home."

"Yeah, I think I'll head home soon too. This has been a helluva day." The three of us trade knowing glances.

Regina looks past my shoulder. "Oh, here she comes. Good luck!"

"Don't stay out too late," Father Frankie says as they inch away.

"You talking to me or the suit?" I joke, and he signals that he's got his eye on me.

"Boo!" Shannon pops up next to my ear. She's holding two full shot glasses and hands one over to me.

"How did you get this? I'm still waiting to order your water."

She sends a dismissive wave. "I'll hydrate later. Let's party!" She shoots the liquor back like she doesn't have shit to do tomorrow. But I do. So I hand mine to some stranger standing next to me. Shannon squeezes her eyes shut and smacks her mouth. "You ready to get back out there?"

I stuff my hands in my pockets. "Actually, it's getting late. Why don't I get you home?"

CHAPTER TWENTY-THREE

Wrangling Shannon out of the club is no easy feat. A quick farewell to her friends turns into one last dance, which becomes two last dances. Her intoxication grows more apparent as she moves on the dance floor. When we finally make it out, Shannon stumbles along toward the curb, holding her phone with both hands like it's an old-school BlackBerry.

"I got it!" Shannon flings her arm in the air then flashes the screen of her booked Uber ride. "Four minutes." With another step, she wobbles in her heels like she's going down. I catch her, keeping her upright like the Statue of Liberty.

"You okay?" I ask.

A goofy grin spreads across her face. "I am uh-mazing. Aren't you?"

I can't help but let out a little laugh. "I'm good." Or at least I will be when I can finally get home tonight.

Shannon rolls her head back, gazing at the sky and holding her arms out as if welcoming the fresh-ish air. "This is what I love about New York. One minute you're riding the subway like any old day and the next you're partying with friends you haven't seen in forever! Anything can happen. Don't you love it?"

After today, I'm not sure if I completely *love* it, but it makes for an interesting life.

The Uber arrives and I start toward the car. When I open the door, the driver confirms the ride and I motion for Shannon to stop hugging the city so she can slide in first.

"Hey, Shannon!" a voice calls from down the way. Some guy dressed in a tightly tailored blue button-down and a Hemsworth haircut advances toward us with his chest puffed up. "Where're you going with this guy?"

"Oh, hey, Josh, what are you doing here?" she calls out playfully.

Josh knits his brow. "You asked me to meet you here." I give him a once-over. So this is her fuckboy.

"Oops!" She covers her mouth with a coy expression. If she genuinely forgot about him, it wouldn't be the first time.

He summons her with a wave of his hand as he closes in. "C'mon, honey, let's go back inside."

Her eyes shift my way.

"Shannon, get in the car," I say, gesturing toward our ride.

With clenched fists, the guy comes for Shannon as she climbs in the back seat. "Wait a minute! I came all the way up here, and you're just gonna leave me hangin' like that?"

I block him with a firm hand on his chest, guarding my friend. "That's enough, dude."

He shoots a glaring glance between Shannon and me like he wants some action. One way or another. "And who the fuck are you with your pussy-ass pink shirt?"

Oh, no, he didn't.

"It's salmon, you asshole. And *I'm* the one who's taking her home." My heart pounds in my ears as I take him back a full step, not blinking an eyelash.

He scoffs with a menacing leer. "Is that what you think?"

"Hey!" Shannon's UFC bouncer buddy calls, marching toward us. "Is there a problem here?"

Josh turns and yells back, leaving me to slip into the Uber. I slam the door shut, and with a jolt the car escapes the scene, leaving that douchebag in the dust.

Adrenaline drives through my body as we head up First. Shannon flips around, staring out the back window. "Whoo, he looked pissed." Her wide eyes match mine. "Someone really needs to lock up my phone when I've been drinking."

"Good idea." I snatch her sidekick but she yanks it away, gripping it close to her heart.

"No, I need this. We gotta keep the party going!"

"Did you say party?" the driver calls back.

"Yeah!"

The driver holds up a tiny remote and with a click of his thumb, colorful rope lights strobe along the roof. Splashes of purple, blue, red, and green illuminate Shannon's freckles in the dark car. What kind of Uber is this? "Here, crack these." He passes back a couple of plastic glow sticks, and Shannon bends them in half until their pink fluorescence radiates. How'd he know our color?

An electronic beat pumps through the speakers and our driver-slash-DJ cranks it up. "Oooh!" Shannon whoops. "This is my jam!" The bass drops and Shannon waves the glow sticks around her face like it's a wild rave.

Why didn't I take that last shot?

"Come on, Richard! This goes with your outfit." She hands me her party favor and grabs my wrist, waving my arm back and forth like hey, ho! With Shannon, the party never stops.

Another hot song later, we're heading uptown on FDR along the East River. With the city lights reflecting off the water, the river is as lit as this ride. Shannon freezes for a second and gasps. "I have an idea." Whatever it is, nothing good can come of it. "Let's get Taco Bell!" Her wide-awake expression is totally serious. And she's probably starving. I can't count how many late-night crunchy tacos we ate on the 1 train back to our dorms. Is she still doing it after all this time?

I catch her tapping away on her phone. "Who are you texting now?"

"What, are you jealous?" She looks up with a teasing smirk but I don't play back. "I'm not texting anyone. I'm ordering some tacos." She pronounces *tacos* like she just returned from spring break in Cancún. "Delivery in thirty minutes!"

I pop my head in between the front seats. "How do you stand drunks on your ride when you're stark sober?"

He shoots me a side glance. "Who says I'm sober?" Uh-oh. "I'm kidding, man. Your girl's just trying to have a good time. She's cute. Enjoy it while it lasts."

I lean back in my seat, rest my hands on my Gucci, and watch Shannon bounce around for the next fifteen minutes.

After what feels like the longest car ride ever, we pull up to

Shannon's apartment building on the Upper East Side. I follow her upstairs, trying to ignore the fact that she's swaying her hips for me. Or for Richard. What she doesn't realize is she's so tipsy it looks more like she's just wobbling around on a swaying cruise ship. Her apartment door swings open, and I get a waft of something citrus—like the leftover scent of an orange and bergamot candle.

"This is it," she announces and flips the hallway switch. Light spills into her studio apartment—revealing her velvety emerald sofa and fish-scale-patterned divider screen behind it. I set my Gucci down on the narrow entryway shelf next to a vase of silk magnolias. Must be nice to comfortably afford her own place.

She pushes at the heels of her pumps, leaving them toppled on the wood floor. "Why don't you come in and make yourself comfortable?"

"Do you have any aspirin?" I step into the six-foot galley kitchen and peek inside the five cabinet doors, hunting for a water glass.

Found one.

She pouts. "Oh, no. Do you have a headache?"

"No," I say, filling a glass from the water pitcher on her counter. "It's for you."

"But I feel fine."

"You won't in the morning." I return to the hall and reach inside my Gucci for a tiny travel bottle of whatever painkiller I've got and sprinkle two pills in my hand. "Here," I say, holding my hand out. "Take this, then go to bed, and don't forget to set your alarm, okay?"

Her fingers tickle my palm as she takes the meds. I better get out of here before she gets any more ideas. "I'll see you later," I say and turn back toward the door, but she pinches my jacket and pulls me back.

"Wait. You're leaving?"

"Yeah, girl, it's late."

She sets her water down and waves a dismissive hand. "Pff! The night is young and so are we. Plus, I wanted to give you a little birthday present." She grabs my belt and tugs me close. So close her boobs press against my chest. She slides them down my body, lowering herself to her knees.

Is this girl for real right now?

"Whoa. What are you doing?"

"Don't you want to show me your little Richard?"

I shake my head, jerking back. "Nope. Nope." I knew she was assertive, but damn!

She relents, rising to her feet, and whispers in my ear, "What's the matter? Are you shy?"

Flinching at the feel of her breath on my neck, I can't help but giggle. "Shannon, come on."

"Let's not play games." She slides her hand down my tie. "My body wants you. And I know your body wants me. I felt it on the dance floor. What's the big deal if we hook up?" My old college pal wraps her arm around my neck and pulls me in, parting her mouth against mine.

I twist my lips and turn away. "Shannon, stop! We can't do this."

"Why not?"

"Because I'm Delia!" I blurt out.

"What?" Horror blackens her eyes while the color drains from her flushed cheeks. "Delia?"

"Yeah." I gulp hard, wishing I could swallow the truth too.

She gags and slaps a hand over her mouth. "Oh, no, I think I had too many cocktails." Shoving me out of the way, she bolts to the bathroom. The sound of her retching echoes into the hallway.

This is a mess.

Knock, knock.

"Seriously? What now?" I open the front door half expecting it to be Jerk-Off Josh, but it's the takeout guy with Shannon's tacos.

"Delivery for Shannon?" he asks, holding up the plastic bag. The smell of spiced beef and melted cheese seeps into the apartment.

Shannon yaks again, and the splash of vomit sloshing in the toilet is clearer than Mr. Delivery and I would prefer. He cringes. "I'm guessing she's not hungry anymore."

I grimace and take the carryout bag. "Thanks."

He waves, flashing me a sympathetic look, and I'm tempted to follow him wherever he's going if only to avoid what's next.

"Shannon! Are you okay?" I call, setting the food down while making the short journey to her bathroom.

Shannon's long red hair drapes around her face as she reaches for the handle, flushing her mess. If it weren't for my dick, it'd be just like college. She tears some toilet paper from the roll and wipes her mouth.

"Better?" I ask.

With her legs curled in, she pushes herself up and leans back against the tub. I brace myself for the million questions that are about to spew from her mouth. "Why didn't you tell me you were in love with Delia?"

Huh? "*In love* with Delia?"

"Yeah, that's what you said, isn't it?"

It is now.

I clear my throat; time for some more make-believe. "I didn't tell you because I haven't told her yet."

She looks even more confused. "Then why did you come home with me?"

"I didn't *come* home with you. I was making sure you got home. And not with some guy like Josh. That's what Delia would have wanted." Which is what got us into this mess in the first place.

Her expression softens. "Still. That's very misleading."

I cross my arms and lean against the doorframe. "Yeah, I can see that now."

"So, she really doesn't know how you feel?"

Actually, she knows everything I feel. And think. And do. "I'm sure she knows in her own way."

Shannon seems to take a minute to consider this, then looks at me like she's put it all together. Can she see through to the truth in her drunken state? Then again, being intoxicated may be the only way to comprehend it. "Wait, you said you worked at HBG, right?"

"Yeah . . ."

She gasps, covering her mouth. For a second, I think she's about to puke again. "I think you're the guy she's been crushing on for years." Her pale hand slides down to her heart. "Sorry, I shouldn't have told you that."

"It's okay."

"I thought his name was Eric. Or did she say Rick? I dunno. Rick, Eric—I guess that all kinda sounds the same."

Her lubricated logic isn't too bad. If it gets me out of explaining that *I'm* Delia and gets her off my dick, then all the better.

The smell of fried tortillas wafts nearby. "You in the mood for some tacos?"

She shakes her head. "I'm in the mood for bed."

So am I.

I help pull her up but she manages to walk, hunched over, to her partitioned room while I retrieve the water. "Here. Drink this."

She sits up and takes a big gulp of water, then lets out a satisfied sound.

There's a good little drunk girl.

"You good?" I ask, and she nods, sinking back beneath the covers, pulling the sheet to her chin. "Okay. Good night, Shannon." I leave my friend to sleep it off.

"Wait!" she calls. What now? A bedtime story? "I'm sorry if I ruined your birthday."

I breathe out an exhausted laugh. "Trust me. You didn't ruin my birthday."

"Okay, good. Because listen, I know Delia and I'm positive she doesn't know how you really feel. You really should tell her. I know she'd love to hear it."

I smile at her kind gesture to the real me. "I will. As soon as I see her, I'll make sure she knows how special she is to me." Because she is special. And it took all of this for me to realize it. If only I had shown myself more compassion, showered my body in appreciation, and found the courage to believe in myself unconditionally, then maybe I wouldn't be in my friend's apartment in the middle of the night pretending to be someone else. Maybe I'd actually be happy. Even if life isn't perfect.

The hall light flickers then goes dark. I whip my head left then right, waiting for the light to return.

Still dark.

"What the . . . Damn, girl, did you spend your electric bill money on cocktails?" I retrieve my phone and turn on the flashlight.

She slowly climbs out of bed and peeks behind the thick fabric of her drapes. "No, the entire city's out. Even the traffic lights."

"A blackout?"

"Yeah, I think so," she says, squinting in the torchlight.

How can this happen two nights in a row? And on the opposite side of town? I let out a fatigued sigh. There's no way I'm walking seventy-five blocks home in the dark. "Do you mind if I hang out until the lights come back on?"

She tosses me one of her pillows. "Go for it."

I lower my phone to guide the way back to her sofa. Five minutes later there isn't a speck of light in the room. Guess I better get comfortable. I shrug my shoulders out of my jacket and kick off my shoes before settling into the vintage-style cushions. Breathing in the lingering scent of Shannon's shampoo on the pillow is almost comforting. This morning I thought this would be the worst day of my existence, but all things considered, I guess it wasn't so bad.

"Good night, Richard," Shannon says through a yawn, and I catch it too.

"Good night," I say, letting my eyes close for just a minute.

CHAPTER TWENTY-FOUR

A thundering clatter from the street jolts me conscious, but my eyelids are too heavy to lift. Do they have to collect garbage this freaking early? I adjust my body against the bed, trying to sink into it as if it will silence the horrendous drone.

It doesn't.

Groaning, I fold my pillow over my ear. Just five more minutes. Please! My bladder's buzzing like an alarm—the kind without a snooze button. Ugh. What's today anyway? It's gotta be . . .

The memory of yesterday rushes back like an outlandish dream: me waking up with a penis; overhearing Todd Fairbanks; talking my way into a position at Monty Fuhrmann—twice; everything Eric confessed . . . my pulse quickens.

Holy shit! That actually happened.

I'm a man.

A man named Richard.

My eyes shoot open and I pat gently between my thighs, taking stock of my schlong. Huh? Where is it? I cup my hand against myself.

Wait . . .

I dig into my loose pants, feeling the shape of my precious labia. While one hand reunites with my lower half, the other slides across the hills and valley of my chest.

My breasts! A full B cup. It's all here!

I gasp and rub my blurry eyes. "Ohmigod, ohmigod, ohmigod." My familiar womanly frame is completely intact—everything from the peaks of my chest to the tips of my toes in Frankie's dress socks. When my vision doesn't clear with a few more blinks, I know it's me. It's really me!

I'm back, baby! Whoo!

Never have I appreciated being a woman as much as right now. I reach for my glasses on the nightstand, and the rest of the room catches up to me.

Hold up.

This isn't my apartment.

A groggy morning groan grumbles on the other side of the room divider. My hand leaps over my mouth as I freeze, cringing and holding my breath. Shit! How would I ever be able to explain Delia waking up here when Richard slept on the couch last night? I have to get out of here.

Now.

My escape is twelve feet away and fuzzy as all hell. I hold my breath and swing my feet over the edge of the sofa, landing on the slick hardwood. This isn't the first time I've crept out of someone's place after a sleepover, but it was nerve-racking then and nearly unbearable now. I collect Frankie's jacket and shoes, listening for

Shannon's sleepy breaths. Strong and steady; she's still out. As I tiptoe toward the door like Elmer Fudd hunting wabbits, the floor creaks beneath my feet and I stop dead.

Slow, Delia. Take it slow.

If I make it out unnoticed, it'll be the second miracle of the day. And it's only the ass-crack of dawn.

With every move, my trousers inch farther down my hips. I crouch down, clutching the shoes and jacket against my waist to keep them from falling completely. Carefully, I peek around the divider and can just barely make out Shannon buried in rumpled white sheets. Still sleeping.

Whew.

I lift my Gucci off the entry shelf like it's a sleeping newborn and hold it close. With my arms full, I struggle to reach for the door handle without a sound. My heart races faster and faster, wanting me to get the hell out with the same speed. I hold my breath and manage to turn the knob with a slick, sweaty palm.

Almost there.

"Richard, is that you?" Shannon croaks from her bed just as I slip out. Damn, she sounds like shit.

"Fuck," I mouth to myself. Then, in the manliest voice I can muster, I say, "Yeah." Just go, Delia. Just get out of here! "Gotta run." I sound like every woman I've ever heard doing a shitty impersonation of her dumb boyfriend.

I slam the door shut and hurry down the stairs, which is no easy task with socked feet, ill-fitting clothing, and blurred vision. But I make it to the foyer and huddle next to the mailboxes.

Okay, jacket—check.

Shoes—check.

Gucci—check.

Breasts—check!

I hurry into Frankie's gray jacket and black shoes, glancing behind me in case Shannon's on my tail. But knowing her, she won't leave her bed for at least an hour. What time is it? I reach inside my sagging pants and pull out my phone. Dead again. I force a frustrated sigh and pull Frankie's belt tighter, but there aren't enough holes to secure it. Figures. The one time my waist is too small. Plan B. I tug off the leather and it jingles like fucking Santa Claus is coming to town, pants slipping down faster than a cookie addict can slide down a chimney.

The sound of footsteps echoes in the stairwell. Uh-oh. I look up just as a woman in a sleek ponytail and skintight yoga gear passes by, shooting me a nasty look.

"Well, good morning to you too," I say under my breath as I yank at the pink paisley tie. The knot releases, and I thread the silk through the belt loops, cinching it until it fits right. Okay, now I'm ready. Ish.

Outside, the sun is just coming up behind the buildings. I start trekking downtown, my heart pounding fiercely in my ears. There's no way I'm riding the train like this but there isn't a cab in sight. At least I don't think there is. All I can make out are blurry blobs of color passing along the road. It takes two more blocks before I see anything that even remotely resembles a cab. I step off the curb, waving it down. "Taxi!" But it passes right by me. Then another. And another. I'm sure I look ridiculous wearing a grossly oversized men's suit.

Worst walk of shame ever.

Just as I'm about to give up and find the closest subway, a yellow car pulls over and I hop inside as fast as my feet in these big-ass shoes can carry me.

"What happened to you?" The driver's gruff voice grates on my ears.

"You wouldn't believe me if I told you."

He turns back with a crooked expression. "I'd believe you have cab fare if you showed me."

Understood. For all he knows I'm an escapee from crazyville. I reach inside my Gucci and whip out my magic plastic card, flashing it in front of his face.

"Where're you headed?" he says, satisfied.

I exhale. "East Village."

CHAPTER TWENTY-FIVE

rush up the stairway to my apartment, forgoing quiet courtesy as I thump my oversized shoes on each step. My keys jinglejangle as I drill one in the keyhole and push the front door open. A second later, the sound of Frankie's feet stomping along the old wood floor booms from his bedroom.

"Delia? Is that you?" He turns the corner to the living room then stops short at the sight of me. Out of breath, and practically drowning in his suit, I stare back at him. "Oh my god! You're back! You're really back! I was so worried about you!" He plows into me and wraps his arms around my shoulders.

I hold on to him tightly, relief expelling from my lungs. I'm home. "It really happened, right? I had a dick yesterday?"

Frankie pulls away, flashing a smile as big as his heart. "Either that or you pulled off the most ingenious hoax I've ever seen."

"If only I were that clever."

His eyes scan my entire frame as if he's looking for cuts and bruises on his suit. "Michael Kors still looks good, but Delia . . ." He cringes. "You're a hot mess."

I lower my blurred gaze and lift my foot a few inches off the ground. Frankie's black leather shoe slides back to my ankle, while my fingertips barely peek out of the jacket sleeves. "I feel like a fucking vaudeville clown. I need to get out of this getup." I slip easily out of my roommate's shoes, looking forward to walking in my own again.

"Is that Delia?" Regina's voice barrels down the hallway before she does. She rushes to me but stops short of an embrace, holding on to my shoulders tightly while looking me up and down. Her eyes light up like it's Christmas morning. "Holy shit! You're back!"

Yes, I am.

She wrangles me into her arms, squeezing all the air out of my lungs.

"I . . . can't . . . breathe." I barely manage the words.

She releases her grip. "Sorry! I'm just so glad you got your body back."

"Me too. I can't tell you what a relief it is," I say.

"Did you spend the night at Shannon's?" Before I can answer she gasps, covering her mouth with her hands. "Ohmigod. Did you change back in front of her?"

My stomach twists, matching the expressions on Frankie's and Regina's fuzzy faces. "Not exactly. I slept on her couch because of the blackout."

"*Another* blackout? Frankie, did you see the blackout?" Regina seems more surprised by the second blackout than my second miraculous body change.

"I don't think so."

"So what did you tell Shannon this morning?" she asks.

I shrug innocently. "Nothing. She was still in bed when I flew out of there like a bat out of hell."

"Aw, you poor thing," Frankie says with a pouted lip. "Why don't you change? So I can have my suit back."

I roll my eyes, shrugging the jacket off my shoulders. "You want the underwear back now too?"

"Um, no . . ." He gently lays the fabric over his arm.

"You guys want coffee? I could use some coffee. I'll go make some coffee." Regina backs away, blabbering like she's already had three espressos.

"Yes," I say with an exhale. "Make it strong. Like, grows-hair-on-your-chest strong." The moment the words leave my mouth the three of us freeze, trading cautious glances. "On second thought, regular's fine."

"Comin' right up!" she says and disappears into the kitchen.

Frankie inches close like he wants to tell me a secret. "So is, ah . . . everything back to normal?"

"Yes, Frankie. Now you're the only one in this apartment with a dick."

"Just checking. Will you come to the hospital for another blood test today? I've *got* to compare the two samples."

"Absolutely."

I schlep my Gucci to the bedroom, trousers dragging at my feet along the way. Closing myself in my room, I lean my head back against the door, letting the pants finally fall at my feet. My apartment. My room. My body. Appreciation for this moment wells in my chest. "Thank you," I whisper to whatever gods changed me back again. For the first time in so long, I not only know what I want, but I know who I am. Cleaning toilets for months scrubbed away my memory of what I'm capable of and what confidence affords.

I wiggle my feet out of the fallen fabric, unbuttoning the salmon shirt enough to shimmy it loose. Frankie's striped boxer briefs slide down as I walk to find my dark frames on the night-stand. I kick off the undies and slide my glasses on easily. Finally, I can see clearly again. My wall mirror seems to wait patiently for the reveal, and my heart flutters in anticipation. I step in front of my reflection.

Wow!

It's so much more incredible than I remember. I hold my precious face in my hands like a good friend I haven't seen in years. Staring into my own eyes is the best birthday gift I could ever receive. I love it so much that I kiss the glass. Muah! I don't even mind the tiny blackheads on my nose or the stray eyebrow hairs. With a big smile, I whip around to check out my bird tattoo, totally intact. I take a good look at my tush. Faded stretch marks and cellulite never looked so good. I give it a shake and it jiggles around like Jell-O.

So cool!

I slip on a pair of white cotton panties, a comfy bra, an old tee, and my favorite stretchy leggings. Clothes that fit on a body that's all mine! As cheesy as it sounds, I actually hug myself, grinning ear to ear.

Knock, knock.

"Come in!" I say, reaching for my Gucci on the floor. Regina pushes the door open, carrying my mug that reads *This Might Be Wine*. Frankie follows behind, double fisting two more cups.

"Here you go." Regina hands over the hot brew.

"Thanks." I settle on my bed and gesture for them to join me. While they get comfortable, I plug in my phone and take my first sip. The vanilla flavor lingers on my tongue and I let out a satisfied hum.

"So I see you need glasses again," Frankie says.

"From what I can tell, everything survived the change back." Everything but my soul-sucking pessimism.

"Do you think it'll happen again?" Regina asks, as if I could possibly have a clue. The thought of pissing from a penis again gives my coffee a sour taste.

"Fuck, I hope not."

"So what now?" Frankie's worry-stricken eyes burn into me, but the only fire I feel is the one under my ass urging me to take this city by the balls just like I did yesterday. But today, it will mean so much more.

My phone dings an alert, then another, and another. "Hang on," I say, picking up my device.

ERIC: Are you awake? (12:30 a.m.)

FRANKIE: You're still not home. Are you okay? (2:41 a.m.)

OWEN: Where are you? (8:08 a.m.)

"Shit. I'm late." I leave my coffee and phone on the nightstand and climb off the bed.

"Late for what?" Regina asks.

My nerves tingle in anticipation of the unknown. "I was supposed to be at Monty Fuhrmann ten minutes ago. Well, Richard was, anyway."

Regina swings her legs around and plants her feet on the floor. "Wait. You're going back?"

"Of course I'm going back."

"Don't you think that's a little crazy?" she asks.

"What's crazy is yesterday as Richard, it was ballsy. Today as Delia, you want to question my sanity?" *Fucking double standard.*

"That's not what I mean. But c'mon. What are you going to do? March in there like you did yesterday and tell them you're Richard Allen?" Her words give me pause for about, oh, half a second.

"But I am Richard Allen! I'm the one who took charge yesterday. *I* saved that meeting. That's *my* fucking pitch. And I'll be damned if I don't see this through."

"*Chica*," Frankie starts, "I love your enthusiasm and everything, but Regina's right. They're expecting a man. How are you going to explain any of this?"

I bite my upper lip, thinking back to the moment before I walked into Becker's office. My lie hardly made sense to me at the time but I had one thing going for me. Valuable information. Facts that their precious prospect confirmed when he called in. I'm the only person on the planet besides Owen who knows this pitch backwards and forwards. It's the only card I have to play. And I'm doubling down.

"I'll figure it out as I go, just like yesterday," I declare. "What good was this whole experience if I don't at least try? I'm done waiting for permission. Waiting for some man to give me a chance. Today is my day to finally woman up."

Regina takes my protest in for a moment as she draws in a long breath. "You're right, Delia."

"Yeah." Frankie claps his hands, then points a vehement finger my way. "You go show 'em."

"Okay, we're with you," Regina says. "How can we help?"

I beam at them both, grateful that I found such supportive friends in a city of nearly nine million strangers. "Pick out something for me to wear. Something that says, *I don't take shit from nobody.*"

"On it!" She snaps her fingers and immediately begins digging in my closet.

"I need to freshen up." I point a hitchhiker's thumb toward the door.

Frankie raises his brow. "Freshen up? You need a serious scrub-down."

"There's no time!"

"You better make time 'cause you rank." Frankie pinches the tip of his nose.

I raise my arm and take a whiff. "Ugh." It's like Old Spice and old onions had an all-out battle. Old onions won.

"Told you."

"Fine. Quick shower and I'm out the door." I lunge over my bed for my phone and send Owen a quick text.

DELIA: Something came up. Be there soon.

I tear my clothes off on the way to the bathroom. As the water runs down my back, I notice how much lighter my body feels. I may not look as muscular or as physically powerful as Richard, but

I feel just as strong. The scrub-down hardly lasts the length of my favorite song. I quickly towel off my soft, familiar skin and smear my hand over the steamed mirror before popping in my contacts. Looking into my own eyes, I'm reminded that I'm more than a man.

I'm a woman.

W-O-M-A-N!

I'm Delia-fucking-Reese, smart as the rest of those guys at Monty Fuhrmann, and capable of anything. All I have to do is say yes.

"Yes!" I say to my reflection. "Yes! Yes! YES!"

BANG! BANG!

"What are you doing in there?" Regina calls from the other side of the door.

Beaming and bouncing around, I yank it open. "Nothing. I'm finished." I push past her, panting from the excitement, and hurry toward my room.

"Wait. I have something for you," she says.

I stop in my tracks.

She hands me a bold pink blouse from her wardrobe. "Wear this."

I take it, feeling the fine fabric on my fingers. The hue is so bright it almost lights up the dim hallway. "It's beautiful, but . . . I don't know if it says I don't take any shit."

"Sure it does." The corner of her mouth turns up into a smirk. "Show 'em that pink deserves respect."

I look into her brown eyes, smiling back. *The Pink Ranger is just as powerful as the other Rangers.*

"Pink deserves respect," I say.

Regina has laid out one of my gray suits on my bed. It's the closest thing I have to Frankie's Michael Kors. She's threaded the pink paisley tie through the loops of the waistline. I shake my head, letting out a little chuckle, then dress swiftly, making sure my collar is straight and the silk belt is secured. My reflection reveals something different but also recognizable—a revitalized confidence. Looks like the tie isn't the only token remaining from my day with dick. I slick my hair back in a ponytail, throw my makeup bag in my Gucci, and straighten my spine. "Okay, Delia. Let's do this."

CHAPTER TWENTY-SIX

At 9:06, I push through the revolving doors of Monty Fuhrmann Tower and rush along the marble floors with my Gucci along for the ride. No curious looks from the guards when I use Richard's keycard to get through security. I squeeze my way into the packed elevator. My stomach tightens with every level we climb. The constant stops don't help—third floor, eleventh, twenty-fifth, and finally the thirty-second floor. Owen's assistant is just walking back to her desk when I approach.

"Good morning, Ashley," I say, bypassing her for the boss's open door.

Her voice trails directly behind me. "Excuse me? You are . . . ? Is Mr. Campbell expecting you?"

Oops! I almost forgot. "Oh! Sorry." I extend my hand. "I'm Rich—" Try again. "Delia Reese. Richard Allen sent me to speak with Owen. It's about the ten o'clock meeting with Todd Fairbanks."

She raises a freshly waxed eyebrow. "Your name is Rich Delia?"

No, but I like the sound of that. "Just Delia."

Owen's head peeks out from the doorframe, his eyes shifting left and right. "Did you say Richard Allen?" His brows squish so tightly together they look like one long squirming caterpillar.

"Yes, Mr. Campbell," I say.

"Come in." He waves me forward and slips back into his office.

The morning sun beams a bright orange glare on the wall behind him. I squint, hovering my hand like a visor for a moment, letting my eyes adjust. Owen perches on the corner of his dark wooden desk, arms crossed, tapping his thumb against his biceps.

Squaring my shoulders, I look him dead in the eye, invoking the spirit of Serena Walters. "Richard's been detained. He sent me in his place."

Owen jumps to his feet, balling his fists at his sides. "You've got to be kidding me. Where the hell is he?"

"I wish I could tell you, but I don't have that information." I press my fingernails into my dry palm.

He scoffs. "I suppose you're from the *Zurich* office too." Before I can answer, he walks off to the window, rubbing his hand over his forehead.

I smirk. That Zurich story was pretty clever. Only a ballsy son of a bitch could spin that one. "Actually, I live here in the city."

Aside from a few heavy sighs, Owen's silent for at least twenty-four seconds, staring out at the skyline. "I can't believe I trusted him. Twice! Now what am I supposed to do? Fairbanks will be here in less than an hour."

I step up to him. "Mr. Campbell, I know we just met, but Richard sent me here to replace him because he knows I'm the best person for the job."

Owen whips around, his face so red I'm afraid he might have a heart attack too. "Replace him?"

"Yes," I say, as if it's the most natural thing in the world. This would be a much easier sell if I could just tell him that I am Richard Allen. But he'd never buy that.

"I don't think so." Owen stomps to his door. "Ashley! Get Darren in here now!" he barks.

"Darren quit this morning, Mr. Campbell. He's not here. I sent you an email," she responds without hesitation. Damn, Darren. That was fast.

Owen smacks his palm into his forehead. "You have all got to be fucking kidding me. Is this a joke?"

I straighten up, widening my stance like a superhero. "Mr. Campbell, I'm fully prepared to execute this meeting with you."

"I doubt that's possible," he says, dismissing me with a slight scowl. Whether he's saying that because I'm a stranger or because I'm a woman, he'll eat his words soon enough.

I rest my hand on my hip and swivel my neck a little. "Well, it is. Plus, I know you want to show Fairbanks the new young blood on the team. Who's newer and younger than I am?"

He checks his watch and shakes his head like he's about two seconds away from a total hissy fit. "Exactly. That's the problem! What could you possibly know about this deal?"

"I know that Monty Fuhrmann helped Ezeus acquire Smark-Tech, taking it from an unknown tech company to over fifty million users in the U.S. and more than a quarter of a billion worldwide."

"So what? You read the *Wall Street Journal*?"

I walk toward him, head up, not taking shit from nobody. "I do. But what the *Wall Street Journal* doesn't know yet is how Monty Fuhrmann was purposefully left out of the Ezeus IPO due to some . . . ethical differences."

He stands tall, almost casting a shadow over me. "Is that *all* you know?"

"No." I hand Owen the neatly folded list that he gave me, I mean Richard, last night. By the look on his face, it's clear when the sell starts to settle in. I rattle off each of the items in order, then start back at the beginning, expounding on each one as if I were giving a dissertation on the entire pitch. I'm not even halfway through the third point when he raises his hand.

"Okay," he says. "I've heard enough. How do you know all of this and how the hell have you managed to memorize it in less than twelve hours?" Strangely, the more anxious he gets, the more settled I feel. Someone has to keep it together for Fairbanks.

I shrug. "I told you, Richard reviewed everything with me. He knew I could handle it because . . ." I smirk. "I'm just that good. Now, the way I see it, you can kick me out of the building and pitch to Fairbanks *alone*, which I know you want to avoid, or you can take a chance on me, which really isn't a risk at all. Given the circumstances, I'm your ace in the hole."

"You? I don't even know who you are!"

I can feel my cheeks blush the same shade as my shirt. Shit. How could I have forgotten to introduce myself to him? "I'm Delia Reese," I say, offering a firm hand. He doesn't take it. Instead, he gives me the third degree about my history: where I went to college, how I obtained experience, other companies I've worked with in the past. I tell him everything. The truth.

"Sounds a lot like Richard's experience. You two are practically twins, huh?" He walks over behind his desk. "Is that why you both have a tendency to bust into offices wearing pink shirts?"

I follow him, taking a seat in front. "No, that's just a coincidence. Besides, he wears salmon, I wear pink."

He breathes out a bull-like sigh. "Listen, Ms. Reese—"

"Delia."

He gives me a pinched look. "Delia. As much as you might be the solution to my problem, I don't know you well enough to let you into *any* meeting that's this important. There's too much at stake. I'm sorry, but unless you know someone whom I trust that can vouch for you, I'm going to have to ask you to leave."

I bite my upper lip. There is someone, but I'm not quite ready to tell him I've returned. Oh, well. Desperate times . . . "Eric Walker. He can vouch for me."

Owen's lips flatten and he looks at me sideways while picking up his phone. "Ashley, I need you to get Eric Walker in here ASAP. If he's *here*, that is." He slams the receiver down and rubs his face.

Okay, now my pulse is racing. The man I'm crazy about is gonna walk through that door any minute.

My leg starts to fidget. "By the way, how's Curtis? Any word on his condition?"

He shoots me a squinty stare. "Are you sure you weren't here yesterday?"

I hint at a smirk, raising an eyebrow. "I think you'd remember something like that. Don't you?"

He breathes another deep sigh. "I don't know anymore. It's been a really weird couple of days. Becker's going to pull through, but his doctor's recommending early retirement."

"Let's hope he takes that prescription," I mutter beneath my breath, a little louder than intended.

Owen's mouth starts to curl up in a smile, but he quickly adjusts.

"You wanted to see me?" The familiar voice seems to sing to my ears. Eric's standing in the doorway with his hands on his hips, slightly out of breath. My heart pounds wildly at the sight of him in the dark gray suit that I love. Then again, I love him in every suit. "Delia!" A smile springs from ear to ear. "What are you doing here?" His ol' blue eyes lock onto mine as he walks toward me. For a moment, it's as if we're the only people in the room, and I know he's thinking the same thing I am.

"Oh, good. You do know her," Owen chimes in, breaking the spell between Eric and me.

"Yes. Well, actually. What's this about?" Eric shifts his eyes between Owen and me, his cheeks growing flushed while he bites back a grin.

"Apparently, Richard Allen has been . . . detained, and he sent Ms. Reese to fill in for him."

Eric tilts his head. "You know Richard?"

That's one way to look at it. "Yep."

"Somehow she knows everything he knows, including the pitch, but I need you to tell me honestly if she's competent enough to do this." Owen looks as serious as POTUS addressing the public before sending troops into a war zone.

Eric wrinkles his brow and points to himself. "Me? Why me?"

"Because you're the only person who actually knows anything

about her. So, I'll ask you *again*. Do you think she's competent enough?" Owen's irritated tone is totally justified, but I don't like him talking to Eric like that. He's blameless in this dilemma.

Eric gets past his confusion. "Yes. Yes, definitely, she can do it. She's as smart and as skilled as anyone on the team, if not more so. She's the best person for the job." Eric looks to me like I'm the greatest girl he knows, and my heart skips a beat. "You'd be lucky to have her in that meeting with you, sir."

Would I ruin my chance at this pitch if I kiss him right here? Right now?

Owen lets out a sigh. "Thanks, Eric. You can go."

He nods to the boss and sends me a bemused wave. There must be a million questions he's dying to ask. I just hope I have enough clever energy left to answer them when this is all over. As Eric turns and heads out the door, I can't help but stare.

Oh, yeah. That's why it's my favorite suit.

I shake off my Eric-buzz and focus on Owen's wall clock behind his desk. Only twenty more minutes before Fairbanks arrives.

Owen clears his throat, getting back my full attention, and crosses his arms over his chest. "Okay, Delia Reese. You're in. We need to finish preparing, and we need to do it quickly."

I did it?

My stomach does a double flip. No, that was a triple.

I did it!

Talking my way into this pitch for the third freaking time has got to be some kind of record. Holy shit, this feels good! In twenty minutes, I'll be sitting across from Todd Fairbanks, closing the deal of a lifetime.

Owen and I use every remaining second to go over all the key points and how we'll field potential questions. Every so often he gives me a surprised gawk when I note some special fact from yesterday's meetings.

He gives his Rolex a quick glance. "Are you ready?"

I tilt my chin up. "Do you really have to ask?"

"I guess not." He walks toward his door without a word, and I follow close behind. I'm almost too close, because he quickly turns back, almost bumping into me. "Is my tie straight?"

I step back and give it the slightest adjustment to the right. "Yes."

He looks me over, giving my waist a double take. "Are you wearing a tie as a belt?"

I look down, smiling at my special souvenir. "I am."

He narrows his eyes. "Isn't that the same tie Richard was wearing yesterday?"

"Like you said, practically twins."

CHAPTER TWENTY-SEVEN

As we approach the conference room, I peer through the open blinds that line the glass wall. Bright morning light pours in from the wide windows, reflecting off the dark lacquered table. A carafe of ice water and glasses, notepads, and pens sit on top. All but three chairs have been removed. They're strategically arranged around the table for negotiation, but otherwise the setting appears conversational. Todd Fairbanks stands just inside the door, his gaze fixed on his cell phone. He's already dressed for the Hamptons in a casual white polo, light-colored jeans rolled at the cuff, and Sperry boat shoes with no socks. Ashley sets a tall bottle of Voss on a coaster. He smiles, looking as if he's thanking her, and she nods before exiting swiftly.

Now that I think of it, I washed those jeans the other day.

After all that's happened, nothing should surprise me, but I

Amanda Aksel

still can't believe I'm here. As Delia. I flash a toothy smile, wishing
I could jump for joy. I'll save it for later.

"You're not nervous, are you?" Owen asks, and I have a feeling
his confidence is still a little shaken. Good thing I've got enough
for the both of us.

"Not at all. I'm excited."

He stops a few feet from the doorway and buttons his suit
jacket. "Well, don't get too excited, Delia. We haven't convinced
Fairbanks yet."

The moment the words leave his mouth, I regain my *this is
business* composure. My heart begins to race, quicker and faster
with each step we take into the conference room. But I'm also hit
with a keen sense of knowing, a foresight. No matter what happens
here today, this won't be the last big deal I ever get to pitch. I can
feel it.

"Todd!" Owen greets with a great big smile, showing off his
bleached dental work. "How are you?"

Fairbanks steps over to shake his hand, but with a much more
reserved, almost nonexistent smile. "I'm very well." He acknowledges me, and his mouth turns up a little more.

Fairbanks in the flesh. Again. My stomach tightens and I immediately check my palms for leaks. Nothing more than a slight
misting.

Just be cool, Delia. Remember you've already seen this guy's
underwear.

"Todd, this is Delia Reese. She's stepping in for Becker today,"
Owen begins, and even though he's acting all loose and easygoing,
his jaw tightens after every remark.

I reach for Fairbanks's hand. "Nice to meet you."

He finally gives me a full-on smile. "You too, Delia. It's good to see a woman calling some shots around this place."

I totally agree.

Fairbanks's smile fades and he tilts his head. "Hmm, that's unusual."

Uh-oh. Have I turned back into Richard? I give my hands a quick glance.

Nope. Still me.

"What is?"

"That's the second time I've heard that name in the last two days, and I've never met anyone else with that name before."

Nothing gets past this tech genius.

I coolly shrug it off. "Me neither."

"Well, unless you're a housekeeper on the side, there's at least two of you in the city," he jokes with a slight chuckle.

I let out a nervous high-pitched laugh, then immediately tone it down. Owen shoots me a knowing look. My body begins to recoil, but I shake it off and take my place at the table.

Todd follows my lead and pulls out his chair. "Sorry to hear about Curtis."

"Um, yes, thank you, Todd." Owen returns his attention to Fairbanks. "He's doing better. I'm sure he'll pull through just fine."

Todd nods slowly and silently, as if paying his respects to Becker's heart attack. Then, his expression completely shifts. "Wasn't there supposed to be someone here from the Zurich office?"

My partner and I exchange glances. "Unfortunately, he needed to return to Switzerland this morning." I squirm a little in my seat at Owen's lie. "Would you like anything else before we start?" he asks, pointing to Fairbanks's full glass bottle.

"No, thanks. I'm good with this." Todd leans forward, resting his forearms on the table. "I do want to say that up until yesterday, I had no intention of letting Monty Fuhrmann work on this offering. And while I wish that Curtis hadn't suffered a heart attack, I'm somewhat relieved that he's not here."

I look for Owen's reaction, but he and Fairbanks are completely focused on each other.

"I know that this firm has bent over backward for me in the past," he continues, "so it was difficult to make the decision to exclude you, understanding what that might mean for your firm's reputation. But I want you to know that it's very unlikely you'll be able to propose a deal that I'm comfortable with. I don't know if that changes your pitch, but I just wanted to put it out there. No bullshit."

"Mr. Fairbanks," I start before Owen can utter a single syllable.

"Call me Todd."

I smile politely and set my hands on the table, fingers interlaced, palms mist free. "Todd. We're well aware of why you have doubts about working with us. I believe that during this conversation you'll find we understand you and Ezeus better than you realize. This is an important milestone in your business. We agree: no games, no bullshit."

The tech mogul narrows his eyes and folds his arms as he rests back in his chair. After a few seconds, he nods as if we've come to an understanding, a level playing field. "So, Owen, Delia, whatcha got for me?"

I glance at Owen on my left and he sends me a subtle wink. He grabs his notepad, and I pull out three freshly printed pitchbooks. They seem to sparkle in the light-filled conference room. Fairbanks asks a ton of questions as we go through the document, interrupting at every turn, but Owen and I maintain our equanimity. After his opening statement, I expected Fairbanks to remain guarded throughout the full presentation. But with every response we give, he seems more and more receptive. Satisfied even. I'm completely engrossed in the pitch, yet underneath that focus I hear a bit of a whoo girl cheering me on. This is the best day of my life. I'm finally where I belong.

Fairbanks's questions stall, so I sneak a quick glimpse at my watch. It's been an hour and a half since we sat down, and I was sure he'd give us less than forty-five minutes.

"So what do you think?" Owen asks.

Our potential client sits back and has his first drink of the bottled water. And it's a long one. He swallows and takes in a deep breath. Then says . . . nothing. My mind starts to race, debating if that's all this meeting will amount to, contemplating what move I can make to change his mind if he says no. But right now, I just really want him to say something. Anything.

Fairbanks clears his throat and stands. "I can't believe I'm saying this, but . . . I think we have a deal." He grins and extends his hand to Owen.

Owen jumps to his feet. "That's great!" he says, pumping the handshake harder than seems necessary.

I join them, resisting every urge to spring onto the conference table and scream, "I'm queen of the jungle!" while pounding my fists against my chest. But instead of shouting at the top of my lungs, I'm cheesing so hard my cheeks hurt.

"Great job, Delia. I'm really looking forward to working with you," Todd says, giving me his hand.

"Thank you," I say, hoping that Owen heard that last part. But even if he doesn't give me a permanent position on this, I'll always know that I was the one who created Monty Fuhrmann's plan for the Ezeus IPO, and I helped seal the deal. And that feels pretty damn good.

We walk Todd out to the elevators, confirming our next meeting, and tossing mock apologies for delaying his weekend at the beach. As soon as the steel doors close, I turn on my heel to face Owen, smiling so much that I'll need to book a face massage. "That was incredible!"

He looks pleased and breathes a sigh of relief. "I have to say, it was better than I expected."

"I knew it would work," I say with wide eyes, and he wrinkles his brow. "I mean, when Richard told me about it, I knew it was the right plan."

His pleased expression returns. "You kicked ass in there, Delia. It's not something I can forget easily."

"So what's next for me?" I ask, clenching my hands together.

"You impressed Todd Fairbanks, gave him confidence in the firm. We can't let you go. What do you think about working for us? It's got to be better than cleaning his apartment, right?"

My jaw drops and my face heats up like a July afternoon in Boca. "I . . . um . . ."

He raises an eyebrow. "You think you're the only sharp knife in the drawer around here?"

"Well, I certainly hope not," I say, not meeting his eye.

"Delia, it doesn't matter." He places a hand on my shoulder in a fatherly way. "You're exactly what this team needs. We could use more upper-level female perspectives around here."

I finally look at him. *Upper level?*

His kind smile turns into his serious-negotiator stare. "And it looks like we have a VP position that just opened up. Why don't you start there, and we'll see how you do."

VP? Did he just say he'll start me as VP?

Hell yeah!

Finally, someone in charge sees my potential. "Thank you, sir." I reach for a handshake. Now I'm the one pumping it more than necessary.

"C'mon, let's go tell the others." He motions for me to follow him, but my feet remain planted.

"Wait," I say, and he turns back around. "Are you hiring me *just* because of my female perspective?"

"No. I'm hiring you because you nailed it in there. The perspective's just a bonus." True. I did nail it, and I didn't need a dick to do it. "Now, I've had enough questions for today. Let's celebrate!"

As we head back down the hall to the conference room, Nicole zips by. "Hey, Nicole!" Owen catches her. She turns back, sporting a pair of hot pink frames in the same style as yesterday. "Would you mind calling the team into the conference room and getting us all some champagne?"

She stares at him over the rims of her glasses. "Does that mean . . . ?"

"Yes, it does. We closed Fairbanks." Owen pats her on the shoulder, grinning like a kid on Christmas morning.

"Ah, that's great news!" she says, shifting her eyes my way.

"Nicole, I'd like you to meet Delia Reese. She's our new VP."

I extend my hand like an olive branch. "Hi, Nicole."

She takes it, her expression totally transforming from *Who the hell are you?* to *You go, girl!* "Good to meet you, Ms. Reese. Nice blouse."

"Nice glasses." I smile. "And call me Delia."

"I'll get the guys." She nods before heading off, no eye roll necessary this time, and Owen excuses himself for a minute.

I wander to the conference room by myself and gaze out the window overlooking the city. I'm literally on top of my world. My dad's never going to believe this, but I hope in time he'll see that pink deserves respect. I breathe a sigh of gratitude that something in my life changed. Besides my genitals.

I made it.

Nicole pops in carrying a chilled bottle of bubbly and pulls a set of flutes from a cabinet behind the conference table. Is that Dom Pérignon? The guys appear, one after the other. I glance around behind Brian, Mike, and the others. Where's Eric?

Owen saunters in, practically floating on air. He grabs the bottle of Dom from the table and peels back the black foil paper.

"Are we celebrating?" Mike asks.

"We're celebrating," Owen says, twisting the tiny metal cage loose. "We closed the Ezeus deal!"

The guys shoot curious glances my way as they hoot and cheer, dodging the flying cork that nearly takes out a ceiling tile. I applaud with them, though not as boisterously. Owen pours the foamy spirits into each flute, and Nicole disperses the glasses around to everyone, keeping one for herself.

"I'd like to propose a toast." Owen raises his glass and we follow. "To Richard Allen, wherever he is, that crazy son of a bitch." I'm trying my best not to laugh my ass off. "It's because of him we saved this deal, and with our newest VP. Please welcome Delia Reese!"

The guys raise their glasses, cheering and smiling as they shoot the thin flutes of champagne. One by one, the guys approach, congratulating me on my position even though none of them know who I am. The welcomes are warm and I thank them, wanting to relish the moment. I sip from my glass, glancing at the door for Eric. He's the one I really want to celebrate with.

"Would you excuse me for a bit? There's something I need to take care of," I tell Owen.

He tilts his glass to me. "Of course!"

"Thanks."

I dash out of the room to call Eric. After three rings I'm convinced he's not going to answer. Has something happened to him? Just as I think it's going to voice mail, he picks up.

"Hey, where are you?" I ask.

"I had to run to another meeting. I'm about to pull up to the tower." He sounds as eager as I feel.

"Don't move," I say. "I'll meet you outside."

Before he can say another word, I hang up and take the elevator down to the lobby. I pull my hair free and check my makeup in the reflective doors. The instant they slide open I fly out of there so fast, feeling so light on my feet that my heels hardly touch the ground. A taxi pulls up to the building just as I approach the entrance. Eric steps out with another gentleman in a suit. The guy says something to him before leaving him on the sidewalk.

My man is waiting for me. I take in a deep breath and push through the glass doors. The butterflies in my stomach come alive again, but this time I'm not nervous. I'm confident.

Eric sees me now, his smile widening as our distance closes.

"Hey, Sinatra." It's all I can manage to say. I want to talk about everything—what happened yesterday, what he said to Richard, the pitch we just landed with Todd-freaking-Fairbanks. All those things I wanted to shout from the rooftops yesterday, and now nothing comes out. All I can do is stand here looking at him, looking at me, Delia.

"Hey." His eyes sparkle as they take me in. "I can't believe you're here."

"Neither can I." I lock onto his gaze. My hair dances on the breeze, and I tuck it behind my ear. "Honestly, you have no idea."

As if in a trance, neither one of us can turn our eyes away. I lower my hand and he finds it, tracing his thumb over the tops of my delicate fingers. His touch sends an electrifying tingle throughout my entire body, and I'm completely transfixed by the way he's looking at me. It's the same way he adored the photo of us on his phone last night.

"Delia . . ."

Hearing my name roll off his tongue sounds even better than before.

He pulls me so close, his suede cologne replaces the scent of the city. "I'm crazy about you."

Finally. I close my eyes and press my lips to his. His mouth is more delicious than all the Sassicaia in the world. His hands grip my waist as my body, my Delia-body, melts into him. An intoxicating wave floods my brain as his kiss pulls me in deeper and deeper.

I take a breath and draw back, knees so weak it's a miracle I'm standing. "I . . . I've been wanting to do that for so long."

"Then why didn't you?" he asks with the same ache from time wasted.

I shake my head slowly and lower my eyes. "I wasn't sure you wanted me to."

"Delia." He leans in, lifting my chin. "I've always wanted you to."

He kisses me again like I'm all he craves. If we weren't standing on the front sidewalk of Monty Fuhrmann Tower while bankers and cabs bustle by on Broadway, I'd yank off his tie.

And mine too.

Eric rests his forehead on mine, tickling the tip of my nose with his. "When I got your text yesterday, I thought I might never see you again. That I'd missed my chance to be with you."

If only I could bottle up his words, his kiss, the way it feels when his body is pressed against mine. I'd drink it on my living room floor every time I missed him.

I let out a small laugh. "Well, luckily you'll be seeing a lot more of me now."

"Mmm, sounds good to me." His hands gently stroke my sides, until he catches my expression. He raises an eyebrow as a smirk tugs at the edge of his sexy mouth. "Wait, does that mean . . . ?"

I beam as bright as the sunlight atop the city. "We just closed the Ezeus deal."

"Are you serious?" Eric's jaw falls for a moment before he embraces me in a tight squeeze. "Oh my god! That's amazing! I knew you could do it!"

"Oh, and . . . they just offered me a job."

He pulls away, eyes wide and gleaming. "I'm so proud of you, Delia."

I bat my lashes. "I'm proud of me too."

He smiles, caressing my cheek with his fingertips, and gives me another sweet kiss. "Then I guess this means you're staying in New York."

"Of course. There's no place I'd rather be." A lightness swirls in my chest, and I find myself grinning for all that's happened and all that's yet to come.

Eric's arm slinks around my waist, pulling me in again. "You know, I've got some time for lunch, and my place isn't far from here."

I let out a wispy breath. "You read my mind."

"I'll get us a ride." He takes my hand and we walk side by side off the edge of the curb. Holding me close with one arm and signaling for a cab with the other, he lands soft kisses on the top of my head. My eyes close as I sink farther into him. This moment is more satisfying than a Brooklyn blackout cupcake. Now I've really made it.

CHAPTER TWENTY-EIGHT

A fter an incredible . . . um . . . lunch with Eric and some paperwork at Monty Fuhrmann Tower, both having been long overdue, I head home to my apartment. Along the way, I stop by my favorite little wine shop. Sure enough, they have a top-shelf bottle of Sassicaia. All is as it should be. I can't wait to celebrate with my roommates tonight. Drinking on the floor will never be the same. I shoot them a quick text.

DELIA: I got the good stuff. Meet you in the living room in twenty minutes.

REGINA: Hell yeah! I'm dying to hear EVERYTHING!

FRANKIE: Is it that wine from Il Vezzo? I've been dreaming about it since yesterday.

As I open the door to our apartment, Regina saunters by with a bowl of hummus in one hand and three wineglasses in the other.

"Hey, girl," she says, setting everything down on the center of the coffee table. That's right—I *am* a girl. A proud one with a *real* boyfriend and a *hella real* salary!

"*Hola, chica.*" Frankie sets a corkscrew on the table before taking my hand and twirling me around like I'm his little ballerina. He grabs the wine bottle from me. "Yes! Where did you find this?"

"In the high-dollar section we never venture into."

His eyes narrow and drop to my waist. "Are you wearing my good paisley tie as a belt?"

"Yes," I say, protecting it with my hands. "Can I keep it? Pleeeease!"

His nostrils flare and I can tell he wants to snatch it off my waist, but then he glances at the bottle of Sassicaia and his expression softens. "Sure, but you're buying me a new one. And they're not cheap."

Regina walks in again from the kitchen, carrying a tray of pita chips, grapes, and brie. "She can afford it now. Can't you, Delia?"

"Yes, I can."

I really can.

"Can you also afford to take my suit to the dry cleaner's? I need it for my date with Martino next week."

"Ooooh!" Regina and I howl, causing his cheeks to turn salmon. I slip off my heels and settle on the sangria-colored rug. "Yes, I'll take it in tomorrow."

"Good," he says, satisfied.

I uncork the bottle and pour evenly between the three glasses, careful not to lose a drop. We each take one and hold it just below our noses, inhaling in unison.

Now I can finally relax after a very long couple of days. Hopefully I'll sleep like a rock tonight. And wake up with my vagina. "This is the best, right?"

"Mm-hmm," Frankie and Regina hum.

Frankie sits cross-legged on the floor next to me, while Regina grabs a copy of *Vogue* and stretches out on the couch.

"So, how was your day?" I ask them, waiting for the wine to breathe. Frankie shoots me a sarcastic look and Regina scoffs.

"Puh-leeze! Nothing compared to yours. Spill it, Post-dick Delia!" Regina says.

I let out a laugh, then hold my head high. "I prefer to be called VP Delia now."

She hoots a long "Oooh!" then settles into a toothy grin.

"Stop stalling! What happened?" Frankie begs.

Taking a slow sip of wine, I savor the refined taste. "Well, I showed up at Monty Fuhrmann Tower just as myself, and proved that I was the best person for the job. And not just because Richard Allen sent me in his place."

Regina closes her magazine. "Geez. They must've had so many questions."

"Yeah, I bet Owen's still trying to figure out how I knew everything I did on such short notice."

"Is that your new boss?" Regina asks.

"Mm-hmm. You should've seen the two of us pitching Fairbanks. We closed the shit out of that deal! It was amazing." My heart flutters at the thought of how it all came together—like I was meant to do that meeting all along. The two of them set their wineglasses down, whooing and applauding a job well done.

"Was Fairbanks as cute in person as he is in pictures?" Frankie asks.

"Cuter." I let out a little laugh and he joins me.

"That's crazy. Your life is nuts!"

"Nuts was yesterday. Today my life is perfect." As hard as it was, yesterday was the best thing that could've happened to me. But damn, what a whirlwind. Wouldn't trade it for the world.

Regina raises her glass. "To Delia, the Pink Power Ranger who dared to do something crazy. And with a dick to boot."

"To Delia!" Frankie joins in.

"Cheers!" I tap my glass to theirs, and we each suck down a deliciously long drag.

"Oh, wait! I almost forgot." Frankie sets his glass on the coffee table and jumps to his feet. "I'll be right back." He shuffles into his dark bedroom while Regina and I share a look and shrug.

She leans in, batting her eyelashes. "So, what about Eric?"

My cheeks blush as I hide a coy smile behind my glass. "I kissed him."

"*You* kissed him?" She gawks at me as if that's the most unbelievable part of my day.

"Yep." I nod. "No fear. No doubt." I'm practically counting the hours before I can do it again tomorrow.

Frankie returns with two handfuls of medical supplies. "Wait, did you just say you kissed Eric?"

"Yes, I did." I run my finger across my lip and my stomach flutters. "And that's not all we did."

"Ooooh!" my friends tease in harmony, flashing big smiles. I shut my eyes just long enough to relive the moment in my mind.

Regina clinks her glass to mine. "When it rains it pours!"

"Congratulations, *chica*!" Frankie says.

"Thank you." I nod. "Whatcha got there, Dr. Ramirez?"

Kneeling down, he carefully places his stockpile on the table, then takes my glass from my hands. "Before you drink too much more, I want to get another blood sample."

Regina groans. "Do you really have to do that now? Can't it wait until tomorrow?"

"It'll only take a couple of minutes. I'm dying to compare the two samples."

I stretch my arm out while Frankie slaps a pair of blue latex gloves on himself and a lime-green tourniquet on me. The alcohol wipe is cold, and my skin prickles as he sticks me with the needle.

"I think we should celebrate with a game of Truth or Dare," Regina proposes.

I shake my head. "No way! That game is dangerous. Potentially."

"Oh, c'mon," Regina whines. "Nothing that crazy could ever happen twice. But just in case, don't say anything about having a dick."

"Yeah, say something you actually want to have happen. Like, I would dare myself to have hot sex with Martino after our date." Frankie giggles, keeping his eyes fixed on my arm.

"Seriously, Delia," Regina prods. "Truth or dare?"

My gaze wanders to the bright pink wings of the butterfly needle in my arm, and I feel a rush, a release as the tube fills with my blood.

The truth?

The truth is that when you dare to be who you really are, a path unfolds where you least expect it. Yesterday was proof of that. I'll probably never be able to explain how it all happened. But there's one thing I know for sure.

You don't need a dick to have balls.

ACKNOWLEDGMENTS

When I first wrote this book, I had no idea that I would be embarking on a five-year journey that would require more courage and determination than I believed I was capable of. There's a serendipitous story behind this book with twists, tears, and inner transformation. It was Nichiren Daishonin who said, "Could there ever be a more wonderful story than your own?" I'd like to acknowledge the most amazing people in mine . . .

Heather Hildenbrand, my elephant friend and fellow author, this book would've never happened if you hadn't insisted I write it immediately. Thank you for your encouragement and support. My friend, *shoten-zenjin*, and dedicated editor, Carine McCandless. Working with you over the years was like writers' boot camp with lots of laughs. I'm a much stronger writer because of you. From the bottom of my heart, thank you for everything. A special thank-you to my agent, Suzie Townsend, and the team at New Leaf Literary & Media. It's no secret that you're the greatest agent an author could ask for. You inspire me more than you know, and I look forward to many more projects together. Kristine E. Swartz and the team at Berkley, from our first call I knew you were the editor I'd been praying for. Thank you so much for your trustworthy wisdom and collaborative spirit.

A very special and sincere thank-you to my husband, Joe. I have the deepest appreciation for your eternal love and support, and for believing in me and my work, despite all of the challenges. You are my greatest friend and ally. To Lani, my sweet little girl who snuggled on my lap through many drafts and edits. You are the treasure of my heart. And thank you, Mom, for always being my biggest cheerleader. Thank you to *all* of my family and friends, particularly those who offered extra emotional and writing encouragement throughout this process—Chantell Morales, Chelsea Fine, Michiko Tajima, Jessica Goldner Bowman, Sara Long, Kristina Robinson, Robert Robinson, Rachel Linde, Mai Lee Aksel, Show Lee and Gil Mendoza, Alice Wilson, Denise Nostrom, the Hampton Roads Writers, Steph Nuss, Kristina Harrison, Imani Pretlor, Nicole Cruz, Judy Glenney, Steve Aquilino, Stacie O'Brien, Daisy Pardasani, Armen Czepyha, Jay Odnant, and all of the Winsletts. Also my teachers who encouraged my writing from the (very) beginning, Peri Kost aka Ms. Smith, and Antonio Zarro.

A heartfelt thank-you to all my fellow members of the SGI-USA, who warmly encouraged me over the years. I could fill the pages of a book with your names alone. A special acknowledgment of appreciation to Chika O'Berry, Ram Surendren, and Moonjung Cho. And of course, all of the infinitely precious YWD of Virginia South Region. Because of each of you, I was able to reach into the depths of my life and keep fighting for my dreams. My victory is your victory, and your victory is mine. Let's keep winning together! Lastly, and most importantly, thank you to my mentor, Daisaku Ikeda. I owe you a tremendous debt of gratitude for your courage, compassion, wisdom, and dauntless efforts for *kosen-rufu*. Because of you, I learned how to be the champion of my own life and dreams.

Amanda Aksel is a West Coast transplant whose curiosity about people led her to earn a bachelor's in psychology. Instead of pursuing a career as a couples counselor, she wrote about one in her first novel. You'll often find her writing stories about fabulous, independent heroines; pretending to be Sara Bareilles at the piano; watching reruns of *Sex and the City*; or sprinkling a little too much feta on her salad. Amanda calls Virginia Beach home but loves to travel the world with her high school sweet-heart husband any chance they get.

Ready to find
your next great read?

Let us help.

Visit prh.com/nextread

Penguin
Random
House